The Family Behind the Walls

BOOKS BY SHARI J. RYAN

The Family Behind the Walls

SHARI J. RYAN

bookouture

Published by Bookouture in 2025

An imprint of Storyfire Ltd.
Carmelite House
50 Victoria Embankment
London EC4Y 0DZ

www.bookouture.com

The authorised representative in the EEA is Hachette Ireland
8 Castlecourt Centre
Dublin 15 D15 XTP3
Ireland
(email: info@hbgi.ie)

ISBN: 978-1-83618-477-5
eBook ISBN: 978-1-83618-476-8

*To the warriors and heroes who take the torch,
passed down from generation to generation,
and carry it forward to light our way.*

I press a stick of white chalk against the center of the blackboard, take a breath, and scratch out a date:

January 27th.

PROLOGUE
DALIA, JULY 27TH, 1943

Hamburg, Germany

In the dark bunker, searing with vengeful heat, twenty-five steps underground, we stand skin-to-skin with neighboring villagers. I hold the children tightly within in my arms as my husband Leo's embrace envelops us all. We stand in stillness, waiting as sweat oozes from every part of our bodies. The rubble beneath our feet continues to shake and jolt us in every direction for what seems like an eternity.

Then it all stops as if it was a figment of our imaginations, as if it never happened at all. Knowing it might start again, we wait until the minutes pass without feeling a nerve-numbing quake.

No one speaks a word but the fear within us is louder than anything I've heard tonight.

"Micah," someone shouts. "Micah, stand up, get up."

Someone must have fallen. We can't see anything, and it would be impossible to light a match with so little space to move.

"Micah!"

"Someone should go up and check the street," a man says from behind us in the back of the bunker. "The air raid is over."

How could any of us be sure it's over? We thought the raids ended with the demolition of the western part of Hamburg over the last few days, but it seems the British and Americans are back to attack the east too.

"It's too soon to go up there," Leo replies. "After the amount of damage done to the west—those fires are still burning. We won't be any better off."

"We can't breathe down here," a woman complains.

There isn't any more oxygen outside than in here, I want to argue. It's useless to reply when everyone's pleading to survive as the world burns above us.

"My elderly parents are alone. I must find them," another voice cries out.

"I don't know what to do," Leo whispers in my ear. He always has a plan, and a backup one too just in case. "The fire won't die down for a while. Even if the last of the bombs have fallen tonight, the damage is done and it's still spreading. These people must realize there's an inferno outside that bunker door."

"It isn't your decision what they do," I whisper back, reminding him he's no longer in charge of a squadron, but just fellow citizens taking cover in this bunker.

Leo sighs with grief and frustration. He can't stand still, shifting his weight from one foot to the other, his ash covered arm rubbing against mine.

"All who want to remain in the bunker move toward the back. Anyone who prefers to leave, move forward," he says, pushing me and our four children backward as we trip over others who are moving in the opposite direction. It's hard to tell how many of us are even in here. We continue shuffling back until we hit a stone wall. Leo then ushers us to the right, farther away from the exit.

Lilli whimpers, "Mama, I'm scared." She's only eight and I can't imagine what's going through her little mind after watching our city erupt into flames all around us.

"It's all right, sweetheart. We're safe here," I tell her. Is it a lie? Am I lying to myself by thinking we're safe?

The metal door squeals and scrapes as it gives way to stone steps. A bright orange glow bursts into the bunker, blinding us. We all shield our faces from the wave of searing heat filling the space. Dozens of heavy footsteps charge up the steps, rushing out onto the street. Everyone who is still down here with us shouts, "Shut the door!"

Someone secures the exit with the metal latch from the inside, closing us back into the darkness.

There's more space to move now, but no additional air, just a rush of thick, acrid smoke cloaking us like a thick blanket.

"There's a lantern hanging from the wall at the bottom of the steps," Leo says. "Whoever is over there, feel around for an overhead shelf and grab the lantern."

The faint rustling of clothing merges with the deep thuds echoing off the stone walls.

"I have it," someone shouts as if they've just won a contest.

"Bring it down this way. Follow my voice. We want to keep the lantern as far away from the exit as possible. The gasses could—"

Leo stops talking, something he does when he's speaking his fears out loud and realizes he doesn't want to scare anyone else around him.

"Over here," I shout, following Leo's stunted comment. Everyone shuffles around as the man with the lantern makes his way through the crowd. I reach out to feel for movement and grab the man's shirt as he steps past me. "Here. Give it here."

Leo feels for my hands and takes the lamp before stepping away from us. His footsteps scratch along the floor then stop.

Within seconds a faint glow illuminates the lantern's glass. "We must keep it dim. We don't want to use too much gas," Leo says.

It's enough for us to see those standing closest to us.

A few people cheer for the simple gift of light. A few cry. And one shrieks, "My Micah...No! He's not breathing. He's... God help me! No!" Her cries echo between the walls. "He's just a child. He's just a child!"

I clutch my chest upon spotting her lifeless son draped in her arms.

What we can't see in the dark can't hurt us...

Alfie, whom I consider my son for the sake of protecting him against German law, is huddling in the corner, holding his hands up to his ears, his eyes clenched shut. Little Lilli is beside him, her head against his arm.

My son Max is by Leo's side, and his younger sister Jordanna hasn't released me from her grip since we made our way down here. We're all covered from head to toe in black ash, leaving only the whites of our eyes to catch the light.

"Can we go back home?" Jordanna asks. With little hope in her question, at fifteen, she's much too aware this won't end without significant impact.

"No, we mustn't go anywhere just yet," Leo says. "Does anyone have injuries? If so, raise your hand."

"Max," I call over to my son. He turns to face me; his child-like eyes have aged with wisdom the last year as he fills into his role as a seventeen-year-old man. With so little to see of his features, it's more obvious than ever before how similar his eyes are to Leo's. He resembles his father in every way. "Take Jordanna over to the corner. Check on Alfie too. It doesn't seem as if he's doing well." Max and Alfie have been best friends since they were in diapers, and now they are more like brothers. "I need to help others."

At least a dozen people raise their hands. Leo starts on one side, and I move to the other.

Charred skin, fabrics burnt into flesh, hair disintegrated. I tear clothes off the uninjured, using unscathed materials to dress burns until we can get them medical treatment.

Burns were common in my time of nursing during the Great War but not as much as gunshot wounds and amputations.

I've barely helped one person when a fist pounds incessantly against the metal door, shocking us all with the reverberation between the walls. Leo stands and makes his way up the steep steps toward the door, lifting the latch before stepping back down toward us.

The door flies open, revealing two Gestapo, disheveled, covered in soot and sweat. "Papiere!" one of them says. "Take out your identifications."

The demand causes a fire inside of my stomach. Leo steps up to the first police officer. He pulls out his and my identification papers, leaving the children's papers in his robe pocket. "Obergefreiter Bergmann," he says, stating his former Lance Corporal ranking as he always does before anyone can read more about him—find out he's Jewish. We've had immunity from deportation because of his achievements and service in the Great War, but it seems we're on borrowed time.

The Gestapo stares at Leo for a long moment then down at his identification, and back up at his face. The silent conversation continues as he confers with his partner, showing him Leo's papers. Their gazes drift in my direction. "Are you a medic?" they ask as I'm in the middle of wrapping someone's leg.

"That's my wife," Leo answers before I do.

"That wasn't the question," the Gestapo grits through his teeth.

"I was a medic on the home front during the war, yes," I reply.

"Both of you, come with us. We need help."

The children will have to stay here, but we can't leave them.

"We should stay to help these people down here," Leo argues.

I continue wrapping the woman's leg, her mouth hanging open, her eyes stark white with red veins.

"It wasn't a question, Ober-gef-reiter Bergmann," the Gestapo snaps at Leo, mocking him, it seems.

"The city is on fire. What can we do?" Leo continues. He knows better than to argue with the Gestapo, but we have no choice.

They storm toward us and Leo drops his robe to the ground, leaving him in his pajamas, just before the police grab his arm.

"Anyone else here have medical training or experience?" the other Gestapo demands. It doesn't take him long to scan the area, finding our children, the elderly, and injured. He doesn't wait long for a response before lunging for me and pulling me up to my feet. "You. Let's go."

I peer over my shoulder, finding Max's hand over Lilli's mouth as she stretches her arms out for me, tears leaving white streaks along the black ash on her face. "Don't say a word. Stay put," I mouth to my children, praying they understand what I'm trying to tell them. Max acknowledges me with a long blink then lowers his head. Thank God. Jordanna's tears follow, her head shaking back and forth, furious and pleading with her eyes for us not to leave.

If there's anything I've been firm about these past few years, it's that the children should always be with either Leo or myself, no exceptions. From our apartment windows, we've seen members of the Gestapo snag unaccompanied children wearing their yellow Star-of-David badges. They've thrown them into lorries, taking them away without warning. There are few Jewish families left in Hamburg now. We're an exception and that privilege can be taken away at any given moment.

I'm grateful the children don't have yellow stars sewn to

their pajamas. Covered in black ash from head to toe, there's no visible way to identify them. However, that doesn't mean much, knowing the Gestapo's capabilities. If they were to find out the children belong to us and are here alone, the privilege Leo has held on to for his military service won't protect them. Most Jewish citizens don't have a moment to explain why they should be treated differently than any other Jewish person in this country. Jews are not wanted here.

I mouth the words, "I love you," knowing it's not enough to keep them alive. I need to shelter my children. The last thing I want to do is go with these mongrels, but if I argue with them, they'll surely realize it's because I want to stay and protect my children. It won't take them long to deduce the children sitting in the corner without adults belong to us. We'll all end up with a target on our heads.

Max and Alfie stare at me with hollow eyes. Max loses a tear and Alfie seems to be losing the last bit of hope he was desperately holding on to. My heart aches, sobs burn my throat, and I try my hardest to swallow the pain because I cannot let these Gestapo suspect I'm leaving anything behind.

This decision is the only one that will protect them right now.

But what if I'm wrong? I could have just unknowingly abandoned them or left them in the hands of more Gestapo. Fear burns in my stomach as I begin to follow the Gestapo up the stairs of the bunker. And as I reach the top, I know it was a mistake.

The two Gestapo step to the side to carry out a silent conversation, leaving Leo and I here waiting and contemplating what's to come for us and the children. The door to the bunker closes and I jump at the echoing clatter.

"I have to go back for them," I utter beneath my breath.

"Sweetheart..." Leo replies in a hush.

I swallow against the dry ashes in my throat before speaking out. "Excuse—I've—I—uh, I've forgotten something in the bunker. May I—" I plead to the two Gestapo across the short distance between us.

One of the men twists his head to the side before taking his time to turn around and stare at me as if I've cursed him rather than ask a simple question. "You forgot something, did you? The four children with tears in their eyes as we took their mama and papa from them?" he scoffs, mocking me.

"They need us. They should be with us. You understand that, don't you?" I ask through chokes and gasps.

The Gestapo is still staring at me without an answer written on his face, then whistles and holds his hand in the air, signaling to someone behind us. "The bunker," the Gestapo says, nodding toward the door we walked out of a moment ago. "Grab the four children from down there."

"Yes, herr," the man replies before his footsteps clunk toward the door.

"Is he bringing them to us," I ask, the words shooting out of me like bullets.

The closest Gestapo takes a long stride toward us, narrowing the gap between us. "Bringing who to you?" he says. He's not confused. He's toying with me.

"My—"

The man coughs and then clears his throat. "May I remind you, for every second longer we stand here, more people are dying. That will be your fault," he says, narrowing his eyes at me.

"But my—my—" I cough too, so hard it feels like knives scraping down my throat.

"We don't have time for this. Not another word from you. And I won't warn you again." He steps behind us and presses his fists into mine and Leo's backs, shoving us forward.

My heart stutters in my chest as I swing my head over my

shoulder, watching another Gestapo reach for the door to the bunker. No, no! *Don't take them. I can't just keep walking not knowing what they might do with them.*

"No! Wait!" I shout at the Gestapo pushing us along.

At least, I think I do. I can't hear anything above my heartbeat pounding in my ears...

ONE
JORDANNA

Eighteen Months Prior

I wish these pretty wallpapered walls—blush-pink with cheerful white flowers in my bedroom blocked out more sound. I've pinned up drawings and clippings from magazines to add another layer of padding, but nothing works. I'm truly fortunate to not share a room with my brother, Max, but that doesn't mean I want to hear him and his friend, Alfie, endlessly talking about a girl from their private Sunday school class. Max, who is only two years older than me and has never even had a girl-friend, is giving Alfie advice. How can he possibly give advice when he doesn't know anything himself? Maybe they've simply run out of things to talk about since Alfie is here all the time.

"Just tell her you think she's beautiful and ask her to go to the theater next Friday night. Perhaps she has a friend, and I could join you," I hear Max say, his voice full of excitement.

"Jordanna." Lilli, the littlest of us Bergmann children, says my name as if it's a statement rather than the start of a question. She's perched up against two pillows on her bed across the room, combing her porcelain doll's deep brown hair. The doll resembles Lilli and I, with her big brown eyes and long dark lashes, pale complexion, and rosy cheeks. Lilli brushes that doll's hair so often, I wonder how the doll still has any hair.

"Yes?"

"Why do you always look so grouchy when Max and Alfie are playing and laughing?"

Lilli is six and wouldn't understand why the constant noise coming from Max's room bothers me. "I'm not grouchy. It's just hard to think when they're so loud."

"Then why do you always smile so big when Alfie is in our room being silly?"

"What are you talking about?" I ask, my cheeks burning hot.

"That." Lilli giggles. "Your cheeks turn red whenever he's talking to you."

"That's nonsense."

"Well, don't you know how to kiss?" Max's voice booms through the wall.

That's it. I roll off my bed and stomp through our bedroom, into the hallway and up to Max's closed door, then knock.

"What is it?" Max asks between rolls of laughter.

I push the door open, finding Max sitting on the edge of his bed and Alfie on his wooden writing desk chair, holding one of Max's old teddy bears in his hand. They're both laughing so hard I don't know how they can breathe.

"It's after eight. I'm tired and I don't want to listen to your noise anymore," I say. "Are you showing Alfie how to kiss a bear?" My question is meant to sound humorous, but I don't think it comes out that way.

Alfie's thick, chocolate brown hair falls to the side of his forehead as his gaze finds the teddy bear. With a brief glance back at me, he tosses the old stuffed animal onto Max's bed. "I should get home anyway," he says. "My father said I had to get up early tomorrow to go down to the emigration office with him and my mother."

"Emigration?" I ask. "What for?"

"The same reason hundreds of others line up there every day," Max says, standing up from his bed and walking toward me. He gives me a brotherly look, the one where his eyes grow wide. Then he mouths the word, "Stop." Max rests his hand on the doorknob while staring down at me, waiting for me to step out of his room. How can any of us leave Hamburg? All I can think about is Alfie and his family planning to leave Germany. They can't leave. I'd never see Alfie again. I shouldn't have come storming in here like a thunder cloud. I don't want Alfie to leave. Max could be quieter and that would be fine, but I don't mind listening to Alfie laugh. "We'll keep it down until he leaves. Sorry for disturbing you."

In the past, I might argue to stay, just to be the annoying younger sister he claims me to be so often, but my stomach hurts, and my heart is pounding hard. I might cry. I back away and Max closes his door. *He can't leave.*

I'm about to return to my bedroom when I hear Papa's low voice coming from the family room. I tiptoe down the hallway, stepping over the one creaking wooden floor plank and press my body flush against the wall to listen in on their conversation.

"I understand those aren't the exact words he used, but he said the topic has been very secretive," Papa says, his voice a quiet hush.

I know better than to eavesdrop after all, it didn't help me just now with Max and Alfie but if I don't, I'll never know what's going on because Mama would prefer to keep the evils of the world a mystery to us.

"Then what are we supposed to believe?" Mama asks.

Papa exhales heavily and clears his throat. "Well, he also mentioned a report that was released in Minden recently, outlining the process of deporting Jews to Warsaw in cattle cars where they're then sent to work in factories. And if they can't work—if they're old or ill—"

"If they're old or ill...then what?" Mama replies, her words pinched.

Papa clears his throat again, a tell-tale sign that he doesn't want to say anything else. I don't think I want to hear anything more either. I knew I would have been better off not listening, but it's too late now. "The report stated they're shot if they aren't capable of working."

"This is already happening here then. How can you be sure we have nothing to worry about? What are we going to do? We can't just sit here and wait for this to happen to us..."

There's a moment of silence and my muscles tense, waiting to hear what Papa thinks.

"Dalia, I understand this relentless fear of the unknown. I feel it too, but my former deputy officer reassured me just today that my—I mean, our immunity to the Jewish deportations is still in place. I'm a decorated war veteran who fought for this country, Jewish or not, and I'm a descendant of a mixed marriage. Both of those statuses will protect us."

Mama explained the mixed ancestry Nuremberg Laws to me with a visual chart not long ago, showing what grade-level of Judaism our family is since different laws apply to different grades. She said Papa is half Jewish, but since he married her, who has two Jewish parents, his status is no longer considered mixed, only Jewish. Then the three of us were born with seventy-five percent Jewish blood, which makes our entire family Jewish, plain and simple. I don't think Papa really has any form of protection because his parents come from a mixed marriage...

"Leo, you know that isn't true. We as a family are Jewish."

Papa huffs with frustration. "I know. I'm clutching at straws, but we *can* rely on my immunity from the Great War, though."

"How long before the rest of the Jewish people in our

community are taken away in cattle cars too?" Mama asks, her voice shaky.

"Darling, my focus is on you and the children, as selfish as it might sound. You are all more than enough to worry about right now. It's hard to predict how horrifying things might become here for others. It's a terrifying thought and I'm sorry, but we must keep our heads down, follow the rules, and pray it's enough to keep us all well."

Pray it's enough? Papa has never relied on prayer. He stands by facts as he's said many times throughout my life.

"We mustn't tell the children any of this. It will only scare them," Mama says.

"Avoidance won't help. They need to understand the reality of what's happening around them. They know they've been home-schooled for years instead of attending public school because they're Jewish. The truth is only becoming more unavoidable."

Mama sniffles. "I'm their mother. I want to shield them from it all, and instead I feel as though I'm keeping them held up like prisoners in this apartment. Jordanna is missing out on her adolescent years and striding right into becoming a home-maker next to me. I want more for her. She's so brilliant and strong, and it breaks my heart knowing the restraints are only going to get tighter for her."

"She's like you. Her strength will carry her through this until the end," Papa says.

With a scoff, Mama responds, "What exactly *is* the end, Leo?" A clap against the sofa is Mama's telltale sign of anger. She always slaps the sofa to punctuate her question before her heels clunk heavily against the floor.

I hurry back to my bedroom, knowing she might rush off to her bedroom. I close myself inside, finding Lilli asleep with her doll pinned beneath her arm and the hairbrush on the floor. I pull her covers up over her nightgown and turn off the dim lamp, leaving me in the dark with nothing but terrifying thoughts of cattle cars, forced labor, and people being shot turning over in my head.

TWO

DALIA

The rhythmic claps of boots echoes through the streets, an unceasing fear filling our day from dawn until dusk. From the window of our apartment, we watch the Gestapo patrol in every direction, their dark uniforms in line with the dismal mood of the city. Each of the men carries a neat stack of folded letters—all fluttering like trapped feathers in their gloved hands. Thudding footsteps pound up the stairwell of our building, shuddering the hanging framed portraits on our walls. This is our home, and it can be taken from us in an instant. All our memories live here with us, first steps, first words, and celebrations. It's as if we're watching a terrifying show at the theater, wanting to only peek through the slits of our fingers, fearing what might jump out at us next. Except, we're not in a theater and our hands won't be enough to protect us.

I sit with Jordanna by my side, both of us unnerved, straining to hear which door they'll stop at next. We've been trying to find out what this sudden increase of activity means, but our mirroring silence says it all. I should tell her everything will be all right, but she knows when I'm not being honest. She's only fourteen but as of late, I see her as more of an equal than a child. She's my closest friend, and acts, talks, and looks just like me. People have asked us if we're sisters, which she doesn't find to be a compliment as much as I do. I know her thoughts as well as my own and I hate that she knows mine the same, because I'm terrified.

I didn't question the hushed intelligence Leo received from his former deputy officer this past January, but for the last six months, I've been convincing myself that the rumored agenda to eradicate all Jewish people from Europe is implausible, despite the deputy officer's warning. It's hard to imagine a harsher brutalization than what we're already experiencing.

I wish that was still the case.

"Wouldn't they have knocked on our door by now if they needed to give us something, Mama?" she says.

They're still walking around outside and aren't through with whatever they're doing. "You're right," I tell her.

"Papa and Max will be home soon. They'll realize what's happening," she says in a whisper as Lilli joins us in the family room with her doll clenched beneath her arm.

"What are you watching out the window?" she asks.

"Nothing, just the clouds rolling in," Jordanna says, joining Lilli on the couch. "I thought you had braided your doll's hair. Why'd you take it out?"

Lilli shrugs as a hint of contemplation lines her beautiful face. I can't imagine what she must be thinking. She doesn't understand much of what's going on around us: the new laws of marking all our clothes with a yellow Star of David and the word "Jude"...she thinks are pretty decorations. I've made excuses for why we can't use public transportation or visit parks, and she's already been watching Max and Jordanna learn from a tutor in our home rather than going to school. The curfews don't affect her, but the food shortage does. Each time she asks for a particular meal I can't provide, my heart breaks a little more. All the while, Max and Leo are working through physical labor at the factory for no pay.

We're surviving off what little savings we have left, a thought that constantly gnaws at me like a nagging hunger. Every night I fall asleep wondering how much longer we can hide the truth from our children. And yet, every day we come closer to the edge of a cliff we're nearly promised to be pushed over.

A knock at our door sends my heart leaping into my throat. I clutch my pearl necklace, feeling its familiar coolness against my neck, but it doesn't offer me any comfort, just a reminder of what I could easily lose. My voice shakes as I force the words out of my mouth: "Girls, go to your room and shut the door." I listen for the sound of their footsteps, holding my breath as I wait to hear they're secure in their bedroom. Every step toward the door feels as if I'm walking through thick mud; my body heavy with fear. I'm supposed to be resilient, but I don't know how much longer I can be.

"Mama," Jordanna says.

"Go, now," I say, wishing more than anything I could keep her by my side for a sense of comfort.

Jordanna takes Lilli's hand, tugging her from the couch while keeping her eyes pinned to mine.

I force a smile I'm sure she can see through. "I'll handle everything. No need to worry."

My throat tightens and my chest constricts as I approach the door as another knock follows. With a shaky hand, I unlatch the lock and open the door. A chill of sweat coats my face as I come face to face with the Feinstein family. They're all standing before me, paler than I've ever seen them. Our old friends, Miriam and Ezra, are shaking, and Alfie stands behind his parents, wide-eyed and perplexed.

"Come in, come in," I tell them, reminding myself to take a breath.

I usher them inside and close the door. "We're so sorry to barge in on you like this," Ezra says. "We were wondering if you received a notice today, as well?"

Miriam presses her fingers to her lips as tears well in her eyes.

"No, not yet at least. Have you?" My words are chalky, stuck in my throat.

Ezra pulls a paper from the inside of his coat pocket and hands it over to me. I struggle to separate the folded pieces, trying to steady my hands before reading the typed text:

Geheime Staatspolizei

Hamburg, 8th of July 1942

To: Jüdische Familie Feinstein

By order of the Reich,

You must vacate your apartment at Kanalplatz straße four by the 11th of July 1942 at 17 o'clock. You will report to Hamburg-Tiefstack rail station for resettlement.

One suitcase per person will be allowed, holding only necessary clothing and personal items. All other possessions are to be left behind and considered property of the Reich.

Failure to follow this order will result in arrest and prosecution.

By authority of:

Obersturmbannführer Wilhem Richter

I've read the letter twice, but the words float around in my head, illogical in any sense—or my mind is refusing to understand the truth. My hands tremble so viciously that the paper wrinkles and twists in my grasp. "This can't be," I whisper, but my voice falters, giving away the terror coursing through me. All of us are useless, powerless, and there's nothing more unbearable to accept right now.

A key jangles in the front door lock, followed by Leo and Max stepping inside, both hesitating, wide-eyed, upon noticing the Feinstein family in our apartment. Leo recovers swiftly and composes himself. "I wasn't expecting to see you tonight. What a pleasant surprise," Leo says to them.

I attempt to be inconspicuous as I shake my head at my husband, wanting to warn him they aren't here on happy terms.

"Dear, the Feinsteins received an unthinkable notice today," I say.

Leo spots the paper in my hand and gently slides it out from between my fingers to read. I want to tell Max to stop peering over his father's shoulder, but he's the same height and it's hard to stop him from doing anything he wants now that he's almost an adult.

"No, they can't—they can't leave," Max grunts. "The emigration office denied them visas six months ago, holding them hostage here. They can't just send them away with less than three days' warning now. We have to do something. Papa, there must be something, right?"

"Max," Alfie says. "As Jews, you're aware we can't fight the Reich. We mean nothing to them."

If we don't receive a notice today, it's only due to our immunity from Leo's work in the last war, despite how often I've questioned the reliability of a promise never written on paper.

Leo paces, his nervous amble back and forth as he clutches the back of his neck.

"I couldn't help overhearing," Jordanna says, peeking around the corner. "We must help them. Max is right."

The sight of Jordanna's tears is like a dagger against my chest, knowing how much she has already endured just for being a Jewish girl in this country. How much more of her innocence will she be forced to give up? I want to protect her and pull her into my arms. Even still, I know my embrace isn't strong enough to protect her from the horrors of our reality. My personal feeling of helplessness is so clearly reflected in her eyes. This isn't fair.

"There's nothing that can be done," Miriam says despondently. "No one can fight this."

I stand frozen in place, my heart ripping at the seams while I watch Max gasp for a breath, staring at his best friend who has been by his side most of his life. And Jordanna, who has secretly been in love with Alfie since she was old enough to notice that spark inside of her chest, but hasn't noticed his lingering gazes at her when she walks past him. My motherly instinct has always told me those two would end up together someday. Now, I don't know what to think. The thought of young broken hearts adds to the misery of knowing how little control we have over our lives. All I can think is that I'm failing everyone by not having the right thing to say, or offering a solution, especially my children who are staring at me now with heartbreak in their eyes.

"You can all stay with us," Leo says. "I don't know how long we have before we'll receive a notice too, but until then, you will stay here."

Ezra shakes his head. "No, no. That's impossible. If we don't show, they'll find and arrest us all."

"What about Alfie? He could stay, couldn't he?" Jordanna asks. "His name wouldn't be on the apartment registration, right?"

The Reich has access to far more information than most of us could imagine.

Ezra and Miriam stare at each other, sharing a look I can't decipher. The air within the apartment has become stale with all of us breathing so hard, coming to understand there isn't one right answer.

Miriam presses her hands against her chest. "I suppose Alfie could stay. We'll tell them we don't have a son and their records are incorrect," she says through a sob.

"I have connections through—uh—through an old comrade that might be able to help me obtain new papers for him. If I'm able to, we could switch Alfie's last name to ours. I'll see what I can do as quickly as I can," Leo says.

Alfie hasn't had a word of say in the matter and he's left staring back and forth between his two devastated parents. "How will I find you?"

"We will find you when it's safe," Miriam tells him, grabbing his chin between her fingertips. "You are our world, and we will write to you every single day, telling you we're doing well. My heart says you'll be safer here with the Bergmann family."

I can still picture Max at ten or eleven, begging both Miriam and me to let Alfie sleep over for the night, pleading with his hands pressed together. Alfie would do the same at their house the next weekend. Neither of the boys is pleading for anything right now, because no one knows what's safe.

THREE
JORDANNA
JULY 27TH, 1943 – HAMBURG, GERMANY

I stretch my feet up the length of my pink walls, my head hanging backward off the side of my bed, thinking about the fact it's been an entire year since the Gestapo handed out hundreds of deportation letters in just our community, Alfie's parents included.

I stare at Lilli, belly down on the ground, her feet swaying from side to side as she draws a picture with one red crayon. Mama has suggested I find a hobby too, take up knitting, writing, drawing, reading, or just anything really to occupy my time —the endless minutes we all wait for the war to come to a close. It's already been four years. I want to live beyond the walls of this apartment, experience a life without so many laws, where we're not afraid to walk outside. Nothing can distract me from knowing how much we're all missing out on.

This excruciatingly hot July marks one year since Alfie's parents were forced out of their home and made to face the decision to leave their son behind. We all thought the move would only be for a short time, but that hasn't been the case.

"Jordanna, I asked you to sweep the floors before your papa

and Max get home," Mama calls out from the kitchen, her voice ringing down the hallway.

My feet slide to the right, landing on my bed and I roll off the side, forcing myself upright then down to the family room where the broom awaits. No one comes to visit us anymore and I don't know if Papa or Max notice that the floors are clean after working in a factory all day, but Mama wants to keep our life within our space the same as it's always been, with the addition of Alfie, of course.

I'm unsure if there are any other Jewish families left in this city now, and if there are, they live as discreetly as we do. We hardly ever leave the apartment. If we do, we're forced to walk around with the Star of David branded to our clothes and Mama says any unnecessary public appearance is just asking for trouble.

I grab the broom and start to sweep. The smooth swish of the bristles gliding over the floor hardly form a pile worth brushing into a dustpan. *If the Nazis come for us, our apartment will be spotless.* Mama wouldn't appreciate that thought, but it's true.

What if life stays this way forever? We'll be left just watching life exist from the inside of our windows. Other non-Jewish citizens carry on as normal. Despite the country-wide food rations and financial burdens, they still walk around freely without fear of the Gestapo stopping them for questioning and proof of identification. They go to the theater, swim in the canals, visit friends, and wait out the war in the company of others. It isn't fair.

I still thank God every day that we have a roof over our heads and have enough food to survive thanks to Papa's connections at work, but we're simply helpless in the middle of a war— at least that's what I've heard Mama tell Papa more than a few times these past months.

It's hard to distract myself from wondering when things will finally change. Either our luck will run out or the war will end. If the war ends and Germany comes out on top, there will be no one left to protect the Jewish German residents from the Fuhrer pursuing German racial purity of the Aryan race anyway. And if Germany were to lose the war, the Jewish people will be the ones to blame again, just as we were after the First World War. The antisemitism will only become worse here. I'm unsure if there is a third option that would somehow give us our lives back.

But maybe everything will just turn out for the best. Alfie's parents will return, hatred will disappear once and for all, and I can live as a normal teenage girl. My days of sweeping might turn into dancing around a ballroom. Alfie would ask me to dance, perhaps. I wonder if he knows how to dance...I imagine he does.

"Perhaps you'd like to kiss the broom now," Alfie says, walking past me with a snicker. He pauses to peer over his shoulder at me, his hair flopping to the side of his forehead—a gesture that makes me suppress a drawling sigh. Then he sticks his tongue out at me, reminding me that I'm just Max's little sister to him.

My face burns with embarrassment, as usual, which has been hard to hide while he's been living with us. I can't let anyone know about my feelings for Alfie, especially Alfie. I'm sure he's already uncomfortable living here without his parents as it is. I wouldn't want to make the situation worse for him.

I grumble and pull a handkerchief out of my pocket to dab across my face, neck, and arms—the sweltering sticky heat and Alfie's tease bringing me back to reality. The hot temperatures seem never-ending and it's impossible to do much, even sleep. Mama said distractions are the best way to ignore the heat, so she's been playing the most romantic, classical music on the phonograph all day. It worked; I was distracted, but now I'm not.

"How dare you make fun of me," I scold Alfie. "I don't see you tending to chores, and the toilet desperately needs a good cleaning."

"Jordanna," Mama snaps from the kitchen. "Alfie isn't responsible for cleaning the toilet. He just finished ironing a pile of linen for me. That's enough."

Alfie isn't responsible for as much as I am around here since he's just our "guest."

And of course, Lilli is still seen as the baby of the family, even at eight, and has yet to pick up a broom. Mama doesn't have her do much of anything aside from making her bed and tidying up after her pretend tea parties. While Max and Papa work at the factory all day, Mama and I tend to the apartment and care for the others.

The heat is getting to me. Usually, I'm not so sour.

"Has the post come today?" Alfie asks Mama as he turns into the kitchen nook around the wall that separates the two main living spaces.

Mama pauses before responding. I think she's trying to find the strength to keep giving him the same old painful answer. "I'm sorry, sweetie, nothing came for you today."

Alfie steps back out of the kitchen, teetering between the separated rooms. He can see us both now, but he's still focusing on Mama. His shoulders fall and he presses a smile onto his lips. "No, no, it's all right. You don't have to be sorry," he says, his voice pinched with disappointment.

A twinge of pain flutters through my heart, the same feeling I always get when I hear him ask if there are any letters for him. He never complains, just relentlessly holds on to hope while wondering if his parents are still well. They promised to write to him every day, but he hasn't received one letter from them this whole time.

I can't help but wonder where they were sent and the real reason they haven't written to him. I've overheard Mama and

Papa talking about rumors of Jewish people being sent to ghettos and labor camps as a form of punishment, but they never talk about what that actually means.

The only reason we haven't been forced to resettle is because Papa's former deputy officer from the army was able to convince a higher power of the Reich to grant us immunity from deportation. So long as Papa continues his labor work at the factory, supplying ammunition to the army, he said we should be safe.

Alfie twists on his heels to return down the hall toward the bedrooms but stops and turns back to face Mama. "Actually, may I help you prepare dinner?" he asks her.

The clinking of the ceramic casserole top shimmying into the grooves of the dish seems to answer for her. "That's very kind of you to offer, but I'm just about done and only have to slide the casserole into the oven."

"Of course. I'll see if Lilli has any space at her tea party for me today. Yesterday, she told me I would need to leave my name, and she would send for me if room became available."

I stifle a laugh; grateful my little sister is turning out to be just like me. She can be a royal pain much of the time, but these moments outshine the rest.

"She couldn't have put you on a waiting list," Mama says following a gasp, comically stunned.

"It isn't the first time, I'm afraid," Alfie says with a sigh, sounding defeated by an eight-year-old little girl.

The two of them laugh, followed by Mama releasing a heavy sigh. "I don't know what I'm going to do with my little Lilli."

Alfie holds his hands out to the side. "Oh, I say just let her think she has all the power in the world," he says.

His statement hits me like a dense patch of fog. He's right. Soon she'll understand the world she's living in—the one where we have little to no say or power over our lives, never mind the fact that we're a Polish Jewish family living in Germany.

Alfie travels back through the main living room, scuffing his socks against the worn wood where I'm still mindlessly sweeping a spotless floor. He stops, spins around and points to a spot on the floor in front of the coffee table. "It seems you've missed a spot," he says with a chuckle and wink, causing sparks in my belly.

I release a quiet hum as he closes himself into the room that he and Max share.

It isn't long before the heavy thud of boots vibrates the walls around me. I know the rhythm of their footsteps, almost in sync, but not exactly. Papa and Max are home earlier than usual. I can't imagine working in a factory in this heat. They must be sick.

They walk in through the front door, their shoulders heavy, knees bent, hair soaked and cheeks burning red. "I'll get you glasses of water," I say, dropping the broom against the wall and rushing to the kitchen to fill a pitcher of water.

Mama passes me, wiping her hands on a dishrag as she tends to Papa and Max. "You poor things. Sit, sit. How about some damp rags?"

"We'll be all right, Mama," Max says.

Papa doesn't say the same.

I pass Mama once again as she returns to the kitchen for rags as I bring them water, the tin pitcher and glasses clattering in my overfilled hands. I place everything down in front of them on the oak coffee table. "Can I get you anything else?"

"No, no, darling. We're fine," Papa says. "Come." He holds his arm out to the side, over the arm of the sofa, and I run to give him a hug and a kiss. Papa presses a kiss to my cheek and the heat from his body swelters over me. He reeks of burnt rubber, sweat, and nicotine. I'm sure Max isn't much better.

Mama returns with wet rags, placing the first over Max's head, despite him refusing it a moment ago, then Papa's.

"It isn't healthy to be working in this kind of heat. I don't know how you two even made it home in one piece," she says.

"Dalia, have you listened to any broadcasts today?" Papa asks, brushing off the topic of a hot factory.

She shakes her head. "We've had records playing to—"

"Yes, I know..." he says, not allowing her to finish her statement explaining why she's been distracting us.

"What were the broadcasts about?" I ask. I thought the music was to distract us from the heat.

"Jordanna, sweetheart, could I have a word with your mama for a moment?" Papa asks.

"Well, how about Max? Does he get to stay and listen?"

"Jordanna," Mama says, her voice stern and also full of concern. "Go to your room, please."

He's only two years older than me. Why is he treated as an adult and me as a child? It's not fair.

I make my way toward my bedroom down the hall, slowing my pace once I'm out of their sight and around the hallway wall.

"The firecrackers we saw on Saturday and Sunday night, the whistles—"

"The western part of Alster Lake is in ruins. The Brits and Americans have already obliterated the industrial side of Hamburg," Max says. "Entire buildings and city blocks are in ruins. There was talk today that many of the residents who made it out of the fires are fleeing in our direction for safety."

"Max," Papa says. "Lower your voice, son."

Mama gasps, but the sound is muffled. "Well, we must be safe here if others are heading in our direction, yes?" she asks. I can tell she just wants to believe it. She has a point, though.

"The city's gauleiter declared a state of major catastrophe on Sunday morning. So, moving the residents in this direction must be a part of that plan. I prefer to assume it's safer here. One can never be too sure, though," Papa says.

I continue down the hallway into the bedroom I share with Lilli, finding Alfie patiently waiting for her attention on the desk chair between our beds. "Have you seen a goblin?" she asks from a spot on the floor she's sprawled out on between our beds.

"A goblin?" I reply, closing our door slowly, hoping to avoid making the hinges whine too loudly. There's a fine art to eaves-dropping, and though it's my worst habit, I can't get myself to stop. I just want to know what's happening outside of this building.

"You look as though you've seen a goblin," she repeats.

"No. There are no such things as goblins," I remind her.

"Why do you look so scared then?"

"I'm not," I reply.

She shrugs and returns to her game of jacks and bounces the small rubber ball, causing a clatter between the porcelain tea set she's yet to clean up. "Lilli, you're going to break your cups. Why don't you take a break and have some tea with Alfie. It seems he's been patiently waiting quite a while."

She flips her long dark braids, tied off with red ribbons, behind her shoulders. "No, not yet," she says with a sigh.

I wonder if the people of Western Hamburg will try to live with us. Where will they all go here? Surely people can't just sleep on the streets.

"Did something happen?" Alfie asks, staring at me as if he's trying to read the thoughts inside my head. But when Lilli stares up at him with a curious squint, he clears his throat. "Never mind."

I swallow the lump in my throat while trying to make something up. "It's nothing," I tell him. "Max was fooling around at the factory today. They're giving him a lecture." I lift my brows, hinting to him that there's more to say, but not now in front of Lilli.

Alfie stands from the chair and makes his way toward me. "Well, what was he caught doing?" He must not have noticed my gesture, hinting at making up a story. Or he does and wants me to make up more.

"Uh—he was, um—reading a bulletin instead of working. He read some nonsense and stirred up a commotion among the other workers."

"Nonsense..." Alfie repeats, but not as a question.

"About a fireworks show that upset villagers who were trying to sleep."

I don't know if my made-up story is making much sense to Alfie. The creasing lines between his eyebrows tell me he is confused.

"How did you learn all of this?" he asks.

I stare at him for a long moment, knowing he knows I have a tendency to eavesdrop. He's caught me before. "I—I just over-heard on my way to my room."

"Hmm," he says, his gaze floating up to the ceiling as if lost in thought. Then his eyebrows do that thing again where they crinkle. When he breaks his stare from the ceiling and looks back at me, he presses his hands against the sides of my arms and whispers, "That must be why your mother was playing records all day." I can hardly breathe from his touch, or from the fact that he's reading between the words of my story and still putting the pieces of truth together. It's too much to wrap my head around.

He's right, though. Sirens must have been blaring in the distance all day. Mama tries to drown out the noise when possi-ble. They occur so often it's impossible to always avoid.

"Sir Alfie, I have decided you may have some tea now," Lilli says. Alfie doesn't respond right away, but he steps away from me and folds his hands around the back of his neck as he walks toward the window, covered by thick drapes. "You know, it isn't polite to refuse tea."

Alfie shakes away his heavy thoughts and turns back to face Lilli, clears his throat and prepares a suitable response for the princess. "Accept my apologies, Fraulein Lilli," Alfie says with a curt bow as he flashes me a glance. The passing look causing a flurry of heat through my body. Alfie shrugs to the ground, leaning against Lilli's iron bed frame. He looks silly sitting in front of a little girl's tea set, yet, quite charming at the same time. In any case, Lilli is content and hopefully unaware of what's happening in our city. That's all that should matter right now.

A heavy knock on our front door rumbles through the apartment. "Bulletin!" someone shouts from outside. "Important bulletin! All city water has been poisoned by the enemy! Do not drink the water!"

My heart sinks to the bottom of my stomach, realizing I've just handed a glass of poison to Papa and Max.

FOUR

DALIA

"What in the world is that boy shouting about?" I say, rushing toward the door. He must be terrifying everyone in this building. *Contamination?*

"Don't open the door, dear. Let him be," Leo says, seeming less concerned than I.

Max places his water glass down on the table, the soft clink echoing louder than it should in my ears.

Once the newsboy's voice stops bouncing through the corridor, Leo raises an eyebrow and holds his glass up closer to inspect and I press my hand to my chest, anger consuming me.

"Contaminated water," Leo repeats the warning, then clears his throat before standing up from the sofa.

"How would we know?" I ask. My strained muscles fail me as my wrist shakes and my fingers tremble. We're always waiting on the precipice for more terrible news to hit. This fear lingers like a foul odor, stuck to the walls and ceilings as a constant reminder that we will forever be living in some form of fear and doubt.

"Someone must have gotten sick. It could just be a rumor.

There's no way of knowing for sure. We'll be all right. Let's just boil some drinking water to be safe."

Neither of them had much since being home, but I don't know what they consumed throughout the day.

With a house full of children depending on me, I'm stunned by indecision. Every choice feels as if it's a wager made on their lives. We could run and end up without shelter. By staying, we may become the next target for these endless air raids. The weight of the responsibility weighs on my soul. I'm supposed to protect them, and I don't know if I can.

My heart lodges in my throat, as dread consumes my every thought. "Did you buy a newspaper today?" I ask.

"There's no point, Dalia. You know that. They contain nothing but tales, propaganda, and exaggerations. With that said, there were no attacks last night. The raids could be moving on, but the water might in fact be polluted."

"I'm not certain I believe that," I reply. "How could our well water be affected by the western half of the city?"

"The network of wells can run into each other. It's possible. The attacks were targeting factories and we don't live near any. We should be safe here," Leo says. I can see the uncertainty in his sea-blue eyes as he fidgets with his small compass hanging from a chain on his belt. The compass has always been his source of comfort—a good luck charm of sorts.

"Of course," I say, wrapping my hand around the back of my neck. "Dinner won't be ready for a bit. The two of you should wash up and change into clean clothes. I'll put a pot of water on the stove to boil."

I watch out the window above the faucet in the kitchen, studying the neighbors coming in and out of their apartment building across the road. No one appears concerned, but they may not be aware of what's been happening these last two nights. As Leo said, the newspaper is full of exaggerations.

I peer up toward the sky, noting the cloud coverage hasn't

changed at all today or yesterday. It's been gloomy despite the intense heatwave. Wouldn't we smell smoke here if the west was burning? The sirens have been ringing in the distance but not in our precise region of the city.

Dinner time in our home was once filled with laughter, playful bickering, and the comforting chaos that makes up our family. Tonight, though, everyone is eerily quiet. The clatter of knives and forks against porcelain feels like nails against a chalkboard. The silence otherwise is heavy, a weight sitting on my chest making it hard to swallow my food.

Lilli's pushing around groups of peas on her plate, lining them up one by one along the edge of her heap of potatoes. Jordanna is nibbling, her head leaning against her fist, elbow anchored to the table, and a look of boredom, or spiraling thoughts of concern, masking her face.

Max, Alfie, and Leo can't seem to get the food into their mouths fast enough. I'm forcing food down my throat because I know better than to let a meal go to waste when there's a countrywide shortage. "Girls, you must eat your food," I tell them.

Jordanna stares up at me, and I can tell there is something she doesn't want to speak about at the table. She likely overheard Max talking when he got home or turned a radio on when I wasn't paying attention. She knows how to find information.

"Is the water cool enough to drink?" Lilli asks without shifting her stare from her artwork of peas and potatoes.

"Should be, yes. I'll fill a pitcher." I excuse myself from the table.

"Why did Mama have to boil water before we drink it?" Lilli asks.

No one answers right away. I'm struggling to think of a reason she might understand too.

"With all the airplanes in the sky, some of their fuel floats to the ground and can fall into our well water. It wouldn't taste very good but if we boil the water, it burns away anything nasty that might have fallen into the water," Leo says.

"Oh," her sweet little voice replies.

The apartment isn't large enough to miss the sound of Jordanna sighing in response.

"Papa, is the heat going to stay the same all summer long?" Lilli continues with her usual nightly questions. At least she's bringing the normalcy back to our typical family dinner.

"I'm sure the heat wave will end soon, my little darling."

* * *

An infant's shrill scream in the middle of the night will startle a sleep deprived mother like an electric shock to the heart. I survived those tireless nights three times, and until this past year, had almost forgotten the painful jolt of panic when awoken from a dead sleep.

My eyes flash open as the air-raid siren shatters through the silence, the sound ripping through me like a jagged knife. I gasp, fumbling around our dark bedroom trying to grasp at the darkness around me as I try to determine if it's today, yesterday, or tomorrow until I spot the bedside clock. It's just before midnight. The children have become all too used to the sirens in the middle of the night.

At this hour, I shouldn't be able to so easily spot Leo sitting upright in bed, staring toward the window on his left side. "Dear, what is it?" I ask, my throat dry and scratchy.

He doesn't respond except to hold his index finger up to me as he stumbles out of bed and runs for the window, tearing the drapes apart.

"They've returned. The Allies," Leo says. "Dalia, grab the children. We must go at once."

"Where will we go?" I ask.

"We don't have time for a discussion. Hurry. Hurry, sweetheart!" he shouts. In a frenzy, I grab my thin robe and boots from the closet, the crack and clatter of the wooden floor parting adding a layer of seriousness to the moment. Leo snatches his compass from his nightstand then collects our family papers from beneath the bed.

I open the door, finding Max with Lilli in his arms, Alfie in his shadow, and Jordanna slipping her arms through her matching robe to mine. "Put your boots on quickly, all of you," I say, trying to balance myself against the wall while slipping mine on.

"What's happening?" Jordanna cries out as Leo rushes past her to collect their boots from their bedrooms.

"Here we go," he says, handing them each their boots. "We have to move."

"I'm scared," Lilli whimpers, nuzzling her face against Max's neck.

"They've returned for another round, haven't they?" Alfie asks, the fear in his voice ever so present despite what he's been through this past year. We didn't realize how much he knew of what was happening in Hamburg the last few days but maybe we should have been more forthcoming.

"We must leave at once. Everyone get to the door," Leo shouts. We haven't made it out of the apartment building when the ground beneath us begins to shake, throwing us off balance. We step outside, blinded by flames roaring around us, licking at the black sky. The air is thick with smoke, stinging my eyes, nose and throat. My senses are suffocating and all I can think about is the children—keeping them close and safe. I need to shield them, but even with my body in front of theirs, I'm powerless against the wrath of our world burning before us. The mass of destruction takes more of my breath away.

"Let's head for the canal," Leo shouts, coughing against the infiltrating smoke. "We'll wade through the water until I can spot a bunker with a clear path." He charges ahead, sure of his plan, as always. Except Leo would never suggest us stepping foot into a bunker as a family of Jews. Maybe no one will know us; who we are. I have faith Leo knows what he's doing. He spends his life preparing for catastrophes, or so it seems. A soldier is never truly at rest, he's told me before. I thought it was from the nightmares of blood and gore, but I realize now, it's to prepare for whatever might come our way.

Thick smoke wafts around us. The chemical smell of melting tar, and the acrid whiff of fuel mixed with burning wood burns my nostrils and throat. Up ahead, a plume of fire drops from the sky. A second doesn't pass before the ground rumbles at the same moment winds howl in a vortex surrounding us. The sirens are mute in comparison. With the smoke growing closer, blocking our visibility, Leo wraps his arms around me and Jordanna then pulls us to his left side. Max hoists Lilli up on his right hip and grabs a hold of my arm with his free hand as Alfie clings closely to his side. We're all running, following Leo as he compulsively checks his compass for direction.

"I can't breathe," Jordanna shouts.

"Hold your robe over your face," Max tells her.

"No, don't! No fabric on your face," Leo grunts. "We're almost to the water." The canal is just two rows of apartments away from us, but the short walk feels much longer when we can't see where we're going.

I wouldn't question my husband, but I can't imagine why we wouldn't cover our faces from the smoke.

Leo stops running and we all crash into his backside as he keeps his arms out to the side. "Halt! Wait here." He skids down a short hill in front of us. It's the drop to the water but smoke is floating over the canal too. "It's boiling," Leo shouts. "This won't work. Napalm. Bloody hell."

Another ball of fire drops from the sky, the flames clearing a way through the smoke just long enough for us to watch it land in the canal.

"What are we going to do?" I ask. A gust of sharp, gritty dirt coats the inside of my mouth, the taste of rust and charcoal coating my tongue.

"Come along. Stay with me." He's breathless, but his determination never wavers.

We are running back toward our apartment. All the children are coughing and choking with each step. The longer and further we run, the more I question how we're still upright with so little air to inhale. I don't know whether to focus on that thought or the bloodcurdling screams in the distance. All I know is, stopping isn't an option.

The smoke hovers overhead as we run between two buildings, one side charred, the other intact.

A scuffle of feet followed by Alfie tripping and catching himself against the asphalt, forcing us to stop. "I'm so sorry," he says.

Not to us, but the person melted against the road, skin black as tar and clothes grafted to bones. Alfie screams, followed by Jordanna and Lilli. We all stand frozen for a moment in horror, the gravity of what we're fleeing weighing us down. Alfie's face is pale, his eyes wide with terror, as if his mind can't process the nightmare unraveling in front of us. A second passes before I reach out and grab his arm. "We have to keep moving," I say firmly, trying to pull him forward. His feet seem stuck to the ground, but he reluctantly begins to move again with heavy, stumbling steps.

Down another row of apartments, we forge on, keeping a grip on one another.

"Where's Alfie?" Max shouts.

We stop and search around our small area of visibility.

"Max!" Alfie shouts, his voice echoing around us.

"Where are you?" I call out.

"Stay here, all of you," Leo says. "Alfie, keep talking so I can find you."

"Leo...Leo," I cry out, pointing to the sky, unable to form any more words or scream.

I push the children to the ground, tossing myself over their bodies. Max fights his way out to wrap his arms over me. "I am your mother, stop it," I shout at him.

A howl blares overhead, crashing with a static burst and the ground trembles beneath us. A high-pitched squeal pierces my ears, shooting in through one and out the other, drowning out all noise. Debris falls over us and I continue to cling my arms over my children, praying Leo and Alfie are all right.

A vortex of heat strikes us from beneath, forcing us all up at once as if we've been lying on hot coal. "Dalia!" Leo screams, his voice muffled and soft.

"I'm here. We're here," I call back. I don't see him anywhere.

From a cloud of smoke his silhouette appears, Alfie with his arm in Leo's hold. "This way. We need to run."

The smoke clears in our path, but it's not clear why. We're able to see more of the street we're running along but also, people burning in flames, screaming through bloodcurdling cries. My tears and cries are silent among the rest. Trees ignite around us, windows explode from the buildings, cars burst into flames. The heat from the gravel is searing through my boots.

Another explosion blasts through the path, dizzying and shoving everyone in a different direction. Flames creep up from up behind, reaching out as if to seize each step, forcing us to run harder and faster.

In the near distance, all I see are black shadowy figures with flames sprouting from their bodies.

With one more turn around a corner, we spot a short line of villagers shoving their way down a set of stone stairs beneath a building. "There. Right there," Leo shouts, "a bunker."

By the time we reach the top of the descending steps, the metal door is closing. Leo throws himself down the stairs and into the door, forcing it back open. "Just six more."

"There's no room," someone shouts.

"Make room," he growls.

We make our way down the dark, narrow stairway, deeper into the ground than I was expecting. I have Jordanna and Max in my grip, knowing Max has Lilli and Leo has Alfie. There's no visibility. There's no telling how large the space is or how many are down here. Faint cries, whimpers, and prayers are all I hear.

"Are you all right?" Leo asks as we reach solid ground in the middle of all these people we may or might not know.

"Yes," Jordanna squeaks.

"I'm scared," Lilli says.

"Everything is fine," Max assures her.

"Yes, sweetheart. We're safe here." I always tell her we're safe, but there's no such thing as safety anywhere in this country.

"Alfie? Where are you?"

"I still have a hold of him," Leo says. "Are you all right?"

Alfie doesn't reply.

"Alfie, sweetie, what's wrong?" I follow Leo's question.

"What's wrong with Alfie?" Jordanna cries out with panic.

Again, he doesn't reply.

FIVE

JORDANNA

JULY 28TH, 1943 – HAMBURG, GERMANY

The Gestapo, in their black, ash covered uniforms and with their threatening demands ripped Mama and Papa away from us just a moment ago. We'd only been down in the bunker a few minutes when they burst in through the door. Now, we've been left with only their cries echoing between the walls before they stepped back into the inferno. The orange flames outside the bunker door dance across the stones lining the top steps and cast a daunting glow over all of us down here.

The air becomes thicker by the second with fumes from burning wood and melting metal. We're all coughing, gasping for air.

"We need to shut the door!" someone shouts.

"I'll handle it," another person says. "Give me a second to cover my face."

They're closing us back in, without Mama and Papa. They might not be able to get back in, and could be stuck outside.

"Don't worry, they'll be back," Max says, trying to calm us down. Lilli continues to cry for our parents though—her emotions are my thoughts, ones I'm trying to keep inside.

"Mama," Lilli continues to cry. My hand grips onto Lilli's,

her small fingers intertwine between mine as her clammy hand trembles.

"We need to be brave right now. They'll be back," I tell my sister.

We are all trying to be brave, but the taste of bitter tears seeps into my mouth. Max knows how to keep his emotions to himself, something he's just managed to learn over the last few years. Alfie, though, he's standing still, staring toward the stairs that lead up to the shelter's exit. His eyes aren't moving—it's as if he's paralyzed by fear. I reach for his arm, grabbing him to pull him back toward the three of us. "We'll find them," I say, gasping for breath.

Alfie doesn't turn to look at me or shift his stare from the steps. It's as if he's turned into stone.

"Alfie, look at me," Max says, grabbing his shoulder, shaking him a bit.

"Why isn't he responding to us?" I ask.

"I don't know," Max says.

I take Alfie's hand. It's burning hot, and tense. I tighten my grip, and he closes his hand around mine. I don't understand what's wrong. "Are you hurt?" I ask him. Still no response.

"Why won't you answer us?" Max asks him again, stepping in front of Alfie, forcing him to look at him.

Alfie swallows hard and searches around the space, his eyes wide as if he's looking for something. The lack of verbal response to Max's question is enough to make me realize something is very wrong.

He pulls his hand from mine, shakes his head and grits his teeth then presses his hands to his ears. He clenches his eyes shut and yanks on his earlobe. His breaths become heavy, and he begins slapping the sides of his head repeatedly.

I clutch my chest, watching in horror, not knowing what's happening. "Stop it!" I tell him. "Alfie!"

Max takes me by the arm and pulls me away, stepping in front of me so Alfie only focuses on him.

"Talk to me. Does something hurt?" Max continues his best efforts to find out what Alfie's going through.

Nothing works. Alfie only glares back at him with an unblinking stare and a look of sheer horror.

Max rests his hands on Alfie's shoulders. "Everything is fine. We're safe here. You have us."

No response.

With frustration coursing through Max, he scratches his fingers through his ash-coated hair and steps away, trying to make sense of everything. He stops short in his step, the rubber of his boot scraping against rubble. I move in toward him to see what's caught his eye and find Papa's robe, which he left behind just before the Gestapo made him leave.

Max throws himself to the ground, thrashing at the fabric before pulling out a rolled-up tube of papers. "Our papers. Papa has left them for us—I think I know what that must mean," Max whispers then swallows so hard, I can hear the gulp. I can see he wants me to read the look on his face and understand what he's thinking, but I don't want to. Papa must not have been sure if he could come back for us. He wouldn't want to leave us without our papers. But I don't want to think that way too. We'll find them. We must.

Max mutters and shoves the rolled-up tube under his waistband then pulls his shirt over it.

The bunker door creaks open, the metal thuds echoing between the walls along the descending steps. Maybe Mama and Papa have returned.

Please. Let it be them.

"You, children," a Gestapo shines a light on us, causing us to recoil and cover our eyes. "You're here without your parents?"

"One of you already took them," Lilli shouts. "I want Mama and Papa."

My heart shatters, knowing Mama and Papa didn't want us to say a word when they left. A cold sweat creeps down the back of my neck as I stare through the blaring light.

"Ah, I see," he says, pulling me up by my arm and dragging me to the stairwell. Max takes Lilli, and Alfie stays close to me, taking my hand back into his—his grasp feels as if *he* needs *me* this time. He's never seemed to need me.

"Our parents will return soon. We should stay here," Max says.

The Gestapo growls and shakes his head. "You're not staying down here. Raus! Get up! Let's go. Up the steps."

"Are you taking us to our parents?" I ask, pleading through every word.

"Halt die Klappe!" he shouts at us.

"Don't say anything else," Max whispers in my ear. "He won't warn you to be quiet again."

Once more, we walk through tunnels of black smoke, unable to see anything on either side of us except each other. Alfie is staring ahead, not once blinking, and Max is carrying Lilli. Alfie squeezes my hand, sending me a signal of the terror he and I are both feeling.

We step over charred bodies, dogs and cats flat as pancakes, and other unrecognizable objects along blocks of cement from collapsed buildings.

Everything in the distance is still burning despite the cease of explosions, but no one is fighting the fires. Even cars are sinking lower toward the ground, the rubber from tires melting like wax. Will we melt too? A sunburn is nothing compared to the searing heat against my skin.

Every muscle in my body aches and my head is foggy. I can't stop coughing, causing a sharp pain in my lungs and I don't know how much further I can walk.

Max pinches his fingernails into my palm. "Keep going. Just keep moving," he whispers.

"Papers!" someone shouts in the distance. "Papers. Show your papers."

How could they care about identification at a time like this? With people charred to pieces on the ground.

Max jerks my hand to the side, but not to get my attention. I turn just in time to watch him whip the rolled tube of papers against a burning car—our identifications are reduced to ash within seconds.

"There's no proof of who we are now," Max mutters.

"Take these children," the Gestapo in front of us calls out. "All of them. Their parents have been put to work."

SIX

DALIA

JULY 28TH, 1943 – HAMBURG, GERMANY

Black raindrops, heavy as tar, fall from the opaque sky ahead as we move farther away from the burning streets. The Gestapo in front of us holds on to a crackling torch—the irony of fire being our only source of light. Above the cries and screams surrounding us as people try to run to safety, all I can hear are the echoes from the Gestapo telling his comrade to collect the children from the bunker.

I've begged with him to let me go back but only to be warned not to say another word. To the two Gestapo, we're nothing more than nagging flies swooping over their shoulders. One is in front of us and the other behind, both with rifles that keep us from running off. We know they won't hesitate to use force. We've witnessed it done to others before.

"I plead of you—tell me where the other officer is taking the children from the bunker," my voice breaks as hot tears sting my eyes.

"Dalia," Leo utters again, just as he did the last few times, taking my arm into his grip.

"We can't leave them! We don't even know where they're taking them," I shout through my ragged breath.

"I know, darling. I'm—trying to find a way—I'm trying."

Leo has asked them to release us just as many times as I have, except he has been able to remain calm and composed. All they're doing is ignoring us. Begging them won't work.

Leo stops walking and puts his hands up in the air. "We can't walk any further until you tell us where the children are," Leo demands.

The Gestapo in front of us comes to an abrupt halt, draws his pistol and aims it at Leo's head. "You didn't worry much about leaving them in the first place—I should assume they mustn't belong to you, yes?" the Gestapo shouts. "Look around you. A soldier of your status wouldn't argue with commands. I assume this isn't an issue for you—" Spit flies from his mouth as he shouts at Leo.

We thought we were protecting them.

"There's no issue," I cry out, afraid of what Leo might say. We're no use to our children if we're dead on the street, and the Gestapo already know we're Jewish. It's best that they don't know the children belong to us—it's our only sliver of hope for them.

"Your wife has more sense than you, Ober-gef-reiter Jude-rattenam," he snarls with a sinister chuckle. "A Jew dumb enough to fight for the German Army. You must think you have some kind of special treatment, don't you? We've heard it all before."

With each syllable, his words pierce the narrow street and tighten around my heart. I always anticipated this day, the day when someone would ridicule Leo's supposed immunity. For years, I've lived in fear, deprived of sleep, hoping we would never have to question the promise made to him.

This officer is too young to have any memory of the Great War. If he did, he'd understand why Leo had no choice. We grew up in a small town near Warsaw, and in 1915, the Germans marched in, claimed our town, and called it theirs.

After years of violent conflict, their manpower dwindled. At just eighteen years old, Leo was conscripted and given a rifle to fight under a foreign flag. The unforeseen consequence was that he was seen as a traitor, collaborating with the occupiers of our homeland. Our once peaceful home became a hostile place, consumed by whispers and threats. Amid indifference, Leo's Army deputy officer emerged as a decent man, guiding us to Hamburg. He assured us of a fresh start, a well-compensated civilian job, and freedom from scrutiny and judgment.

Yet, as I observe the smirk on this officer, I'm left wondering if it was all part of a trap.

The Gestapo shifts the barrel of his pistol to my head, staring at me for what feels like the longest moment of my life. My heart falls to my gut, my body flushes with ice despite the burning of the boiling asphalt gnawing on the rubber of our soles.

I'm afraid to swallow, blink, or breathe. Leo might react. I'm surprised he hasn't already. *Dear God, spare us, spare our children. Bring this war to an end.*

The Gestapo narrows his eyes and drops his weapon by his side. "Move," he snaps, turning around to lead us in the direction we were walking.

I peer over my shoulder in search of any sight of the children but the street behind us is lit by a dark orange glow through the smoke.

It feels as if we've been walking in circles, trying to find the open roads, continuing through the fiery tunnels of the city burning around us. We move across cement blocks of terrain from fallen buildings, camouflaged bodies molded to the crags. It isn't long before agonized screams pull us toward a clearing between burning trees and buildings where so many people are pleading for help. In front of us, the St. Nicholas' Church, a Gothic Revival cathedral and historical symbol of our city, is lit up like a bonfire, burning as if it were made of paper. We aren't far from home, yet I feel as though we're worlds away in this nightmare.

The light from the fire creates spotlights across the incredible damage and destruction, people included.

The Gestapo stops once more and turns to face us. "You," he points at Leo, then me. "Find the living and send them toward the brigade of vehicles off to the right for evacuation. We need to help these people make their way out of here before the entire city burns down."

Those who are still alive are screaming, burning, dying... there's no way we'll be able to help them all.

"What about us?" Leo asks. "We need to be evacuated too." Leo holds his hands up as if asking for peace. His words are careful, calm, and pitiful to any Gestapo.

"What about *you*?" the officer asks, laughing once again. "I thought I made it clear—you're nothing but a Jew. There is no immunity here. Find the living ethnic Germans so we can save our people."

* * *

The rising sun reveals the truth of the devastation. Thick smoke lingers in the air and it's clear that our efforts have only made a small dent in the carnage surrounding us. A numbness has crept through my nerves while I continuously convince myself I'm not in a horrible nightmare. A nightmare that has become a reality I won't ever unsee. Bodies, burned and mangled, cover every square surface of the area. We're surrounded by destruction, with no buildings left standing except the skeleton of St. Nicholas' church.

Exhausted from carrying bodies from one end of the square to the other for hours on end, I can barely muster up the strength to keep moving. My lungs burn with every cloud of smoke I walk through. I can't take much more.

I've watched most of the other residents get evacuated. I heard they're being sent somewhere safe or to a nearby hospital that hasn't been affected by the fires. But there are still some of us here, and it doesn't seem as if we're ever going to be evacuated or rescued—just forced to keep working.

Leo is missing. I last saw him when he was told to assist with some bodies down one of the dark side streets, but he never returned. As the hours drag on, the level of panic ebbs and flows. I keep telling myself he would come back if he could. He would never leave me without warning unless he wasn't given the option... This thought carves a hole into my chest.

Despite the horrific scene of people burning to ash, SS officers are joining the Gestapo, parading around in front of the blackened church, holding handkerchiefs over their noses and mouths. They bark orders at us to continue our grim work of gathering bodies in the center of the clearing.

Each time I peer around, I see men and women covered in ash, some with very little clothing, burns and wounds alike, struggling to follow the orders with what little strength they have left. Another SS officer blows a whistle, communicating silently in a way that strikes us all with fear.

My knees buckle as I go to lift yet another body—a woman left in only her undergarments, her legs and bare feet burnt to the bone, cradling a charred child in her arms. I check her pulse, knowing there won't be one. Tears blur my eyes, and my throat tightens around a shuddering sob as I move behind her. I scoop my arms between hers and drag them across the jagged road toward the other bodies, whispering a quiet prayer for her and her child. "A heroic mother you are, long beyond your final breaths. God bless you," I say, whispering the broken prayer. "I'm so sorry." Tears burn my eyes, mixing with the ash covering my face.

Within minutes another brigade of vehicles pulls into the city square, except no one calls for order or to form a line.

While I'm struggling to understand what's happening, someone takes a hold of my arm and yanks me across the sharp terrain toward the vehicles. "Name?" The question is shouted into my ear.

I try to swallow the lump in my throat before responding. I'm not quick enough and I'm jerked around. "Da-Dalia Bergmann, wife of Obergefreiter Leo Bergmann. We were both brought here, but we must get back to the bunker."

I know better than to speak too much to an SS officer or a Gestapo, but it may be my last chance.

"The bunker is gone, now nothing but a black hole in the ground," the man says with a sneer, peering down at a crumpled paper in his hand. "Jüdin?" he asks.

"Yes, but my husband and I have immunity—" I know that means nothing now, but there's nothing else to say.

"Where is your badge?" he asks, poking me with the end of his torch.

"We were woken from our sleep in the fires," I cry out as he jostles me towards the back of a truck.

"Right. I have another!" he shouts to someone before turning back to me. "There is no immunity for Jews." He spits then grabs me by the arm and throws me into the back of the truck with others piled on parallel benches. After the door slams shut, we're enveloped in darkness once again. This time, it feels suffocatingly final.

Intense hacking and gasps fill the air as we're jostled along on this unforgiving rough ride. My lungs ache with every exhale, expelling the remnants of Hamburg—our home—flattened into ruins and ash, hidden beneath our sorrow. Silent cries are swallowed by the rumble of the engine.

"Where are they taking us?" a woman's voice breaks through, a hoarse whisper, more air than sound. Her words tremble like the wheels beneath us.

"God only knows," someone mutters back, but there is no

comfort to be shared. Just a hollow truth, echoing off the metal walls. Then a voice begins the Hebrew Shema—an ancient prayer. It quivers in her throat, her words faltering.

"*Shema Yisrael, Adonai Eloheinu, Adonai Echad.*"

More voices join in, one after another, until the prayer becomes a soft murmur that unites us. Their lips move with mine, the words barely forming. Is this a plea for peace in our final moments in this world?

My heart beats frantically, desperate for relief. I suddenly understand, with a chilling clarity, that we are all Jewish. Maybe even the last Jews left in the city. That is why we are here, crammed together in this metal containment.

Has Leo already been taken to wherever I'm going? My mind keeps spiraling. Did they drag him away from the square when my back was turned? Or is he out there somewhere looking for the children, and now me?

My babies. I don't know where they are. My God. I've never spent a day without them. They could be screaming for me, trapped like I am, scared and alone. My breath catches in my throat and I choke, spit spewing from my mouth as I claw my way to the ground, trying to climb over legs. "I need to get back to them!" I bellow.

Hands pull me back, preventing me from reaching the back doors of the truck, which block our way out.

"You'll only get yourself killed," one of them says. "Or worse, all of us killed."

I gasp for air, my voice scraping against the soot in my throat. "I need to get out of this truck," I whimper through an unintelligible mutter.

What was the point of it all? Leo's acts of self-sacrifice, the endless hours of factory work, taking in another child, and the constant fear that plagued our sleepless nights—for what? I struggle to hold back tears, clenching my eyes to block out the others around me.

SEVEN

JORDANNA

JULY 28TH, 1943 – HAMBURG, GERMANY

It must be a nightmare. Please, let this all be a nightmare. I want to wake up in my bed to the sound of Mama humming in the hallway, and the scent of fresh bread baking.

A fog of smoke burns my eyelids and I can't move. I blink repeatedly until my vision clears. I'm outside and the heat is still as blisteringly hot as it was yesterday. Even worse, I'm on a woolen blanket, sweating while Lilli's overheating body is curled into a ball under my arm. I sit up, feeling an ache in my ribs. We've been asleep on a road alongside a building, and I don't know what time it is. The clouds are so dark above us. Max is awake, sitting behind me, and Alfie is awake next to him.

"Where are we?" The words bleed out as memories from last night dangle in front of me, just out of reach.

Max places his hand on my shoulder. "We're still within Hamburg. The Gestapo wanted to get us away from the active fires last night. The smoke is just masking everything around us —nothing looks familiar. That's all. The three of you have been asleep for hours since we got here," he says. I remember the Gestapo hollering at us last night while we walked past collapsing buildings and growing fires. It was hard to breathe, and my head was heavy. Everyone stopped walking at once last night and I must have collapsed because I don't remember much more.

I glance around, finding only more children surrounding us on a city block.

"Alfie, are you feeling any better?" My words are nothing but a rasp that causes me to cough up soot. I watch him for a response, hoping the shock or whatever was happening to him last night has worn off.

"He still can't hear anything," Max utters.

"What do you mean?" I ask, keeping my scratchy words quiet so Lilli stays asleep longer.

Max stares at me with mirroring hazelnut eyes to mine. Lilli is the only one of us who ended up with blue eyes like Papa. His lip quivers and he bites down on it, hard. "He, ah—I think—"

"What? What's going on?"

"You remember just before we went into the bunker, when Alfie was separated from us?"

"Yes, of course," I say.

"After you and Lilli fell asleep last night, he tried to talk. He was confused because he couldn't hear what he was saying, but he managed to tell me he thinks he was too close to the explosion that took down the building on the corner. We were just out of range, but he was too close. He said he felt a lot of pressure in his ears. Instead of the air being sucked out, it was pressed in. After that his ears popped like a balloon. Now every sound is very soft and muffled."

Max's explanation sends a wave of nausea through my stomach. As if there wasn't already enough to be terrified of, Alfie's hurt and it's obvious there won't be any medical aid to help him, not with the amount of injured people still scattered along the roads. My chin trembles from the ache in my heart. *I must hold myself together*.

Since I can't move from my spot on the blanket because of

Lilli's position, I twist around as far as I can to see Alfie. The tremble in my chin returns so I bite the inside of my cheeks. He's staring straight out into the road where other children are shuffling around. I lift my hand to get his attention. It can't be permanent. His hearing will come back. It must.

He doesn't look at me, no matter how hard I try to get his attention. I drop my hand to the edge of his knee, and he jolts. The moment his eyes meet mine, tears well, trickling down my cheeks, one at a time, leaving a cool sensation behind.

I press my hand to my heart and mouth the words, "I'm here."

His chin trembles and his nostrils flare. He gasps for air and presses his head back against the building. "He's terrified," Max says.

"Did he tell you that?" I ask as if it's not already obvious from the look on Alfie's face.

"He was confused when he woke up, started talking but realized he couldn't hear himself. He kept talking until he broke down. He kept mumbling that he was scared. I think he had forgotten about his hearing." Or he thought it was all a horrific nightmare just as I did.

Alfie holds his hand up from the cobblestone, just enough for me to see. He tucks his thumb into his palm and straightens his fingers, gesturing a salute. Then, he curls in his fingers, all but one and slides it across his throat.

I don't understand what he's trying to tell us.

"Those with disabilities are not accepted as citizens," Max whispers. "They may not have physical proof that we're Jewish, but it's clear he's deaf."

His words spark an anger that rages through me. I could be fooled into believing a lifetime has passed since the start of this war, and the brutality and hatred only grow worse every single day.

"No one must find out," I seethe.

I reach back to touch Alfie's knee so he'll look at me again. He's sluggish about it, but does. I point at him, then Max, Lilli, and me, then interlock my fingers to show in any way I can that we'll protect him. I cross one wrist over the other and shake my head. I point to him. I need him to understand me. He looks confused.

I search my body for a way to be clearer when I notice soot smeared across my arm. I drag my finger through the thick black dust and spell out the word protect on the stone between us. I point back and forth between Max and me, point to the word, then again at Alfie. I mouth the word: "Always."

Lilli squirms against my lap and presses herself upright. "What's happened?" she asks, her voice squeaky and tired.

"We're staying here where it's safe from the fires," Max tells her.

"What about Mama and Papa?"

Lilli stands up and looks down at her feet, her body covered in black ash. She glances at me and again at Max and Alfie. Her chest bucks in and out and her bottom lip pouts before she begins to cry.

"I'm sure they're fine, Lil. The police needed their help last night. That's all."

Max holds his arms out for Lilli, and she runs to him, dropping herself into his lap. "You're not alone. We're together. Always."

"Now we're like Alfie?" she asks.

I close my eyes, taking in the harshness of her question, the truth neither Max nor I want to assume.

"Not exactly," Max says. "You don't need to worry."

"Alfie, do you think you'll see your Mama and Papa again?" Lilli has never asked Alfie this question. She also doesn't realize he can't hear her, but she's about to find out. "Alfie?"

He doesn't budge, keeping his head resting against the building, avoiding us all.

She leans over and slaps his arm. He startles and flashes his eyes to her, wide and surprised. Lilli holds her hands out to the side. "I asked you something."

Alfie stares at her. "I'm fine," he says, not answering her question.

"That isn't what I asked," she presses.

Alfie glances between Max and me. "I don't think he wants to talk about his parents right now," Max tells her.

"That's not it," she says. "Alfie, can you hear me?" She leans toward him, bringing her face closer to his. "Remember how he was covering his ears last night?"

Alfie lifts Lilli out of Max's lap and brings her to his, holding her head against his chest, lowering his cheek to her head. "I'll be fine," he utters.

"Alfie," she cries. "Can you tell me where it hurts?"

"He can't hear you, Lil," Max says. "The big explosions hurt his ears."

"But will he be able to hear us again?"

"We aren't sure," I tell her.

"Oh, no. No," she whimpers, reaching up and placing her hand on one of his ears. A tear slips from Alfie's eye and a silent sob follows. "I love you, Alfie," Lilli says. "You have us."

Her words, which only we can hear, break my heart.

"All Jewish children, line up!" a Gestapo shouts from the street.

"Don't move. Just stay still," Max whispers. "They might not know who we are. I don't see the Gestapo who brought us here."

I try to swallow the knot forming in my throat, watching the Gestapo scan the area. "Jewish children of Hamburg, line up!"

"It's all right," Max says.

I drop my stare, not wanting to make eye contact with the

shouting Gestapo, but only seconds have passed before I hear the clacking hard sole boots coming toward us. "You four children too, up, get up, *mach schnell,* and form a line behind the others," he says, pointing directly at us.

Why are they sending us too? We haven't told anyone we're Jewish and we have no papers...

EIGHT

DALIA

JULY 28TH, 1943 – BERLIN, GERMANY

I've been sitting on a splintered wooden bench in this military truck among fellow Jews after being taken from Hamburg. We've been pinned side by side for hours, bouncing around like worn rag dolls. Now, we're being unloaded as if we're no more than a pile of rubbish being dumped into a waste pit at a train station in Berlin. A Berlin sign was all I could make out in the little time we had before being shoved into a cattle car, attached to an endless line of others in front and behind.

They want us to step inside faster than our bodies are capable. Therefore, each of us shove forward and are forced to claw our way up and in. More people follow me, burying me deep into the center of the already filled car. I'm too short to see over the heads in front or behind me. There might be hundreds of people in this one wooden car. We're all shoved backward once more as a long baton waves over our heads to clear the doorway. The crash of the door securing vibrates through my ears and limbs. To think I was struggling with the lack of air just a moment ago gives me little hope of staying upright with how much less there is now.

We're shoulder to shoulder, tighter than sardines in a tin.

Amid the acidic stench of urine, vomit, and body odor, sweat from the person beside me is dripping onto my skin, his breath a heavy fog carrying the odor of sour milk. The people in front of me are banging on the walls, screaming to be let out. I could be screaming too, but I've already seen what that does.

The rhythmic sounds of the train rumbling along the tracks is a constant reminder to wonder what our destination will be. The longer we travel, the further away from Leo and the children I am. I'm not whole without them—I'm no one if I'm not a mother and wife. I need them. They need me.

The train leans to one side, forcing me to lean against the person in front of me. Long hair sweeps across my hand, the silky texture similar to Jordanna and Lilli's. I struggle to lift my arm that's been pinned between my side and the person next to me, but wonder if I'm leaning against a child. I find the top of her head, gauging her age by height. She's about Lilli's height. I hope she's here with her mother or father, but I haven't heard any form of a conversation in front of me.

I bend my knees, crouching ever so slightly. The pain is excruciating after keeping my legs locked for so long. I touch the girl's shoulder and whisper, "Are you alone or with your parents?"

She sniffles and her body shivers. "I—I don't know. Mama was here when we got to the train, but—but I don't know where she is now."

"What's your name, sweetheart?"

"Sonia," she says.

"Is anyone in this car a mother separated from her young girl upon entering the car? Her name is Sonia. She may be eight or nine."

"I'm eight," she utters.

"Eight?" I repeat. "Anyone?"

I hear others repeating the question. Based on how far the question circulates, I have a better sense of the size of the space we're confined in. It's hard to imagine more than half a dozen people fitting either side of me, but that's not the case with how we're standing.

The little girl in front of me whimpers. "Mama's not here. She's gone," she says.

"Oh goodness. It's all right, sweetheart. You know what? She might be in another car, right? Maybe I could help you find her as soon as we—" We're released from this moving prison... "As soon as we get outside."

"How do we know when that will be?" she asks.

I place my hand on her head once more. "I don't know, sweetie. Try to stay strong."

The car jolts violently, throwing us against each other as if we're weightless. Cries echo through the tight space and I reach for the little girl again, unable to find her this time. Panic crashes through me and I reach down, feeling for a head of hair. My fingertips sweep across her head, and I squat down just enough to take a hold of her arm and pull her back up to her feet.

"No, let me stay!" she cries. "I can't stand up any longer."

"Sonia, listen to me," I tell her. "I'm a mama, too. My children have been separated from me. Since I'm a mama, I'm sure yours would tell you how important it is to stay on your feet right now, no matter how hard it is to hold yourself up."

"But why?" she continues to cry.

"People can't see very much with so little light when you're down there and you might get stepped on. It would hurt terribly." I picture far worse than being terribly hurt from someone stepping on her. Any one of the people around us could fall on her with their dead weight and crush her.

Sonia's body is leaning against my legs, her head heavy on my stomach. Her breathing slows and I think she's asleep. I wish I could sleep this experience away too, but I refuse to close an eye, not knowing what's ahead—not knowing what's happening to my poor children at this very moment.

I pray Max knows what I would tell them to do. I pray he's taking care of the others. Jordanna, she's my fightershe will push through whatever force she's put up against, and that thought scares me too.

My Lilli, though, I can hear her telling me she's scared. She's terrified of thunder, loud rain, howling wind, loud knocks on the door, and pure darkness. I'm always with her when she's afraid. Maybe it's my fault she has so many fears. She's my baby and part of me didn't want her to grow up so I didn't force her to face some realities of life. I should have known better.

Without windows, I have no sense of awareness. I don't think I'd have an inkling of how much farther we're traveling, but standing upright like this for much longer—I don't know if any of us will make it. We're verging on suffocation as it is, and anyone from Hamburg already has a lung full of smoke.

* * *

Twenty coughs, six whimpers, two bawling sobs, and an episode of sickness have marked the time since Sonia fell asleep. I may be imagining the change of speed, but I think we're coming to a stop. *Let us out. Please.*

Metal against metal, creaking wood, squeals and grinds, confirming a stop. I wrap my arms around Sonia to gently wake her, afraid she'll get trampled. "We're stopping, sweetheart. We might have to move."

Her head shifts around just as we come to a complete stop. The cattle door slides open and the pressure of pushing hands from behind us builds, shoving us forward. The cool night air swooshes in between the crevices of bodies. I could drink in the fresh air.

It shouldn't be long now until we're outside.

Except, a storm of heat presses against us, a force physically pushes us backward and I spin Sonia around to shield her face.

No sooner than we've stopped, the doors close again, locking us back in with another round of people who do not fit inside any more than we did when we first stepped onboard.

With that last thought, the train jerks forward and speed presses us in yet another direction, all of us swaying in one fluid motion.

"Maybe my mama will be waiting for us at the next stop," Sonia utters. "She might be with your children, and then we'll all be together again, right?"

"Wouldn't that be the most wonderful sight to see," I reply. I close my eyes as tears well. My lashes sweep them down the sides of my cheeks. I can't cry. I can't. I must be strong.

A round of gasps and shrieks spiral over our heads as we're shoved toward a corner. "He's dead," someone yells. "There's no pulse."

Sonia clutches onto me with a tighter grip as an infant's crying wail storms through the car. A mother hushes her baby, but the cry isn't of mere discomfort, it's a sound of pain. Sonia covers her ears from the noise, and I reach forward to tap the mother on the shoulder. She can't move. None of us can.

"Your baby's ears are hurting." With the flashes of light filtering in through the cracks between the wooden slab walls of the car, I find snippets of surrounding imagery. "He was holding his ear a moment ago. Your hand is likely hotter than a warm compress. Press your palm against his ear. The heat will reduce the inflammation."

The woman does as I say and within moments the baby's cry weakens, then comes to a stop.

"Thank you, thank you," the mother cries out.

It's a temporary solution. Like this train, keeping us from something much worse.

"Are you a doctor?" Sonia asks me.

"No, but I was a nurse many years ago."

"How many years ago," she presses.

"During the Great War, before you were born. Many people were getting injured every day and I was there to help mend their wounds."

"Why did you stop being a nurse?" Such a simple question full of complex answers.

"I wanted to be a mama," I tell her. Even if I desired to go back to work after Lilli was born, it was no longer an option. Jewish nurses were turned away from every hospital in Germany after 1933. Regardless of how many lives I tended to in our darkest days, I became worthless to our country.

NINE
JORDANNA
JULY 28TH, 1943 – HAMBURG, GERMANY

I'm trying to keep myself composed as we stand in line in front of the Gestapo who just forced us to go along with the other Jewish children even though we have no identification classifying us. We don't know why we're being sent away, which is almost worse than knowing. My body is shaking out of control. I grab Lilli's hand and she squeezes back hard, her paper thin nails scratching the inside of my palms. We all cough and gasp, trying to breathe through the patches of drifting smoke. The inside of my mouth tastes like burnt paper and we all need water. We've been exposed to a lot of debris and I'm scared to think about how sick it could make us if we don't leave this city soon. There were no fires in this square but by the thick ash falling over the roads and surrounding buildings, it's hard to imagine we're more than a street block away.

Papa used to tell us stories about his days in the trenches during the Great War. He would tell us there were some days he would wake up knowing there was only a fifty percent chance he'd survive the day. Other days, the percentage was less, but never more than fifty. His certainty of this topic confused me much of the time, but I think I understand better now.

"Papers," the officer says again after the person in front of Max steps to the side.

"We ran from home too fast to take anything," Max tells the man. "But we're not Jewish—well, our father isn't Jewish. So, we're—" Papa is half Jewish, but he's a practicing Jew. On paper, he's considered Mischlinge—somewhere in the middle— maybe safe, maybe not. The rest of us are considered Jewish, plain and simple because of Mama having two Jewish parents. Maybe we could convince them we haven't been raised as Jewish children, but it will be hard to prove either way without our papers.

My stomach pinches and cramps as I stare at the officer's stern expression, his blue eyes glinting beneath the shadow of his cap, his lips sneering into an undecipherable intent. He either doesn't believe us or doesn't want to.

"Are these your siblings?" he cuts off Max's rambling and points to the rest of us hiding in Max's shadow.

"Yes," Max says.

"Give me each of their names and birth years."

The officer stands with a clipboard in one hand and a pencil in the other, the point pressed to the paper waiting for Max's response.

"Max Bergmann, 1926."

"The others," the officer presses.

"Alfie Bergmann, 1927; Jordanna Bergmann, 1928; Lilli Bergmann, 1935." It's still startling to hear Alfie referred to as a Bergmann. We've never addressed him that way. Papa had his papers altered to have our last name replace his natural identity. He thought he'd be able to keep him safe when his parents had to leave. Without our papers, they can think what they want.

"What is your ethnicity?" the officer says, pointedly.

"Our father is a former German soldier and our mother, a

nurse. I'm sure they've been helping where needed. We must find them," Max is spitting out statements as if his words are our last chance to save ourselves.

"Ethnicity," the officer demands again, continuing to ignore Max.

"German," Max says without blinking an eyelash.

"Not your nationality, your ethnicity," the officer says, his head tilting to the side.

"German," Max says again.

"Your parents were born in Germany?"

"No, herr. They were born in Poland, but their region was occupied under the German Empire at the time." The Gestapo holds his hand up to Max's face.

"Enough. Take your family and wait over there," he says, pointing over his shoulder and to the left where other children are waiting.

I take Alfie and Lilli by the hand and follow Max across the road.

"All I've done was buy us time," Max utters as we near the other children.

"Time for what? To run?" I ask.

"What's happening?" Lilli asks, tugging on my hand.

"Perhaps we *should* run," Max says, running his hand down the side of his face, sweat pooling under his chin.

"Where will we go? They have our names now," I press.

"Well, if they find us, then they will hopefully bring us to Mama or Papa. That's what we need," Max says.

"And if they don't bring us to them?" I ask.

"It will be because they don't have records on them, which means they won't know anything more about us," he hisses. "Surely the police can't be as organized as they usually are, not with this unforeseen chaos of the city burning down."

"You still gave them our names—and lied about us being Jewish," I utter.

"I half lied. I forced them to put a question mark next to our names. It's better than marking us with a 'J' for Jews right now."

I don't know what decision I would have made if I was the eldest, but I'm positive Max only wants to keep us safe. I'm also aware Papa was the only one of us to have immunity against Jewish laws because of his time in the German service, and we were under his umbrella. Without him, we're no different than all the other Jewish people they've already deported from Germany. Our papers clearly define us as Jewish citizens. Just Jewish—not a mixed-race from a mixed-marriage like Max told the Gestapo. We have three Jewish grandparents, defining us as entirely Jewish per the Nuremberg Law. "The Reich has made it clear that they can find whatever information they desire. Even if they don't, they will make their own assumptions," I say.

"And as I said, the truth will point to Mama and Papa. That's what we need."

All I hear is there is no way out of whatever the Gestapo plan to do with us. "The truth? Alfie is not our brother, and we're Jews. Our immunity has been based on Papa's service to the German Army. None of it is enough to keep us safe now. That's why you got rid of our papers, isn't it?"

"Do you have a better idea?" Max asserts, exerting his words through a sharp whisper.

I don't know if there is a better idea to be had.

Lilli is sitting on my feet as we stand here among the other silent children, waiting for our next direction. Alfie isn't talking much, but keeps rubbing at his ears. He doesn't even know what might happen right now since he can't hear the commands.

A group of SS officers pile into the center of this small village, wherever we are, and huddle together for a private conversation.

One of them whistles and waves his hand toward someone around a corner, who we can't see from where we're standing.

Military vehicles pull forward through the center, alongside the SS.

"They're going to take us somewhere else now," I whisper to Max.

He doesn't respond.

Two of the SS officers make their way toward the group of children we're standing among. "Delinquent orphans!" one shouts. "Here." He points to the ground next to his black boot.

Orphans? "We are not delinquents—we've done nothing wrong. We aren't orphans either. They must have us mixed up for another family," I tell Max.

"Then show me your papers?" the SS officer presses.

The crowd of children pushes forward, none of them questioning being classed as parentless. Quiet whimpers and sniffles linger between us all. Should we all be questioning what happened to our parents last night? Were some of these children orphans before yesterday?

"We don't have them, but I believe there's been a misunderstanding," Max speaks up as we approach the SS officer, a tall man dressed in an ash-covered uniform. "My siblings and I aren't orphans. Are we in the wrong place?"

The officer smiles, a condescending grin that burns me from the inside. "My comrades wouldn't make such a mistake."

The heat inside me dissipates into a chill, one physically impossible to feel in these temperatures.

Another whistle blows, signaling yet another direction to follow. "Single file line, move!"

"We're not orphans," I utter to Lilli, unsure what she's thinking or hearing.

We're nearly thrown into the back of a covered wagon, crammed in next to each other without a chance of moving a muscle. Lilli is on my lap and Alfie and Max are to each of my sides. "Where are we going?" Lilli asks, speaking into my ear.

"Away from the fires," I tell her.

"What about Mama and Papa?"

"We'll find them," I say.

Everything coming out of my mouth is a lie and I don't know when I should start telling her the truth because none of us can predict what's ahead.

Alfie takes a turn at whispering Lilli's first question. I turn to him and shrug, shaking my head so he understands I don't know anything more than he does.

* * *

Three crowded transports, each more suffocating than the last and still no clue where we're going. It must have been over twelve hours of traveling by now. We arrive at what seems late in the afternoon judging by the sun hovering over the horizon. Adults and children alike are split into lines that wind around a wooden gate topped with barbed wire. I glance up at the sign above us:

Wohngbiet Der
JUDEN
Betreten Verboten

Residential Area of
JEWS
Entry Forbidden

My heart pounds against my ribs. "What's going to happen?" I whisper to Max.

He tilts his chin toward the sky and straightens his shoulders. "I don't know." Is this place similar to the Warsaw Ghetto, where they've been assigning Jews to laboring jobs just because they're Jewish? Again, I wish I had never listened in on Mama and Papa's conversation that night when I heard about the cattle cars taking Jews away. "I'll tell them we need to find our parents and that we don't belong here."

Except, we do, don't we? "I don't think that's a good idea," I argue under my breath. "Haven't you heard what they do if you question their decisions. We're together and whatever this place is, we'll be able to collect our thoughts and come up with a way to find Mama and Papa."

Max's shoulders don't relax. The sharp crack of a gunshot splits the air. Screams follow. A body hits the gravel, and blood oozes around a man's head, the puddle trickling toward us.

I flinch, shoving Lilli to my other side, ensuring she doesn't witness what's happened. She fights to move back, wanting to see what the commotion is about. "What was that?" she asks.

"A warning shot for us to be quiet," I lie, and yet, it's the most honest I've been with her in days. She doesn't believe me. Her face goes pale in the glow of the orange streetlights above us, and her small hand grips mine tighter, her palm wet with sweat.

The line moves forward and we're face-to face with an SS officer. Acidic bile burns up to my throat, my stomach threatening to purge despite being empty.

"Papers!"

"Don't say a word," Max utters.

"Papers!" the officer shouts at us again.

"We were taken from a bunker during the air raids and fires in Hamburg. We don't have our papers."

"Surname and address," he demands.

"Bergmann, Kana—uh—gege-nd, straße twelve of Hamburg," Max replies, stumbling over his words. Because that's not our correct address. The officer searches through a list he has grasped in his hand, scraping the tip of his pencil down a column.

"Who sent you?"

"I'm unsure. German police. We were mistakenly separated from our parents," Max continues.

"Are you Jews?"

"Are we what?" Max repeats.

"Bergmann," he mumbles and shakes his head. The officer grinds his jaw back and forth, his stare jolting from side to side with a look of indecision. My heart thumps so hard I'm afraid it can be seen through my nightgown. He should have lied about our last name too, but I can't expect him to think that fast when I wouldn't have been able to do better. "How many are with you?"

"Three others, my siblings. We're looking for our—"

"And you're the eldest?" the officer continues, not allowing Max to speak.

"Yes."

"Date of birth?"

"The second of September 1925."

The officer signals something to another guard, his pen scratching on the clipboard. "Not a child."

"Transport him East," the other guard shouts.

The officer huffs and mutters something unintelligible then looks over his shoulder before shaking his head once more. He takes a long look at the four of us as if trying to decide what to do with us. "Up the stairs and over the bridge—deportation orders will be given once we acquire your proper identification," the officer tells Max, pointing to the stone stairwell behind him.

"Come along," Max tells us, stepping forward.

"Not the others, just you. Go," the officer snaps at him.

"I can't leave my siblings. I'm all they have," Max cries out.

He's shoved forward by someone passing by, separating him from us and the officer. He told us not to say anything, but I can't just stand here in silence.

"We must go with our brother," I speak up.

"Of course," the officer says, standing to the side to let the three of us by. But as I step forward with Lilli in hand, someone grabs hold of my arm and pulls in the opposite direction.

"No, that's my brother. We're together," I cry out.

"You three are Jewish Polish orphans, yes?" the SS officer who's grabbed my arm says.

"No, no, we're not!" I squeak, trying to sound believable despite the truth they're shouting.

"And you lie," he says, clucking his tongue. "Do you know what we do with lying children?" They don't know we're lying. They're trying to scare us. It's working.

"They aren't orphans. Our parents are alive! Don't take them. I'm responsible for them," Max argues, shouting from the stairwell now.

The sound of a rifle loading shudders through me, and I can't tell where it's coming from, but I imagine it's being pointed at Max. "No, don't hurt him!" I shout.

"You three *are* Jewish Polish children without a proper guardian," the officer states affirmatively.

"No, and we were born in Germany," Lilli argues, and I want to clap a hand over her mouth.

"Where are you taking them?" Max continues to yell from a line of others pushing their way up the same steps he's climbing. He's pushing his luck too far. Something's going to happen to him.

Tears blur my vision as I mouth the word, "Stop!" to him. I'm unsure if he can even spot me in the growing crowd.

Another officer barrels up the stairs, pushing others to the side until he reaches Max, then shoves the heel of his hand against his shoulder, screaming at him. I watch him fall but I don't know if he gets back up.

"Take them to Little Auschwitz—we have three Polish orphans without proof of race, said to be Mischlinges. Mark them to be screened for Germanization," he says to a nearby officer, waiting for direction.

I try to spot Max on the bridge despite the crowd bulging between us. All I see is an officer spit at him and scream in his face before shoving him once again, harder this time. The sight tears my heart in half as the three of us are dragged to another line surrounded by children.

"Max," Lilli cries quietly. "I want Max."

I try my hardest to force a smile, but my lips tremble as I try to calm Lilli. "Shh, shh. You'll see him again soon," I tell her.

"You said that about Mama and Papa too. Are you going to leave me next?"

Her words are daggers. "I won't leave you." What if they pull us apart? I can't leave Lilli. I won't.

Again, we're brought to another group of children waiting in a line. So-called orphans too, I assume. I've lost track of how many lines we've had to stand in today—all of them spinning us around in dizzying circles to make sure we have no clue where we are.

Alfie keeps looking behind us, looking for Max. I need to come up with a way to tell him he can't be with us. I take a hold of his arm and intertwine it with mine. "Where is he?" Alfie asks, peering down at me.

I drop my gaze and shake my head before pointing up to the bridge he had to cross.

Alfie takes in a shuddered breath and wraps his arm around me. "I've got you, and Lilli. Max will find us."

He presses my head to the side of his chest where I feel his heart racing, a pounding hammer. His attempt to comfort me is something I've only dreamed of before today, but I'm too numb and terrified to feel the warmth of his embrace.

Every second we stand still feels like an eternity and all we're doing is waiting for whatever we'll face next. Hour after hour passes and I can only wonder if people even notice us when they walk by. Children are whining, crying with hunger, and most looking for someone who isn't here. Lilli hears them, sees them and her grip tightens even more. There's no warning when an officer shouts at us to start walking, keeping us in a tight line where we step on each other's tired heels and/or trip from being stepped on. The walk is endless, the barbed wire gate goes on and on, never ending. We turn one corner and find the same gates, same barbed wire, to our left, lining another road. "I can't walk anymore," Lilli groans.

"You must," I tell her. "You have to be the strong girl I know you are. There's no choice. I can do it, and you can too."

Lilli yanks my hand and grumbles—a visible reaction Alfie must notice as he takes her other hand. He holds his finger up to his lips as if he can hear the noises she's making. The two of us hold her tightly between us, walking into the night that may never become day.

Children begin to fall, and struggle to pick themselves back up. I can barely keep myself upright, but Alfie and I seem to be on the older side of the group we're with and try to help anyone who falls before us, draining our strength. It's been over an entire day since we've had water or food. Our bodies are running on nothing.

The streetlights become less frequent, the dark taking a toll on our footings and spatial awareness until two high posted lamps blur in the distance.

I want to hope that's where we're going, but I don't think any one of us is hoping to go anywhere with these officers. I just don't want to walk any further. I can't. I might fall onto one of those children and there won't be anyone to help me up except Alfie, who could so easily fall over too. And Lilli, she'd be alone to fend for herself. I can't let that happen. We pass train tracks, making me wonder why we've been walking all this way.

The wooden barriers to our left become solid walls, reaching high above our heads without barbed wire, an inkling of hope. Beneath the two overhead lights are matching wooden gates, shorter than the walls.

"Once you walk through these gates you will go to registration. Stay in order, in the line you are already in," the SS officer shouts, ensuring we all hear.

Is this Little Auschwitz? If we don't know where we are, no one will ever be able to find us.

The only clue to our whereabouts is an arc of words over the gates that reads:

Polenjugendverwahrlager der Sicherheitspolizei in
Litzmannstadt

Preventive Camp of the Security Police for Polish Youth in Łódź

A street sign below informs us of the exact location: Przemysłowa Street. My heart sinks as the Polish words make it clear we're no longer in Germany. I don't know what they mean by "preventative," and I have no idea if I'll ever find Max again.

TEN

DALIA

The endless train journey from Berlin is taking me farther and farther away from my babies and Leo. We've stopped so many times along the way, I've lost count, and I'm not sure we're still in Germany. Each time the doors open, I hope we'll be let out, but only more people are shoved into the cattle car. There's no more space. We're beyond bodily capacity.

My stomach twists in on itself, aching from emptiness. My mouth is dry and my tongue feels rougher than sandpaper, scraping against the back of my teeth. I fear, when we move, I might collapse, being held up only by the press of wedged bodies against me.

Sonia's head still rests against my stomach, her breath warm, dampening my skin through the thin fabric of my nightgown. I run my hand over her back and peer down at her, staring at the outline of her delicate silhouette. "Lilli?" I gasp and curl over her to get a closer look. "Lilli, is that you?" I blink several times, needing more clarity. What's happening? I whip my head from side to side searching around me. "Jordanna? Max?" My words are muffled against a damp linen covered shoulder—the man crunched against my side. Movement against my stomach pulls me back to...Lilli...no, the glossy eyes collecting fragments of light from the seams of the cattle car's panels do not belong to my daughter. Sonia's awoken from her hazy sleep, waiting for me to say something.

"Are you calling for someone?" Sonia asks.

"Oh, uh—" I take a few short breaths. "No one. It's just—the doors might open again. We need to be ready," I say, forcing sound against my raw throat.

She nods, her movements sluggish. A metallic squeal splits the air, the train doors groaning open with a final, deafening clink. The noise reverberates, bouncing off the walls of the car like a hollow drum.

Shouts fill the air, sharp and urgent: "Raus! Raise Schnell!" The words yank us forward, all of us stumbling from stiff unsteady limbs. It's as if we're caught within the grip of a claw, giving us no say but to comply with the demands.

"I'm going first," I say, speaking directly into her ear above the chaos. "Stay close and I'll help you down."

Moving closer to the exit, I watch as others are slung onto the platform. My knees buckle and I force them straight, pleading with my legs to obey. One step down, that's all it is. Just one step.

A pair of hands grabs my waist from below the step, lifting me off the train. The stranger—a man wearing a yellow Jude Star pinned to his shirt—confirms he's another one of us, a Jew. His eyes are cloudy with something that resembles fear and resignation. We're strangers, yet all bound by the same unspoken dread of what lies ahead.

"Thank you," I utter, though I doubt he heard me. I turn back for Sonia, her slight figure pale and ghostly against the mass of moving bodies. "Come on, I've got you." I take her into my hands. Her weight feels like lead against my weak muscles, but I get her to the ground safely.

She clings to me, her eyes darting through the chaos of shuffling bodies. "I want to find Mama. She might be in the next car," Sonia insists, her voice weak and trembling.

"We'll try to go look," I say, though I'm not certain what we're allowed to do. All that's obvious is that we aren't allowed to stand still.

The sun hangs high overhead, casting everything in a harsh, unforgiving spotlight. And then I spot it—a location marker—a sign, plain and unassuming with black letters that cut through the light.

I read it over and again, tasting the word in my mouth:

AUSCHWITZ

The name might be meaningless, but the thick air of ragged breaths bleeding into the train's exhaust curls around us with ghostly fingers. Violent barks from angry dogs, guards whipping commands, and whistles zing between my ears—making it clear that Auschwitz is anything but just a name on a sign. It's a warning.

The daunting sight of a wide brick structure with an arched opening in the center, topped with a protruding tower, looms in the near distance.

The crowd moves as a rushing tidal wave, as it did before we stepped onto the train. "Let's go there," cries Sonia, pointing in the opposite direction we're pushed.

"If she's there, she'll be coming this way too. Keep your eyes open for her."

Sonia doesn't respond. I'm sure she's upset that I didn't uphold my promise of going to look for her mother, but there's no possibility of moving against this crowd. SS officers line the cement platform we're being ushered along, each with a gun in hand and hounds by many of their sides. My insides tighten as if shriveling up and tugging at all my nerves. Air breezes my face, but fear consumes me as we walk.

Commanding voices shout, directing men left and women and children right.

I watch as the flock ahead diverges, but not without cries and pleas between family members being separated without warning. If I were still with my family, enduring separation would be inevitable. It's inevitable and inhumane.

While in the segregated line, I struggle to absorb the overwhelming surroundings. A Gestapo catches my eye, points, and waves me over. Others are plucked from the crowd and separated; no explanation given.

I hold Sonia's hand and lead her toward the Gestapo with a line in front of him. People are shouting, drowning out the officer's words.

"Your daughter?" is the officer's first question to me.

"No, she's not, but we're searching for her mother. They got separated on the way here."

The sound of a whistle has become the point of a blade stabbing the inside of my ear. "Child separated from mother," the Gestapo shouts, pointing at Sonia.

"They'll help you find her," I say, releasing my hand from hers. My words are likely a lie, knowing they probably won't help her, but it could be her only hope. The other officer takes Sonia by the arm and pulls her away. I catch her stare, grasping for me as if I'm her lifeline, and I just let her down. My chest aches, the pain fiercer than the hunger eating me from the inside.

My grief is heavy, and I consider chasing after her, but know not to move from an officer asking me questions. I should have said something else. I shouldn't have told him she was looking for her mother.

"Name?" the Gestapo says, commanding an answer from me.

"Dalia Bergmann," I say, just not loud enough to hear my voice in the chaos.

"Age?" he presses.

"Forty-two."

"Profession?"

"I was a nurse, but more importantly, a mother, and I need to find my children. We've been separated."

The officer lifts his left hand, a worn slip of paper cupped in his palm. He scribbles out a note and hands it to me before pushing me toward another line made up of rows of women. I lift my fingers just enough to read the writing on the paper that says: "NURSE."

Now I'm left wondering what good this note is without my name attached, or if it will define me in some way here.

We aren't still for long before someone shouts at us to walk an endless walk, it seems. We're guided toward the arched entrance as we watch most of the others being shoved in a different direction around the perimeter and beyond our view.

Upon entering the compound, they take the other women and me to the left. There's no road or marked walkway, just thick, sticky mud outlining rows of shallow buildings with a row of divided windows.

People stand in front of their windows inside the buildings. Each one of them is pale with shaven heads, making it impossible to decipher their gender. Their faces are devoid of expression and all I can do is wonder what they're doing inside, what they've gone through, and if that's what's ahead for me.

On our organized walk along the rows of buildings, I spot a sign notating, "Bla," with no other sign of what the three letters mean. Then another building comes into view. This one resembles a horse stable. Women wearing dark-blue striped dresses with a white armband labeled "KAPO" trade places with the Nazi guards who have led us to this point. The uniformed women jump toward us as if we're pests, shouting profanities, shoving some of us and essentially herding us forward until we reach a long line winding around the stable-like building.

"Strip down and remove all your clothing." The demand leaves us momentarily shocked and uncertain. The individuals ahead and behind me in line exchange long, unsure looks, wondering if we all received the same strange order. "We can move you somewhere else if this is a problem," another woman with a KAPO armband shouts.

I do as I'm told, fearful of the repercussions if I don't comply. It's easier for me to remove my clothing than most others, as I've only worn my nightgown and a thin robe since the night of the fire. Others have layers despite the heat. They dressed in many layers of clothing to keep their belongings. They must have received notice, similar to the Feinsteins. Is this where Alfie's parents ended up, and unheard from since?

Laughter from the male guards passing by is all we can hear while disrobing. Mortification is their aim. At once, we all slip out of our clothes and undergarments, bearing our naked bodies to the world. The sun scorns us, branding us with intense heat, a reminder of the burns inflicted by the fires. I was lucky, but it's hard to believe anyone escaped unharmed, even with minor burns.

Of everything I've seen these last few days, the humiliation I feel now doesn't compare. If someone wants to stare at my naked body, I don't care. The Nazis have already taken everything from me. Dignity means nothing.

The other women don't all seem to feel the same as they wring their hands, contorting in any way possible to cover themselves. We're the same. The Nazis still don't seem to understand this. My naked body looks the same as this brute female officer's. We're people. We're women.

The line hardly moves the space of one person, and when it does, it feels as though a half hour has passed since the last time we moved. Guards walk up and down the line, counting us as if we're part of an inventory, worried they have the wrong number and must recount to double and triple check.

The farther we move along the line, the more forms of assault await. Worse, we watch the others ahead of us endure the torture first. I watch in horror. My heart throbs, a storm inside me as the scene in front of me unfolds—the terror as a laborer shoves another naked woman down onto a metal stool. She stumbles before falling onto the seat then shivers despite the sweltering muggy heat that clings to our skin. Tears stream down her dirt-stained cheeks, her sobs drowned out by the chaos around us. A woman with a black scarf tied around her head, wearing a striped uniform, approaches, razor in hand, and without hesitation begins to strip the woman of her hair. It falls in jagged, uneven clumps, tumbling from her shoulders to the filthy floor, leaving her without one single hair on her head.

I'm next.

My breath catches in my throat as I'm shoved forward, my feet dragging like heavy potato sacks. My scalp buzzes with dread. I've kept my hair pinned up for so long, never appreciating it or imagining it could be stolen from me in this way. I sink down onto the metal stool, slick and sticky beneath my thighs, and clench my eyes shut, refusing to watch as the razor moves toward my scalp.

The first scrape of the blade tears into my skin, a sharp sting that sends jolts of pain pounding through my skull. The woman's grip tightens, her fingers boring into my scalp as if she's trying to peel me away from myself, layer by layer. I bite my lip, the metallic tang of blood striking my nerves as a cool breeze slips through the patchy remains of hair—a nauseating sensation. I hold back my screams as each tug and pull of the razor nips and bites at my skin. My life—my identity, dignity and everything that made me who I am, is gone. My hair falls in clumps like leaves from a tree in autumn, sticking to my clammy legs as a reminder of what's gone. It's just hair, but it's mine and now it's not.

I'm yanked from the stool and forced back into the long line with all the other bald and hollow-eyed women. If I caught a glimpse of my reflection, I wouldn't know what I was looking at or who I am. They might as well have carved out my soul too.

With a clipboard in hand, a Nazi strides toward us, barking orders I can't fully understand despite speaking fluent German. Words are muddling together. I try to pick up on the orders by watching the others in front of me, but all I can do is tremble and struggle to keep myself upright.

As the line shortens, small tables in a row come into view. The visual takes a long moment to register in my head, trying to understand what I'm seeing, but reality sets in as cries of pain rip through the air. More striped-uniformed women are slicing numbers into the arms of those who stand before me, then pouring black ink over the bloody marks.

My stomach churns as I come closer, my steps heavier and unsteady. The wait feels endless, my nerves taut like an over-stretched rubber band. Every second is torture, every breath a struggle against the panic flooding through me.

"This number is your only form of identity now," the woman says as I take a seat across from her at the small table. Her words are stale, emotionless, and detached, as if she's dead inside too.

I clench my teeth and close my eyes, bracing myself to endure the searing pain of a needle dragging across my flesh. Blood trickles down my arm, warm and thick, mingling with the ink that burns as it seeps into the fresh wounds. I want to shove the table, flip it over and scream at the top of my lungs, but my body is numb, my heart broken, and my future shattering like a fallen glass vase. I picture my children smiling and chasing each other around our apartment. It's been a mere few days since I saw them last in the bunker. How could I have let them slip away from me?

A wave of dizziness shakes me, but before I can grasp my bearings, I'm pushed from the stool, knocked down to my hands and knees, staring at the dirt-covered floor. Toes of boots appear beneath my nose and my heart gallops in my chest.

"Get up!" the person shouts.

Someone else pulls me to my feet and swings me around, away from the boots, then shoves their fist into my hand. "You're a nurse. Your paper—it's your job assignment. Don't get it wet."

I'm unsure who's talking with everything around me still spinning into a blur.

The stream of water falling from above grasps my attention. A hand shoves me forward toward a gap beneath the showers. I crumple the paper into a smaller ball, clenching my fist around it, praying it stays readable.

The spray of water stings my body, but I open my mouth wide to drink up as much as I can before I begin to choke. Still, I reach up, cupping my hand to scoop more into my mouth. I have to survive. I need more water. "God, don't let me die," I cry out in just a breath. I must live for my children, wherever they are.

I'm drenched, shivering and dazed as we're shoved toward the entrance of a large adjoining hall where I follow a mass of others, running without instruction of where to go like cattle without a herder. Other working prisoners toss piles of dirty uniforms, blankets, clogs, bowls, utensils, and cups at us—items that are too common amid this madness. None of this feels real —it's a puzzling nightmare that makes no sense.

Another line. Another wait. My legs wobble, and my vision blurs as my body sways from side to side. Hunger gnaws at my insides, and my throat burns each time I swallow despite the mouthfuls of shower water I swallowed.

Are they breaking us down for labor, for death, or for something far worse?

I don't know. I'm trapped, desperately clinging to my identity, hoping against all odds that I will be reunited with my family.

ELEVEN

JORDANNA

The darkness of the sky is like nothing I've seen before. Hamburg at night still offers light, but here on Przemysłowa Street in front of a blockading fortress of walls identified as a *Preventive Camp for Polish Youth* is darker than I knew possible, and not a star in the sky.

A male and female guard step out from a slight opening between the black gates, both with burly chests, and chins that hide their necks. The caps on their heads conceal their eyes. I wish they couldn't see *my* eyes, and the fear I can't hide.

Their feet squelch against the wet gravel as they step toward us. There's silence mixed with faint cries in the distance and the hoot of an owl from above our heads. The air is wet and sticking to my skin, and smells like rotten flowers.

"Line up in columns of four, girls and children under twelve on one side and boys over twelve on the other," the female guard shouts as she steps beneath a glow of light. She must want us to see the gun clenched in her grip.

I yank Lilli with me into a queue, unsure if I should place her in front of me, to the side, or behind. If she's in front, I can keep an eye on her. Alfie steps to my side, into the boys' column, taking direction by sight rather than sound.

With another wave of panic washing over me, I take his hand to get his attention. I point to my mouth and gesture with my other hand to talk. Then I point to my eyes and again my mouth, speaking the words: "Watch them talk," through a breath.

I don't know if he understands what I'm trying to tell him, but he gives me a nod.

Some of the other children in our group aren't following the command to line up, and I can only assume it's because they don't understand German as much as we do. I never considered myself lucky to know two languages fluently until now. I heard a couple of them conversing quietly in Polish, but I thought we were only supposed to speak German.

I twist my head ever so slightly to peer over my shoulder at the children still standing out of order. The SS storm toward the confused young ones and begin shoving them into lines, still shouting at them in German. I turn back to face the front, unable to watch the scene behind me. The horror of hearing the screams and cries is enough to demolish my remaining strength.

I notice Lilli shaking, her soot covered nightgown wriggling like gelatin.

Another SS walks out from within the gated area and waves us in, pointing us toward a white building off to the left.

"This line, move along. The others stay back," the female guard says, her voice stern and final. Lilli and I are shoved forward while Alfie is kept near the entrance. Panic stirs in my chest, my breaths heavy and ragged. I turn back toward Alfie, desperate for one last look. A tear slips down his cheek, his hands trembling by his side as he gives me a subtle, stilted wave. My throat tightens, a scream rising through me, but I clamp my mouth shut, pinching my teeth against my lips. The sharp pain in the center of my chest is suffocating me. Lilli walks ahead, small and frail, yet somehow steadier than me. I can barely hold myself together. I'm falling apart.

"You will sleep in this block tonight, then report to reception in the morning," the guard barks, her words pulsating through my bones. The wooden door slams shut behind us with a deafening thrash, another reminder that I can't wake up from this never-ending nightmare.

"Why won't they tell us where—" Lilli turns to ask, and I cup my hand over her mouth to keep her silent.

"Buckets serve as toilets. You will be woken in the morning. No one is to leave this block. Servings of bread and water will be handed out shortly."

We're scuttled inside, pushed really, some knocked over while entering a smaller area of what seems to be a bigger block from what little we can make out in the dark.

Once everyone is inside, the door closes and locks from outside. Someone daringly flips a light switch, illuminating the space, which doesn't give us any better of a view. A pile of strewn blankets lie in the center of the room, along with a few lumpy mattresses with straw poking out of the sides.

The older children rush to call ownership of the mattresses, leaving the rest of us to divvy up the wool blankets. Wool in high temperatures is unappealing, but a wooden floor is worse.

Some children hesitate to claim blankets. They're younger, closer to Lilli's age. I step forward, taking the bundle in my arms. I distribute them to the children standing alone and those with familiar companions. I hand Lilli the last of the blankets. "Find a spot where we can sleep. I'll be there shortly," I say.

Other girls, with their blankets, remain frozen in place, lost in thought, possibly wondering what might happen next. I am.

Anytime Mama would catch me eavesdropping on her and Papa, she would tell me, *"To know more is worse than knowing nothing."* I wish I had understood how right she was. Mama wanted to protect me from understanding how evil this world can be. Now, I want to tell these children the same. It won't make it any easier on them, though.

I start with the first little girl, asking her if she speaks Polish so I might help her. "Mówisz po polsku?"

"Tak," she says, agreeing. A look of hope brightens her eyes for a mere second.

"Pozwól że ci pomogę?" I ask, gently taking the blanket from her hand so I can help her set up a spot to sleep.

Lilli has already unrolled the blanket and situated herself on one half toward the farthest wall. I bring this little girl's blanket next to ours and shake it out to lie flat.

"Dziękuję bardzo," she says, thanking me with much more than her words as her arms swing around my waist.

"I'm Jordanna and ona jest Lilli," I say, introducing ourselves.

"Jestem...Kalina," she introduces herself with a hint of a smile.

Mama and Papa didn't move to Germany until just before Max was born so we spoke mostly Polish at home, but anywhere else, we've always spoken German. I can help those with language barriers here. It's apparent the guards have no intention of making anything clear in a way the Polish speaking children will understand. It's been four years since Germany has taken occupation in this country.

I ruffle my fingers through Kalina's thick dark curls and make my way back to the other girls still standing about. A few others have followed our lead and situated themselves with blankets. I introduce myself to the girls and arrange sleeping spots for each of them, doing whatever I can to ease their grief. Mama would do the same. Now, among the turmoil, it's clear how hard she must have worked to shelter us from the cruelty taking over our country. Inside our walls, there was happiness, a good life. We were so lucky to be spared from this as long as we were.

Despite the hard, unforgiving floor and the sweat pooling onto the wool, Lilli falls asleep, and I take her hand in mine and give in to the exhaustion too.

* * *

The howling of a trumpet vibrates the glass window and shudders the door, poking the inside of my ears like sharp whittled toothpicks. Lilli gasps and pushes herself up. No longer in braids, her hair is tangled and messy. I can only imagine how mine looks. I push her hair out of her face and help her up to her feet then make my way to the one window. Before I can reach it, the door swings open and a woman in uniform starts shouting and screaming at us. "Up and out. Line up outside," she hollers.

Those who don't move fast enough face immediate consequence, evident of a whoosh and snap from a leather belt. The *whoop* strikes a nerve down my spine. Shrilling screams follow each snap. The girls can't seem to move fast enough for the guard's liking. Lilli, Kalina, and the other younger girls I helped last night managed to make it out faster than I would have figured, avoiding a whipping.

We're all standing in line beside the block, staring ahead at another building. A few girls whimper while one chokes on a stifled breath. "Shh," I say, trying to calm them.

No more than a minute passes before we're following the guard through the maze of buildings before reaching one closer to the entrance. "Inside you go," she says, slapping her hands together.

Other children are already inside, offering us a preview of what I fear is our terrifying future. Their bodies are emaciated, heads shaven clean, heavy sacks of skin drooping below their eyes. It isn't long before I question whether I'm looking at boys, girls, or both. They all look quite the same. Some are dressed in matching gray pajamas, while others are still wearing street clothes. Their eyes share a common look of dread, desertion, desolation.

As the crowd of other children disperses, two older girls in gray pajamas are in the center standing over stools with razors, buzzing the hair off the person in the seat below them, eyebrows and all.

"Get in a line," one of the hairdressers shouts.

Lilli pulls me into the line, yanking my arm to whisper, "I don't want to cut my hair."

"You mustn't say a word. Did you see what happened to those other girls who didn't move fast enough?" I whisper back.

I hear the gulp Lilli tries to swallow. "But Mama said I could grow my hair out as long as I want," she replies, keeping her words softer than a whisper.

Mama used to tell me the same. I've only cut it a few times. She said we looked like princesses. But we aren't princesses. We're rats in an inferior race.

"I'll go first," I say, feeling the burn of tears threaten to fill my eyes. Everything is slowly being taken from us until there's nothing left. Alfie may not recognize us when we find him, not that I'm sure he ever noticed me in the way I noticed every little detail about him. I'll probably look just like him. The thought pushes a tear onto my lashes, but I swipe it away before anyone sees. I have to be brave. I have to be strong. Lilli needs me to be. Mama would do the same.

It isn't long before I'm next in line. I follow the person in front then sit down, hard, and cross my hands over my lap.

Lilli is watching me. She's watching my reaction.

They're stripping me of my hair. It's my hair.

The blade skims along my head and I clutch my hands against my stomach, pushing against the pain burning inside. I force my lips into a smile, knowing she must be calling my bluff.

Whatever she may think, I will keep the smile for her and for the girls standing behind her, facing the same.

They may take my hair, but not Mama's teachingsto care, lead, and be brave for those unable to. Her words constantly echo in my head. She's said them so many times and I understand why now.

The process of shaving my hair off is quicker than I would imagine. My head feels much lighter, and very naked.

I'm pushed aside for being too slow. Lilli is already on the stool, eyes shut tight.

After the first stroke of the blade, a single tear rolls down her cheek and my heart breaks again.

"Next!" someone shouts from around the corner.

"Go!" the hairdresser shouts at me.

I'm trying to convince myself that losing our hair will be the worst part of this registration process seeing as the cold bath that followed was welcome after the heat we've endured, and the ash glued to our skin.

I couldn't have guessed the next room would be some kind of doctor's office. The room is small, enclosed, with stale air. A set of measuring tools next to a stack of papers rests on his narrow wooden desk. The doctor's face is covered in thick puffy wrinkles with a defined grimace. The white sprigs of hair on his head flop around as he mumbles something to a young woman with a clipboard.

"Sit," he grunts, pointing to a metal stool.

I do so while watching him lean over his desk, swab the pad of his thumb across his tongue and snag a paper from a thick stack, titled: Germanization Screening.

The doctor makes his way over to me, hovering like a beast before taking measurements with a cold pair of metal calipers, the metal grinding against grooves along the tool. He doesn't just take the typical growth measurements like our family doctor has always done. Instead, he measures the distance between the arch of where our eyebrows were before shaven being off and the bridge of our nose, then cheekbone to cheekbone, and forehead to chin. Our height from head to toe, arm span, leg length, angle of our lower jaws, and even the position of our ears.

"Hmm," he says, jotting down numbers. "Peculiar."

"What is?" I ask, nervous to know his reason.

He flaps his hand at me. "She isn't Aryan, but these measurements are inconclusive," the doctor tells the young woman assisting him, taking down her own notes in addition to his. "There's no racial data on her record?"

The woman scans the paper clipped to her clipboard before responding. "No, it seems we've sent a request to obtain her identification. However, she's not on the Volkliste."

"Mark her as 'Pending Transfer' until further notice," the doctor says, handing her his sheet of notes.

The sick feeling in my stomach swells, not knowing what anything means, wondering if Lilli will have the same results and hoping the word "transfer" means something in my best interest.

The assistant ushers me to the next room, leaving me unsurprised to find another small space.

This room is also nearly vacant except for an odd chair with a tall flat back and a short metal pole extruding parallel to the metal seat. It looks medieval, facing the right side of the room. Next, I notice an older girl with a head-full of black curly hair waiting behind a camera on a tripod.

"Sit. Press your head back against the metal post," she commands. I do as she says but she hisses and marches toward me, shoving my head back further until the metal post jabs the back of my skull.

She returns to the camera and takes another photo then charges toward me again. This time, she pulls me up from the seat, swivels it around with a shrill scrape between the chair's legs and the floor, leaving me to face the opposite direction. She then takes the second photograph. It's all repeated a third time to take a shot of me facing the left wall.

The bright bulb blinds me for all three shots, the last leaving me with colorful circles floating in front of my eyes.

"Leave now," the photographer demands, pointing to the door as if I'm a misbehaved house pet.

I wish the door would lead me back outside, but there's another room and another angry woman waiting for me at a table. "Come," she orders, snapping her fingers in the air.

The woman grabs my hand, mangles her fingers around mine with a tight grip and jabs each of my fingertips onto a pad of ink then onto a paper.

"Leave," she says through an annoyed exhale, nudging her head toward the door to her right. "New arrivals are to report to the quarantine block for the next few days. Someone will escort you there. Wait outside."

I step outside, grateful to avoid another room, but anxious while waiting for Lilli to step out next.

We've been separated for too many minutes.

I don't know how much longer I can wait.

TWELVE
DALIA
JULY 29TH, 1943 – OŚWIĘCIM, POLAND

Quarantine. That's what the SS officers want us to do. What are we quarantining from or for? I hear some of the others ask, but there were no answers. All we were told is that we'll be living in Block 15 for at least two weeks. I scratch the back of my head, feeling spikes of hair sprouting from my scalp. How could I let this happen to me? I can't stay here for two weeks while my children are alone somewhere. They can't just leave us here to rot...

It's late, after dark, when we enter one of the shallow wooden buildings, finding rows of tiered platforms spanning from floor to ceiling, stretching end to end with a column of latrine holes in the center. The stench could take someone out at the knees.

The building is nearly full already, leaving few empty spaces along the wooden tiers it appears we'll be using as beds, shared beds with several others. With my arms full of assigned belongings, I scuff my clogs along the ground, thinking up a way to make them fit better at two sizes too large for me.

The first open spot I notice is on the bottom tier of wooden planks. I assume everyone is here for the same reason.

"Do you know what we're quarantining from?" I ask a woman closest to me, also staring in my direction.

"Typhus. Or so we hear," another responds.

"They plan to leave us here for two weeks with nothing?"

"No, we'll work and receive a daily ration of food." The one closest to me speaks the most—the one having trouble with her German.

"Silence!" a woman roars from near the front door.

I turn to find another woman dressed as all the others walking around, but with a white armband depicting "BLOCK 15" in black ink. Her sleeves are shorter and I spot her inked numbers on her left forearm. She's been trapped here too, yet works for the Nazis. I can't stop myself from watching her for a long moment, trying to read her eyes as if they'll offer an explanation. But all I see is a vacant stare where thoughts must have once existed.

I'm focusing so hard on what's missing that I fail to see her storm toward me with her hand outstretched, wound up and ready to strike me when she's within reach. The sting of her palm against my cheek radiates with an awful burn through my face and neck, nearly knocking me backward. "I am in charge. Do not disrespect me."

I climb into the shallow hole between the wooden slabs, finding just enough space to lie on my side. The dull orange lights leave us with a glow among the darkness snaking over the compound like a hungry shadow. I take in more of my surroundings, the number of bald female heads, dirty striped pajamas that feel like paper against irritated skin, and the protruding shoulder bones or ankles dangling over edges.

An object falls to the ground not far from my view. My mind may be playing tricks on me, but I see the heel of bread loaf.

No one has moved to claim it. There must be more here somewhere.

I arch my neck to whisper to the woman beside me. "Is there food and water anywhere?"

"I've only just gotten here this morning, but before roll call tonight, I was given bread and a bowl of soup that faintly tasted like potatoes. It isn't enough to fill us up after a long day."

"Roll call?" I ask.

"The gong rang. You must have heard it." That bellowing roar scared the living daylights out of me. I noticed it was the start of everyone rushing around. I could see the action unfold from the line where I was waiting. "You need to be in the line-up before they pass by with the list."

She's much more informed than I am if it's true that we've only just arrived within hours of each other.

"Thank you," I offer before resting back onto my side.

I spot the bread still sitting on the floor beneath a column of bunks.

"Lights out!" the BLOCK 15 labeled woman shouts before turning a corner into what must be a small nook.

I keep my eyes pinned on the bread, holding my stare through the darkness after the lights click off. I shimmy forward, twisting and turning to quietly pull my feet out and lower them to the splintered floor. My feet are raw, burning with blisters as I bear weight on them after a brief break.

I rush past the beds, the smell of vomit and sewerage surrounding me. My throat tightens and stomach twists and turns as I kneel to feel around for the bread, my stomach crying for just a crumb if that's all it is.

My fingertips brush along the crust and I snatch it up, but someone slaps their hand around my wrist, squeezing tightly.

"Thief," she says, her accent undoubtedly Polish.

"No, no I'm not. I was going to ask if it belonged to one of you. I saw it fall but knew better than to call out about it."

"And a liar," she says. "To live or die isn't your choice here, but who you are when you leave Auschwitz, will follow you forever."

Auschwitz. Since arriving here, I've spent enough time with my thoughts to realize the German form of the word Auschwitz translates to "sweat out." I'm afraid to wonder why.

"I'm not a monster. I've been starving for days. I was going to check if it belonged to one of you before helping myself. I know who I am. I'm a mother who needs to survive this pit of hell for her children."

My explanation burns with heaviness, as a brief vision of my sweet children flashes through my mind: Max and his quiet resilience. He always knew how to deal with people better than I. He'd become a friend without flinching somehow. He gets that from Leo. Then the thought of Lilli's sweet little smile, it makes me feel like a beast inside. If she were here and hungry, nothing would get in my way of feeding her that crumb or anything else I could get my hands on. But Jordanna, my steadfast and stubborn Jordanna—she would have some choice words for this woman, despite how often I've taught her the importance of patience and understanding, even for the undeserving. She's seen too much cruelty, and she won't let anyone have the chance to hurt someone she loves. Yet, she's also emotionally sensitive, and I'm terrified just thinking how much she might be suffering now.

The woman laughs with disgust. "Oh, only if your children are still alive, of course..." she utters. "Your hope will fade to black soon."

THIRTEEN
DALIA
JULY 30TH, 1943 – OŚWIĘCIM, POLAND

There's nothing but confusion and relentless hunger coursing through me as I lie on a thin, straw-padded cover between the tiers of wooden bunks. The straw is sharper than needles poking me in every possible location. The straw is just a layer between my body and wood that doesn't give way to body weight. Everything inside of me aches and I can't find a position to rest without breathing into someone's face, or receiving the hot breath from someone's mouth. If I can find just a bit of comfort, sleep should come easy after being awake for so long. Although, I fear what awaits when my eyes reopen.

I think about Leo, my darling husband, and wonder where he is right now. I wish I knew how we got separated. It's been over twenty years since we were last apart. The thought of sleeping in a room without him beside me snatches at my heart.

Leo and I had our future mapped out from a young age after being inseparable since sixteen, but our plans came to an abrupt halt when Germany occupied our home city, Warsaw, classifying us as Polish-Germans. Two days after Leo turned eighteen, the German Army conscripted him to fight in the Great

War. With one letter, demanding his service, civil duty and loyalty, our lives were put on hold.

Unlike me, Leo wasn't afraid or worried. Not as I was. He eagerly did what was expected of him as a young man. With fear in his eyes, he told me not to worry as we said goodbye before they sent him to the Western Front. Three years into the war, worry became impossible to avoid. All we heard was news of young men dying horrific deaths in trench warfare.

No letters, just waiting. That summer, a nearby offensive battle resulted in tens of thousands of casualties. There weren't enough nurses or doctors. The pleas for help rang loudly in my ears, knowing I could either sit and wait, or help. I knew little about nursing, but I was willing to learn on the fly, and I learned quickly. I remained with nursing units through the end of the war until there was mention of the 8th Bavarian Reserve Division being sent home after a deadly battle against the British. A field hospital would be the direct destination for whoever was returning home.

I didn't know if Leo was alive or injured.

Like now.

Except I can't go to a field hospital to find out.

My heart was as cold as ice that day in 1918 as I searched for Leo's name on the admission list. He was alive and my blood recirculated through my body as I ran to find him. I remember walking into a partition of the field hospital, spotting the love of my life with a bandage wrapped around his forearm. He was standing at the foot of someone's cot, giving them a lecture about keeping faith through tough times. He was holding up his compass, pointing to it, saying, "As long as you know the right direction, you can find your way. And you did."

That was him. My Leo. I questioned if I was imagining the sight of him, rugged and handsome as he'd always been, but now older and war-torn, mature, aged.

He spotted me just before I reached his side. I'll never

forget the look in his eyes, the instant tears, the shock—he ran to me, scooped me into his arms and kissed me with everything he had in his body.

My heart pounded against his, internal applause at the ending I'd been dreaming of since he left.

Leo's comrades were hooting and hollering at the sight of our reunion, but everything around us disappeared. At that moment, I knew nothing could ever tear us apart again. I wouldn't let it.

I can still feel his lips on mine. The passion. The longing. The safety of home.

Leo, I need you. We aren't supposed to be apart. The memory of him swooping me into his arms plays, and him wooing me with the words, "You see..." He holds his compass up to me—the one I gave him before he deployed. "I told you this was no ordinary compass. You remember what I told you, don't you?" he asked with a beaming smile.

"You said, '*So long as I'm alive, darling, I'll carry this with me so always find my way back to you*,'" I repeated the words I've never forgotten.

"And here I am, my love. I'll always be with you."

"*And here I am, my love. I'll always be with...*"

Gong [*vibrating rumble*]. *Gong* [*vibrating rumble*]. *Gong* [*vibrating rumble*].

A raucous thunder of rubber against metal rumbles through my head, forcing my eyes open, after refusing to close for hours last night.

Even a dream as wonderful of my love couldn't last forever.

I blink again and again, unsure why it's still dark without an inkling of light from the nearby window.

Everyone scurries from the wooden bunks, rushing out of

the barrack. "What's happening?" I ask, hoping someone will answer me.

"If you don't hurry, you won't be able to use the latrine or washroom before roll call."

I don't know who gave me the information, but it's enough to push me out of my cubbyhole as the blood in my body takes a long minute to rush through my limbs. I straighten my striped pajamas over my shoulders and slip my feet into the clogs. I reach for my head to smooth out my hair, but find smooth, sweat-covered skin. I forgot.

I follow the others outdoors to where they're lining up outside two wide, brick structures. I assume these buildings must be the latrine and washroom. I don't remember the last time I relieved myself. After days with nothing to drink, my body is nothing more than an empty cavity.

The light of dawn teases in the distance, a hazy orange, pink glow promising of a pleasant day—forging a lie. There isn't much of a chill in the air, nothing brisk to send energy through my veins. All I have is fear, keeping me alert.

The latrine smells of sewage, bile, and urine, a stench to make a horse stable smell like roses. Holes in cement, side by side, with barely enough room for our arms to remain square to our bodies. Everyone needs to use the sewage holes at once.

Next are the washrooms, rows of water troughs, filthy black rusty basins with water. I want to drink the water but not in front of a spout filling the trough. I make my way toward the next one in sight, waiting as another woman gulps down mouthfuls of water. My heart races, knowing we could be shoved out of here without notice and I'll still have had no water. I don't even know if the children have a drop of water. The image of them starving to death or dying from dehydration, falling to the ground like the others I've seen here, is wearing me down.

At other spouts, I watch others shoving each other for a

turn. If there were only drops left and the children were here, I would make sure they got the water. I would die for them. But they aren't here, and therefore, I must liveif only for the mere hope of staying alive for them.

I've taught them never to fight with others, never to take from another person. But they might have no choice, like me. That's what we're forced to do here, fight for the bare necessity to survive. I move in closer to the woman, but she doesn't budge. Without another thought, I grab the metal pipe connected to the faucet and shove her to the side, hanging my mouth open to fill it with as much water as I can before she shoves me back.

To my surprise, she walks away, allowing me several mouthfuls before I feel someone walking up to my heels. As I did to the woman before, I should expect to get shoved away when patience runs dry. One more mouthful of bitter water is all I take. The warm trickle down my throat is the most incredible feeling.

No one looks at one another. Everyone focuses on cleaning themselves to the best of their ability with what we're given in the short time we have.

Without instruction, I follow those who seem to know, returning to the barrack for a cup. Some bring a bowl with them too, so I take my bowl, spoon, and cup, then follow the others back outside into a line-up of rows.

A male prisoner drags metal barrels toward our lines, removes the lids and prepares to serve whatever is inside. I don't care what it is, I will eat it.

"Why do you have your spoon and bowl?" the woman beside me whispers.

"I—I'm uncertain what we need," I say.

"You should have your leftover bread from dinner last night. You'll only get coffee after roll call."

The bread. The small scrap of bread that fell to the ground last night was that woman's breakfast. "Oh."

I hold the bowl and spoon behind my back, drowning in a pit of sorrow, knowing I will skip another meal.

The sun is bearing its unforgiving rays of heat overhead, promising another sweltering day. A prisoner walks among the rows with a clipboard passing dozens of frail, tired, and terrified women.

"Who is she? Who are the women wearing prisoner uniforms, seemingly in charge, but with no defining markings like some of the others?" I whisper to the same woman who was kind enough to tell me I didn't need a bowl.

"She's a kapo who reports to an SS officer. All of the people with white armbands that say 'KAPO' are half prisoner, half laboring servants to the SS, but also more privileged than the rest. They receive more of everything, especially when they turn someone in for one wrong step. Then there's the block elder with the armband that has BLOCK and our block number. They also answer to the SS but they're responsible for every person in the barrack they're assigned. They can often be the deciding factor of daily selection—deciding whether you live or die. Use caution."

I wonder how one ends up in that situation, privileged among the rest. Although privilege seems to have a much different meaning here. I wonder what other privileges she receives on that side of these rows.

The kapo calls out numbers, our identities, waiting for each prisoner to confirm their presence. The list must be a dozen pages deep by the time she reaches my number. I call out, "Present," and hold my breath until she moves on to the next number.

"You will report or return to the meadows for your work today and every day you remain in quarantine," the kapo says.

It's the most information I've received from someone in charge, or should I say, since I've been here.

"Move, move, move." Someone shoves me forward toward

the man with the metal barrel. He takes my cup from my hand and fills it with a black liquid. "Move."

I peer inside, wondering what I'm looking at. It's thicker than coffee, darker, and smells sweet and putrid. It doesn't matter. I lift the cup to my mouth and empty the contents, forcing the sludge down my throat. The lumps. I don't know what's in the coffee. I struggle to push it through my throat but it eventually slithers down, sloshing around in the emptiness of my stomach.

We're herded back into the barrack to replace our cup, and for some of us, bowls and spoons, still never touched by food, then rushed back outside back into lines where a kapo leads us to our next destination—the meadow, I assume.

The walk is much longer than it appeared, and the blocks are larger up close, proving a greater distance between one barrack and another from end to end. The walk takes just under twenty minutes. A pile of shovels marks the entrance to the meadow but offer no clue or purpose for why we'll need them. Again, I follow the others who seem to know where to begin. All I can wonder is if I'm digging my own grave. I've heard rumors of Polish Jews being taken into the middle of fields, held at gunpoint and told to dig. They didn't know they were digging their graves until they were lying dead in the holes. I told myself it was just a story—a lie, to make myself feel better.

Kapos, women with white armbands and a glint of authority in their eyes, sprawl out along the barbed wire fencing encasing the meadow. It's clear they plan to stand and monitor us throughout the day. Each kapo looks angry with a sense of brutality in their eyes, and they aren't forced to dig holes. Their only task is to watch us. I shouldn't judge. I don't know what they've already been through or survived. All I know is my organs feel like they're feasting on each other.

I wait for a rare moment when they're all facing a different direction to ask a woman nearby the pressing question on my mind. "Why are we digging?" I ask, keeping my voice low, hoping she can hear me.

She glances at me with tired and forlorn eyes. "No one knows. We were just told to dig. It doesn't matter. We're all going to die soon, anyway. They take what they can get from us before gassing us to death, then cremating us."

Her words slink down my spine, my nerves responding with a twitch. "Ho-how do you...how do you know?"

The woman glances up at me, dark circles underline her eyes, her lips chapped and raw, and her neck covered in insect bites, making me scratch the back of mine. She shrugs before answering. "Others have said so." She nudges her chin to the left toward the barren open land. I find nothing more than grass that eventually meets the sky, though. "When you see it, you'll know—a smokestack of ashes from cremated bodies."

Without the sight of a smokestack in the distance, I should tell myself she's telling stories or repeating false rumors.

Hours pass and my tired muscles ache while continuing to dig in rhythmic motions, a second hand of a clock spinning without pause. All the while I stare off into the horizon, waiting to see a stack of smoke rise into the sky. It could be true. We've been told so little; it makes sense to think the SS would hide the truth of what they plan to do with us. If we knew how it might end, no one would continue working.

I'm strong. I'll fight, I remind myself. If I can imagine a future where I'm back home—we're all back home and together —it must mean it will happen. When I close my eyes, I try to sew these images together—just a daydream—but each time I try, darkness descends. A darkness conceals the unimaginable.

The metal spade of my shovel pings against rubble and dirt, the sound a relentless ringing in my ears. All that changes is the air's temperature as clouds burn away from the sun. I turn around, letting the sun beat off my back rather than my face, trying to ignore the sweat dripping down my spine.

Eventually, a hum of commotion whizzes around me in a ripple of unease and when I look up, I spot the rumored stack of smoke, faint, but distinct, stark against the clear blue sky.

FOURTEEN
JORDANNA
AUGUST 14TH, 1943 – ŁÓDŹ, POLAND

In the kitchen of our apartment in Hamburg, Mama would stand next to the refrigerator with a pencil in her right hand, poking her chin while staring at the wall-mounted calendar. She would always say, "I don't even know what day it is!" when there was too much going on at once. I would laugh because it seemed silly to me, thinking someone could forget what day it is.

I'm uncertain of what day of the week it is now, or the date.

Here within the encasing walls of Przemysłowa Street, minutes can be confused for hours, and days for months.

In the mornings, we're awoken by a trumpet before the sun rises. This morning is much darker than usual. I suspect it's earlier than we've been waking up too. However, as each morning prior, we are still screamed at by women we've been told to address as educators followed by enforced exercise, fights over the use of toilets and running water to wash ourselves, all so we can stand in a double row line for nearly an hour waiting for these so-called educators to ensure we are all in attendance.

Food is scarce, a potato at best, maybe a stale piece of bread if we're lucky. Lilli refuses to eat too often, and I've had to force food into her mouth, fighting her to consume what we're given. She doesn't understand that we'll die without sustenance.

I'm afraid we might die even with it.

Every morning when I stand up, my body feels like a hollow tree trunk, one ax-chop away from falling. The hunger is a growing hole inside of me and when I take in a deep breath, my stomach caves in, the skin slinking against my rib cage.

We haven't seen Alfie. I don't know how he's getting on, his hearing, his chance at making it through a day unscathed in his condition. Even without him here, I can't stop thinking about him. It's foolish, I know, especially with all of us except Lilli and me being separated, but my heart aches for him differently, and I can't stop myself from wondering if he feels the same. I may never find out.

Lilli is wriggling her knees as we stand side by side in this morning's roll call. She keeps scratching her head from the hairs poking up and I'm afraid someone will think she has bugs. I nudge my elbow to her shoulder. "Stop touching your head."

"But it itches," she whines.

"Ignore it," I mutter as an educator makes her way toward us with a clipboard in hand.

"First row, step forward," she says. That's not us. "Grab your belongings and report to Block nine."

"Second row, same, but report to Block ten. You have no more than three minutes before those blocks begin their roll call —you are required to attend the second roll call this morning. They will call on you and if you're not there, you shall receive beatings."

We aren't familiar with the layout of blocks. We haven't been allowed to move far from the block we've been quarantined in since arriving here. We've been in Block 15 so I would think the other blocks must be within this square.

The other girls scatter about, all looking for their assigned block. I watch as one of the other girls from our assigned row studies the number on a nearby block before stepping inside. I guess that must be our block.

With a tug, I pull Lilli in the direction toward the other girl, confirming the number 10 posted next to an access door. "Come along. Let's bring our belongings inside then we'll find the line-up."

I open the door, finding rows of wooden bunk beds, but also what I assume are meant to be mattresses on the ground, made from a paper-like material with straw sticking out of the sides. There's no space within the tiers of bunks, not that I can see, and there aren't many mattresses left on the floor.

"There are so many children here," Lilli whispers, her eyes big and overwhelmed.

"I know. Let's set our belongings down on two mattresses for now." I figure the straw stuffed material will be better than the bare wooden floor.

"What about the bunks?" Lilli asks.

"There are no open spaces. I'll just pull two of the mattresses on the floor next to each other." I grab hold of one to drag it a few steps backward, but end up bumping to someone climbing out of the tier of bunks.

"Watch it," a girl behind me warns. "You don't want to get stepped on, do you?" Her question takes me by surprise, coming from someone in the same situation we're all in. She gives me a long hard stare, and even though I have at least a head of height on her, and she doesn't seem concerned with giving me an attitude.

"I'm sorry," I offer, moving aside to give her more space.

"We were just trying to arrange our beds," Lilli says to the girl.

"I take it you two are new here? Did you notice there are no free beds?"

"Yes, that's why we're moving mattresses on the ground," I counter.

She sneers and shakes her head. "You must be here for behavior correction, yes? Let me guess, you were caught begging on the streets?" she utters, crossing her arms over her chest.

"No, we haven't done anything wrong," Lilli says with hostility.

"Children are only here for a few reasons...You're Polish and either got caught stealing, begging, or helping a Jew, or you're a Polish orphan whose parents refused to sign the *Volk-liste*—the German People's List, which makes you traitors to Germany."

I never heard Mama or Papa discuss anything about the *Volkliste*, but maybe it's because they're both ethnically Polish.

"We shouldn't be here. We haven't done anything wrong. Our parents were taken to help aid injured people during an air raid," I say.

"Well, you aren't wanted here, all the same. There's already no space or enough food for those of us who have been here. You'll just take more from us," the girl retorts. She's around my age, I think, despite her apparent immaturity.

"So, why are you here?" I ask her.

The girl narrows her eyes at me as if I should know the reason. "If you must know..." she laments. "I was with my brother, helping him throw some bread to the Jewish people in the Łódź ghetto. Only, I was caught."

"You're being punished?" I press.

The girl reaches up to grab her blanket from the second-tier bunk and whips it out in front of her so it floats down over the mattress. "Punished?" she says, chewing on the word while unfolding a corner of the blanket. "We sew, harvest, wash, cook, clean, construct pots and pans, and some of us are forced to use tools that could kill us. They hardly feed us and if we don't abide by every rule, we're whipped. I'm sure you've been 'pun-ished' by your parents at some point in your life. This place—

these aren't just punishments. The educators here only know how to torture us."

"How long will we be kept here?" I ask, desperation heavy in my voice.

She shakes her head and groans, highlighting her annoyance with my questions. "You don't know until you're gone."

Lilli grabs my hand, hers drenched in sweat, hot, and her grip tight. "Is there anyone who can help?"

The girl chuckles. "If you find someone, let me know. We're on our own here." She walks out of the barrack, heavy feet stomping across the wood, leaving us staring at the wall.

I peer down at Lilli, finding nothing but fear in her features, the same as I'm feeling inside. Mama would always tell me to look for hope even if it's not something we can see. I realize now, it wasn't a life lesson, it was a way to keep us strong when we might consider giving up. I wonder if she's found any semblance of hope, wherever she is. Even if she hasn't, she would still make sure we did. I need to give Lilli hope, despite everything she just heard.

"Don't listen to her. We'll ask someone else. She doesn't seem very nice, and we shouldn't take her for her word," I whisper to Lilli.

Lilli and I—along with the other girls from the quarantine block—make our way back outside toward the others lining up for our second roll call of the morning. We all try and blend in with one another, but many of the children who were here before us seem to be giving those of us who are new grief, just like the girl from inside the barrack. They must surely realize we're being held prisoner here, and all in the same situation. The least we can do is be kind to one another.

An older girl in gray pajamas, a shaved head, and pale skin makes her way in front of the rows with a clipboard. She's another one of the prison workers and I'm still wondering how they apprehended a job where they are in charge over another.

It's not a job I desire, but I wonder if they're treated differently than the rest of us.

"You," the girl with the clipboard says to a little girl in the front row. She might be the youngest looking child among this group. Perhaps even younger than Lilli. "Step forward."

The little girl hesitates for just a short moment before doing as she's told.

"You soiled the bed last night," the older girl shouts, letting it be known that the younger child had an accident.

"I needed the toilet," the little girl replies, her voice weak and shaky.

An educator steps out from around the building. "This is her," the older girl says. "The bed-wetter."

I watch in horror, my eyes open so wide the air burns, fighting to keep them open.

Lilli used to have accidents too. I often overheard conversations between Mama and Lilli about how much water she had before bed, or if she had any nightmares she could recall. Mama never made her feel like she'd done something wrong, especially since Lilli was embarrassed when it happened. The accidents eventually stopped, but that was only a year ago.

I glance down at her, finding her pale and wide-eyed, horror bulging through her eyes. I take her arm and twist her around, pulling her face into my chest, and cover her ears. She doesn't fight against my hold.

The little girl needs love and assurance that everything will be all right. That's what I would do if I was standing in front of her right now. But I'm not.

The educator shoves the little girl down to the muddy ground, face first, and pulls a whip up by her side. I close my eyes fast, unable to watch what's happening. The slap of leather breaking through the air and the slashing against the girl's backside is the most unbearable sound I've heard in all my life. Until her squealing cry follows, mumbling with apologies.

Slap and slash.

Horrific wailing.

Slap and slash.

More wails.

Slap and slash.

Then silence.

She's been punished for wetting the bed.

Burning acid lurches up my throat and I tilt my head back, warning myself to hold it together. My stomach hurts, my eyes strain. A sob threatens to accompany vomit. It hurts. Everything in my body hurts.

She's a little girl, unconscious with her face in the mud. She might suffocate. I need to help.

I can't move.

I'm not allowed to help or move.

The little girl continues to lie still in the mud as numbers float into the air above our heads. The other girls confirm their presence, while I assume our numbers will be called at the end as new arrivals.

Lilli's number is called first. She confirms her presence.

"Report to the tailor workshop following breakfast."

Lilli stares up at me, fear in her blue eyes.

My number follows. "Present," I assert.

"Report to the front gate for farming labor following breakfast."

We're being separated. I want to ask for a reassignment to stay with Lilli, but I've seen the punishments for any questions asked.

"You'll be safe there," I whisper to Lilli. "Listen to their instructions and do as they say. We'll be brought back together after our work duties, but only if you follow their rules. Do you understand?"

Lilli doesn't respond. I peer down at her, catching her unblinking stare through a gap of girls in the front row.

She's looking at the little girl who's been whipped unconscious.

I take her hand, knowing our seconds in this row are coming to an end. "Please tell me you heard me," I plea in a whisper.

"Yes," she utters.

"You'll be okay. Just follow orders."

The prison girl in charge hands us scraps of bread as she dismisses us to our assigned locations.

Lilli grabs the back of my pajamas. "Don't leave me," she cries quietly.

"We can't ignore our orders," I tell her, taking her hand away from my pajamas. I give her a kiss on the cheek and grab her chin to look at me. "We'll be fine. We have warrior blood, remember?" Papa has always told us this. It was never to make his or Mama's efforts in the war out to be heroic, but to instill in us that we're strong enough to endure more than we may think.

With the girls from our new block scattering, I call out, "Is anyone else going to the tailor workshop?"

No one answers in the rush of everyone trying to get to where they're supposed to be. "I'm going there," a girl says, her voice so soft I wasn't sure she was speaking to us. She's about my height, maybe my age. Her hair has grown out some, maybe a month or two's worth. Her skin is thin along her face, blue veins prominent beneath her eyes and her cheeks make her look like she's sucking on a lemon.

"This is my little sister, Lilli. Would you mind showing her the way to the tailor workshop?"

"Of course," she says. "You can follow me."

She steps ahead of Lilli, her shoulders rolled forward, her head slightly tilted toward the ground.

"Go on," I tell Lilli. "She'll show you where to go. Tell whoever is in charge—whoever has a clipboard, or an educator in uniform—that you were assigned to work there."

"All right," she says, peering up at me with tear-filled eyes.

"You'll be all right," I say, wishing more than anything that she wasn't able to read the truth in my eyes so easily. I don't know if we'll be all right. I don't know much of anything now. I can't tell her where Mama and Papa are, or Max, or even Alfie. I don't know anything more than she does, but I'm trying my best to put on a brave face for her. She just knows me too well to believe it. "I love you."

I'm not certain I remember my way to the front gate, but from what I've been able to gather in the time spent on the outside perimeter of the quarantine block, there are only two roads that make up this walled square of buildings.

"Where are you supposed to be?" an educator shouts at me, standing guard between two blocks.

"The front gate," I reply. "I've just been released from quarantine and trying to find my way."

She steps toward me, shoving her hand against my back, forcing me to trip over my feet as I drag myself along in clog shoes that are too large for me. She keeps shouting at me to move. "Walk faster. Faster! Or are your feet broken?"

We turn a corner onto the road parallel to the one I've been on since arriving. "The line is there," she says, pointing down the road made up of more blocks.

I scuffle my feet, moving as quickly as I can along the rock-riddled muddy terrain until reaching the line of boys and girls. No one turns around to see who has joined the end of the line and that's fine, so long as I didn't miss the departing group.

With a struggle to catch my breath, I find I've arrived just in the nick of time as everyone begins moving toward a truck lined out with the main gate. We're shoved in together like canned meat, children of all ages with the youngest being from what looks to be seven or eight. I can hardly see anyone around me beside the person sitting to my right and the person to my left, and the bald head of the person in front.

My heart thuds and my stomach is burning from the acidity

of the bread as the truck jolts us along the bumpy road. The ride lasts longer than I would have thought, but it doesn't seem we are going very far, rather moving at a slow pace. It gives me time to sit with my thoughts. The "educators", as they refer to themselves here—whoever they are—must not have acquired our proper identification yet, making them categorize us as orphans since we were found without our parents.

The truck pulls up to a farm, acres of land surrounded by trees. As we're pulled off the truck, an older boy shoves the wooden handle of a thin shovel against my chest. The person behind me shoves me forward to move. We walk along another line down the center of the farmland until we reach dirt mounds with evenly distributed green rooted plants.

Others drop to their knees as if already assigned to a section of the crops and I peer around in search of an empty space, finding one at the very end of the row of working children. I hurry by the others so I'm not spotted as the only one not already digging at the dirt, but I'm forced to stop when someone grabs a hold of my pant leg, pulling me fast toward the ground.

FIFTEEN

JORDANNA

AUGUST 14TH, 1943 – ŁÓDŹ, POLAND

Wisps of grass tickles my nose after being pulled to the ground, fast and without warning. For a moment, I'm back at the park near home, resting on a picnic blanket. But then I open my eyes, to the endless field surrounding me. I push myself up to my knees and spot the person who grabbed me—not an assailant at all.

Alfie. His beautiful jade eyes are full of words he isn't speaking. He's here to work too. "Hi," he says with his breath. He recognizes me—even without hair—a face as neutral as all the rest. He swallows hard and his forehead creases with both concern and relief. I want to hug him, beg him not to leave me— make me feel better—but I wouldn't do that even if we weren't under a watchful eye.

"You're here," I say, more for myself, wondering if I'm imagining him.

"Mistakes will not be tolerated," a guard shouts. "Mistakes result in punishment. We work. We don't speak." She leans over another child and screams the orders into their ear once more.

I glance at Alfie, tense, worried how much worse it might be here on the field than in quarantine, but he isn't paying attention to the guard.

I tap his knee then point to my ear, wondering if his hearing is any better. He's quick to wag his hand and whispers, "A little," before returning his attention to the soil.

A smile threatens to tug at my lips, but I can sense a pair of eyes boring into my back. Alfie moves to his left, creating enough space for me to squeeze in between him and the boy on the other side.

"Watch me," he whispers, focusing on the plant. He digs a circle around it, tugs at the stem, and uses his shovel again to widen the hole. With a second pull, a mound of dirt comes free, revealing potatoes. He removes the larger ones, leaves the smaller ones attached, and re-buries the plant.

The field stretches out before us, with rows of green sprouting plants. Others have already moved up a row or two. Another working boy, maybe a year or two younger than me, walks down our line, dropping potato sacks for us to fill. I suppose it's clear what I'll be doing all day.

No one speaks, only works. There are plenty of older prisoner guards keeping a watch on us that it seems impossible to do much else but dig.

"Is Lilli all right?" Alfie whispers as I dig my first circle.

"Yes," I whisper back, but he peers at me from the corner of his eye and I don't know if he's questioning me or isn't hearing much at all still. I nod my head to answer again. This time, his shoulders fall, and he takes a deep breath.

"Thank God."

"We've been in quarantine since arriving," I whisper again, wondering if he'll peer over again.

He doesn't.

There's so much I want to say and he's right here but there might as well be a brick wall between us. I try and focus on digging up the potato roots, avoiding the thought and feeling of the sun bearing down on my pale bald head and neck. I saw some other girls wearing scarves over their heads, but I don't know where they acquired them.

A shriek from down the row startles me into dropping my shovel. I peer down to see what's happening and watch a boy being dragged backward by a guard. He's screaming and crying.

"Don't look," Alfie utters.

What did he do wrong? I need to know. How do we know how to avoid the same mistake?

"This was your dinner, but you left it behind. Now it's gone. Tonight, when you're starving, you'll remember how important each potato is, won't you?" The guard's words are loud enough to hear without watching the scene. Starvation is a punishment. We've all been starving, living off bread and soup water with potato peels, and a thick coffee-like substance. We're allowed to pump water twice a day, never able to be fully satisfied or even a little, really. I keep wondering how long we can survive without enough food.

With each potato I drop into the sack, I consider taking a bite, dirt-covered, raw, and all.

As Alfie is plucking potatoes, I notice a slash on his right arm. My heart swells, wondering what happened, if he was one of the children who had been whipped.

I glance around for watchful eyes, finding the guards focused on others so I reach over and grab his wrist. His gaze falls to my hand then he pulls his sleeve down to cover the wound. "I'm okay," he says softly. We aren't clean here. We're sleeping, eating, and working in dirt.

The thought reminds me of Papa's war stories...Mama would always follow his stories with: "They're trained to survive in inhuman conditions. They know how to take care of themselves in all conditions. It's nothing you'll ever have to worry about, my darlings." She couldn't have known life would lead us here.

The last story Papa told us was more than a year ago now, but I remember the moment so clearly still:

I scowl at Papa, listening to him tell me about the one night they had to sleep in mud. "What's interesting, sweetheart, is that while this story might sound awful, it was the most comfortable sleep I had gotten in weeks that summer. The mud kept us cool. It made me think about the natural resources around me and what else I could take advantage of when we were feeling like all hope was lost for us in our battle. Nature has a way of keeping us alive if we're smart enough to take advantage of what's right in front of us."

"Like what?" I ask him. "Besides mud."

"Eating your greens, catching rain in tins, using vegetables to heal wounds, and leaves—they can do just about anything to help most situations."

I imagine Papa wrapping himself in leaves to stay safe in battles, but I'm not convinced it could work that easily. "You had greens to eat? I thought most of your food came in tins?"

"Sure, we had greens. Dandelions were our favorite snack some days, and a handful of green clovers could be considered eating a mouthful of luck," he says with laughter.

"Leo, what are you filling her head with? She's going to be foraging through the woods eating poisonous berries," Mama scolds him.

"Don't eat berries unless you know what they are. Trust me. That never ends well." His laughter tells me there's a story about bad berries too.

Moving through the field of potato plants, I spot grassy areas in the distance abutted to a line of trees separating us from what I assume to be more greenery on the other side.

I wonder where the trees lead. Is it a way out? A way in? I think I see people between the trees. Could that be? Are they waiting for us? To take us away? I blink and the people are gone. I blink again and they're back.

Sweat is rolling down my arms like raindrops—the thought of rain is something of a dream at this point. My skin is tight, burning, and my heart is throbbing. They haven't given us our daily soup and I don't have a bowl.

Alfie says something to me, but I can't hear what he's saying. His fingers sweep against my face before he lunges toward me as nightfall settles in, blinding me as it does before bed.

* * *

A sting across my cheek rattles my brain around. "Sit up. You have to sit up right away." Alfie is growling at me. Confusion dangles above my head as I'm not quite sitting or lying down, but Alfie's face is all I can see. He keeps looking from one side to the other. "Get up, Jordanna. You fainted. We can't let the guard see you like this. You'll be all right." He squeezes his hand around my knee but all I feel are pins and needles.

"Dandelions would be nice," I say.

He stares at me, his brow furrowing. He points to the sky off in the distance. "Rain is coming. Stay upright."

Rain? It hasn't rained in weeks. My body sways in slow circles, and the sweat on my face catches a slight breeze. It feels good.

With another glance toward the trees, I find Mama wearing her strawberry-pink rain bonnet, staring up at the sky.

"Mama?" I call out, my words struggling for sound against my ragged breaths.

"What's the issue over here?" The voice breaks through the thick air, sharp and biting before a strike to my back forces the air out of my lungs, leaving me to fight for a pinched gasp. Pain shoots through me as my knees give out and I fall forward, my forehead thudding against the pebbled dirt. Again, I stifle a breath, pulling in more gritty dry dirt than air. The dusty substance burns within my dry throat.

"Are you unable to work?" a girl shouts, her voice poisoned with venom and impatience.

My vision distorts with colorful spots, stinging from sweat and tears, but I can make out her figure, daunting and stiff as she towers over me, waiting for an answer I don't give fast enough. She kicks me again, this time to the side of my ribs, and much harder, the force flipping me onto my back before enduring another throb from my head hitting the ground. A burst of light sparks behind my eyes as a sharp pain sears down my spine. For a moment, I'm unsure if I might pass out again.

The ground beneath me is unforgiving, unsteady, and small rocks dig into my palms as I try to hold myself steady. A ringing in my ears silences my surroundings. All I can hear is my pulse pounding against my temples. My breaths are shallow, and my chest is tight. My vision is still blurry as I try to force myself back upright, but the trembling in my hands prevents me from getting up. I slip against the dirt and try again, pushing against the burn in my weak muscles.

Mama's words ring in my ears, *"You are tougher than you give yourself credit for and you can accomplish things your mind would never imagine. Trust me, sweetheart."* Sometimes it feels as if she's spent a lifetime preparing us for what she could never have imagined.

"Yes, I can work," I manage to croak, unsure if my voice is loud enough for anyone to hear. The effort to speak makes my stomach clench, forcing me to swallow back the threat of bile rising up to my throat. I can't give in to the weakness, not here, not like this.

The guard spares me another glance, carrying on down the row of others with her hands clasped behind her back, her chin in the air. I watch as she moves along, waiting for her to turn back and come after me with another strike.

Alfie stands just a couple steps away, his eyes wide and his face pale. He looks at me as if I'm a ghost, and his heavy breaths tell me he's struggling to keep himself together too. He blinks hard, holding his eyes closed a moment as if trying to shut out the scene in front of him. He finally sucks in a sharp shuddering breath and stabs his shovel back into the dirt.

I force myself to stand, my legs frailer than toothpicks as I try to steady my balance. "I want to run away," I whisper, keeping my voice quieter than the passing breeze. "Let's run away."

He can't hear me, and therefore doesn't respond. It's obvious he still can't hear a thing despite what he said earlier. I watch him continuing this tireless labor and all I can do is endure the pang of helplessness in my chest. We're both hurting so much and couldn't be more disconnected, even while standing right beside each other.

My nerves fray as I reach for my shovel, still fighting to hold myself upright. My hands refuse to tighten into a strong enough grip needed to make a dent in the ground. Still, I try the best I can, watching dirt flutter around my feet.

I can't go on this way. I'm away from Lilli and unable to communicate with Alfie. The momentary slice of hope I felt when seeing him here is slipping away, knowing that with only silence between us, our chances of helping each other are dwindling.

The heaviness of despair bears on my chest, holding me back from answers too far out of reach. Even the darkening sky and dense air are against me, making it impossible for me to see past this moment. Alfie and Lilli need me. Mama must have always felt like this about us, but she never stumbled to find a fix for every problem, big or small. What would she do now? How many times in an hour can I ask myself this same question? At fifteen, I should know more. I should know better.

She would tell me *the answer is most often right in front of you*. So, I stare at the pebbles beneath my shovel, watching them bounce from everyone else digging around me. The *ting-ting-ting* from shovels against rock reminds me of—a pattern.

We're in our living room, sitting around our coffee table with Papa on the sofa, leaning in toward us. "Did you hear it?" he asked us.

"The pattern," Mama says, from the corner of the room, watching with a smile. "Listen for the patterns."

"You said...'It's time for Max to go to bed.'" I blurt out.

Papa tilts his head and raises his brow in my direction.

"Not even close," Max says with a snicker.

"Do it again, Papa!" Lilli squeals, bouncing up and down on her knees in her blue nightgown, her coiled pigtails swinging in every direction.

"You don't understand what it means either," Max teases Lilli.

"You know, we should use this to our advantage in class. No one will know what we're saying," Alfie says.

All they need is more ways to keep secrets, I groan to myself. "Alfie, shouldn't you be getting home?" I nudge my shoulder into his.

"Jordanna," Mama scolds me. "Alfie's parents said he could spend the night. Don't be rude to our guest."

"He might as well just live here." I sigh. It wouldn't be the worst thing in the world, but he doesn't need to know I feel that way.

Mama clears her throat but ignores me. "Go on, darling. Show them one more time. Then you're off to bed, little mouse," Mama tells Lilli.

"All right then, let's see here..." Papa says.

He lifts his pencil and begins tapping it against the coffee table.

[— ..— —. / ..—. — — — .—. / —... . —..]
dah dit-dit dah-dah dit / dit-dit-dah-dit dah-dah-dah dit-dah-dah-dit /
dah-dit-dit-dit dit dah-dit-dit

He really did say it was time for bed this round, just maybe not to Max specifically. Max and I have been proficient in Morse code since we were Lilli's age, but she and Alfie have been learning together over the last years.

"Time for bed!" Alfie shouts. That's an easy one for Alfie. He picked up Morse code quickly.

"Time for bed!" Lilli repeats.

"Look at that, honey! All the children know Morse code. Now, if you ever must talk to someone in secret, this will solve all your problems, as long as they know Morse code too, of course."

It's not like we'll be sending secret war codes over a radio during a war, but Papa feels strongly about teaching us skills that he says saved his life when he was fighting during the Great War.

Mama smiles. "I'm sure that'll come in handy when they're asking me for a glass of water in the middle of the night," she jokes. "It's a wonderful skill for you to all have. You never know when you might need it. We should all be lucky Papa has been able to teach us all."

I never thought all those years of learning Morse code from Papa would ever help me in my lifetime. Yet, it's like he knew all along, we might someday be desperate for a way to communicate without speaking, but only if the other person knows Morse code too. Alfie does, thanks to Papa.

I jog through my memory, recalling the patterns that symbolize letters. It hasn't been that long. After a long moment, I begin to tap out the words. "We need to find a way out."

It takes Alfie a few seconds to peek back at me. "How?" he whispers.

He understood. My chin trembles as I fight back tears, knowing I've found a way to talk to him. If anyone was over the age of forty here, I'd worry they might be familiar with Morse code, but no one is older than seventeen. Not here. Only at the barracks.

"What block are you in?" I tap out my next question.

"Four. You?"

It takes me a minute to think about the code in number format. Then I remember how silly it is that the number one and zero are two of the longest tap codes: one short and four long then five long. I tap out the number ten with my knuckle between his knee and mine while continuing to scoop dirt out of a hole with my other hand.

A booming thud follows my last tap, and I whip my head around looking for where it came from. Alfie jumps and looks around too. It doesn't take long before we both gasp at the sight of a girl who's collapsed face forward onto the ground.

"She's dead," someone says, their voice calm and unconcerned.

"You!" another voice shouts. "Take her to the truck and collect her clothes."

She's pointing at Alfie, who's not looking at her because he hasn't heard the guard with a whip in her hand. I keep my focus set on the guard but with subtlety, reach behind me and tap Alfie's knee. He stands up and steps forward in front of me when he spots the guard pointing at him. His knees wobble and his fists clench at his side. *What does she want him to do?*

SIXTEEN

DALIA

AUGUST 14TH, 1943 – OŚWIĘCIM, POLAND

The two-week period of quarantining is over with only question marks on the horizon. We scatter to find our new assigned blocks, dry dirt kicking up into our faces as we shuffle along in our wooden shoes. No one knows what comes next. I expect only hard labor, exhaustion, and hunger. This place isn't for survival...it's a place where death awaits us all.

The new block assignment—Block 13—isn't far from the quarantine block. Upon arriving here, I've found my welcome as non-existent as it was when I arrived in the last block. Similarly, there's no space for additional people here, and many of us have been newly assigned as of today. Block elder 13 shouts rules, ones I've already heard during quarantine.

"You will use the latrine when told. No one is to leave the block after the lights go out or before the morning gong rings. Those of you assigned labor duty in the main Auschwitz camp will need to wake an hour prior to the rest. By four a.m., you will be washed and ready to report for duty. You will receive your assignment location by the transport kapo." This block elder seems more pleasant than the last, but first impressions aren't everything here. "The following numbers, report to me at once for your assignment..."

My number is called as part of the list she rattles off. This morning, after roll call, those of us in quarantine were split into three different blocks, but it seems at least twenty of us have been sent here to Block 13.

I haven't even found a narrow spot on the wooden bunk platforms yet, and I'm still holding my armful of belongings, but I step forward toward the block elder, waiting for my assignment.

It's hard not to watch her face as her gaze darts around, searching for the other women she's called over. This block elder has a yellow Jewish star badge sewn to her uniform despite her semi-privileged role. She's a Jewish block elder working for the SS. I wonder if they're given extra food or privileges. This woman is younger than I first suspected, possibly only Jordanna's age, and by the way she pinches her lips together, I sense a hint of nervousness about her. Her knuckles are white as she grips the pencil in her hand. I also wonder what her story is, who she was before arriving here, why she was selected to be in charge of her own kind, and what's at stake if she doesn't adhere to orders from above.

Her voice grows louder while repeating several of the numbers as not everyone has made their way over yet. A few women stumble away from the wooden bunks and rush in our direction, their clogs clunking heavily. The block elder takes a moment to inspect each of the numbered patches on our chests, narrowing her eyes before staring down at the papers attached to her clipboard.

She points at me with the flat edge of her pencil. "You, Block twenty." She points to another woman two steps behind me. "You, Block twenty-one." Then she adds a mark to her paper, muttering the word "missing." Her eyes refocus on our group, then she cranes her neck from side to side. "And you, Block twenty as well." She points her pencil at the woman to my right. "You will be working at the main camp and will be ready to leave no later than twenty minutes past four in the morning. You are to meet the transport kapo between Blocks three and four."

"What will our duties be, if you don't mind me asking?" the woman behind me questions. My throat tightens, fearing the block elder's response. We aren't entitled to additional information. I think we've all learned that by now.

"The infirmary. You'll be assigned nursing duties."

"Thank you, thank you," the woman behind me cries out. She can't possibly be new enough not to know when to keep quiet. The duration of quarantine is long enough to learn how to attempt surviving, against what seems to be a lack of odds.

"You speak fluent German and have experience in nursing, no?" the block elder asks her.

"Yes, yes, I do."

"Be thankful for that. As for the rest of you who have just arrived, you'll be dispersed in the morning for individual duties."

Each spoken word appears to be a struggle for this young block elder. It would be easy to assume she's never been in charge of anything before. Though someone must have seen something in her that conveyed she would support the Nazis in this capacity.

With nothing left to say, she spins on her heels and exits the block, leaving us new arrivals in a huddled group, and also, the center of everyone else's attention.

"Lucky you," someone says bitterly as we pass by between the columns of tiered bunks.

Without much thought, I stop walking, turn to the woman who called out and approach her at the wooden bunk.

"Where are you from?" I ask her.

"Why do you care?"

"Why wouldn't I?" I ask.

"No one cares about anyone here. Is it not clear to you yet?"

She looks to be between eighteen and twenty, young. "I care about everyone who doesn't deserve to be here. I care about every innocent human being who is being deprived of simple freedoms." I care about finding my family, getting out of here and staying alive all while knowing it seems more unlikely every minute longer that I'm here.

She snickers at me. "You just haven't been here long enough."

What's long enough? My heart bleeds today just as it did two weeks ago when I saw my babies and Leo last, and the torment will continue until I find them.

"Perhaps you're right. That must be it—not enough time."

I place my hand on her wrist and sweep my thumb over her dry skin. I close my eyes and picture Jordanna, forcing a small smile. It's a mere gesture of warmth—the only form I can give this young woman. I would want someone to do the same for Jordanna if she was the one speaking her mind.

A tear falls down her cheek. "I miss my parents and sister. They have me collecting the hair from every newly shaved prisoner, bagging it and bringing it to a warehouse every single day for eleven hours straight. This is what happens when you stay here too long."

When Jordanna would spill her truths, I would search for something positive, a bit of hope, even if it was hard to believe. That's what mothers do: we make everything better in whatever capacity that might be, even if it's just a tale of hope.

"Well, the SS must have seen some form of strength within you," I tell her, swallowing the sick feeling in my stomach, imagining such a horrific job.

"That's it?" she utters, gritting her teeth.

"And I believe you're lucky too," I tell her, feeding the same words she gave me. I realize now, it wasn't an insult, just the truth.

"I'm from Lublin—so, not very lucky apparently," she utters.

"I recognize your accent. I grew up on the outskirts of Warsaw. I'm Dalia. It's nice to meet you."

"Whoever you meet here will be gone soon," she says. "But since you think you're different and I'm lucky, I'm Brygid. Just another name you'll forget."

She rests her head back down on her folded arms and wipes away her tears.

I find a small opening above Brygid two spaces to the left. I slide my blanket wrapped eating utensils into the space, shoving it as far back as I can reach into the second-tier bunk. The woman on the bunk to the right of my newly claimed spot flips her head in my direction. Her eyes are closed, unaware that I'm about to climb up beside her and crowd her space even more. Her skin has a yellow hue, her lips are tinted blue, her eyelids red. My gaze rests on her hand poking out from beneath her cheek, fingernails gnawed down to the skin, bones prominently punctuating at joints.

"She's ill," the woman above me says, hanging her head over the ledge.

"With what?"

Her shoulders shrug, or at least, I think they do. It's hard to see much body movement when no one can move far. "Could be anything."

I press my hand on the sick woman's head, her skin far hotter than an average body temperature. "How long has she been ill?"

"A week," the woman a row down responds. "Maybe a little less than a week."

"Has she gone to the infirmary?"

"I don't want to die," the ill woman rasps. "Don't take me to the infirmary. That's where people go to die."

And it's where I'm being sent to work tomorrow...

"What symptoms do you have other than a fever?" I ask the poor girl.

"I can't keep food down, or inside of me."

It could be dysentery or malaria. I'm sure both are more than common here in these abhorrent living conditions. "Are you able to keep water down?" She doesn't respond. I touch my hand to her face. "Are you still awake?"

"Her name is Magda," Brygid speaks up.

"Magda, can you hear me?"

She doesn't respond, but she's still breathing. I press my fingers to the artery in her neck, and though it's a slow beat, it isn't down to a deadly level. If I'm going to be at the infirmary tomorrow, maybe there's something I can find to help her. Of course, I'm sure I'll have eyes on me for every move I make, even if it is the place where *people go to die*.

The guilt I feel over my reluctance to crawl into the hole beside her gnaws at my stomach. I've always been a helper rather than a hider, but we all need to protect ourselves here somehow. After all, what if she's contagious? But with a quick glance down the rest of the row, it's clear my options are limited to this one space and if I don't take it, I will likely end up on the ground.

I climb up to the bunk base and arrange my blanket then set my utensils by the wooden wall. With every effort to make myself comfortable on my side, facing the opposite direction to Magda, I still pull my smock up above my nose to try and protect myself from contracting her illness. I close my eyes and begin my silent evening prayer: Please God, protect Max, Jordanna, Lilli, and Alfie. Keep my Leo safe, his anger and hatred for Germany concealed, his efforts of finding us less than the risk of losing his life. Bring my family back together. Let this war end so peace can shine over us like an enlightenment from above. Bless us with a new beginning.

Magda's body convulses against mine and I turn over, finding her seizing, foam spilling out of her mouth, her eyes rolling back into her head. I take her hand. "It'll pass," I tell her. "I'm here."

One way or another, it will all pass.

SEVENTEEN

JORDANNA

AUGUST 14TH, 1943 – ŁÓDŹ, POLAND

I keep my eyes trained on Alfie as his are on me, sitting diagonally across from each other in the back of the truck as we make our short return trip to the holding walls of Przemysłowa Street. We stare at each other throughout the endless moments it takes to return to our prison. I wish I could read his thoughts. Though if I could, they might make me cry. The thought of him being in pain—it's agonizing. My heart, weak and tired, still thumps within my chest, feeling too much from just a long gaze. Too much when there could never been anything more, not a world where we barely have the freedom to breathe without permission. There's no order between any of us as we bobble along in the back of an old squeaky. I should be used to the putrid odors of bodily fluids, but the bitterness turns my stomach sour and the resulting acid rising up my throat makes my tongue feel fuzzy.

When the truck begins to move, the bumps along the road shove us in every direction. Somehow, many of the others look to be asleep, but with their eyes open.

Not Alfie. He's still, and somehow holding himself upright. He reaches for my hand and holds it between his as he continues to stare at me. It's as if he wants to share every one of his thoughts with me over the airwaves. He brushes the pad of his thumb across my knuckles, and I close my eyes, trying to imagine we're somewhere else—anywhere else. But the sounds, the smells, the hungry pain in my stomach won't allow my mind to wander far.

We've seen dead people. Too many for children our ages. I've witnessed a Gestapo shoot a Jewish man in the center of our hometown. I've watched other Jewish people beaten to the ground for no reason I could see. In the last couple of weeks, I've seen dead children stacked in a wheelbarrow. We don't hear much about how the children die. We just see them being carted away.

Neither Alfie nor I had ever touched a dead person, until today. Alfie had to drag the dead girl off the field. He had to carry her in his arms, her limp body draped like a rag. When he returned, he was holding a pile of the girl's clothes as instructed.

He knelt back down in the grass to continue harvesting potatoes, and I heard him stifling a cry, gasping for short breaths. I watched him clench his eyes to try and stop any tears from falling. He'll forever feel the end of a young life in his arms, thinking she was robbed of a future, but he doesn't know what I know...what Papa once told me. His story, his words—they mean more to me now than ever before.

Lilli is the biggest offender when it comes to asking Papa for more war stories. Mama would often change the topic or tell us it's time to do something different, but Papa doesn't always listen to her.

"A lot of people died in the war, little mouse."

"But how many were your friends? You said you were friends with a lot of soldiers."

She's six. She doesn't know or remember we aren't supposed to ask these types of questions. Mama has asked us many times to be mindful of what we ask Papa about the war.

"That's a tricky question," Papa says, staring toward the brass horn of our gramophone.

I glance at Mama. Max does too. "Lilli, darling, do you want to come help me sew a loose button?"

"But I want to hear Papa's story," she whines.

"It's fine, Papa. Maybe another time," Max says.

"I didn't even know him," Papa says. "He was right next to me, and something got him. It easily could have been me who was shot, but it wasn't. I recognized the young man, but never had the chance to talk to him. He died quickly, little suffering at least. All I could think was, we might have been friends had I found a moment to exchange a few words. I knew it was too late to learn anything about him, but as it turned out, I was wrong to think that."

"Papa, you look very sad. Maybe we should talk about something—" I interrupt.

"Now, now. Your sister asked a question, and I have a reason for answering it, despite the difficulty. There's an important lesson to take away from this," he says, pointing at the gramophone as if it's another person sitting in our living room. "It was a while before the battle came to a point where I could move the fellow. All I could think to myself was: what was this all for? These are lives, gone for no reason. But when I lifted him into my arms, I noticed a slight smile along his mouth. His eyes were wide open but not with shock, with wonder or a sense of reverence. I was desperate to know what he must have seen in that last second of his life, because it must have surely been something miraculous. We all deserved a moment like that after the battles we were fighting. And it was then that I realized those who died didn't have their life cut short, but instead, were set free—to a place where war doesn't exist, where unimaginable happiness

and beauty awaits beyond the precipice of our fearful last breath."

Max and I don't know what to say. Mama has her hands cupped over Lilli's ears, but tears have formed in her eyes. "So, what comes next is something better than what we know now?" I ask.

Papa's stare finally unlocks, and he glances at me. "Precisely. We're here to find our way to the next place by enduring challenges until we eventually succeed. And we will all succeed at some point. Then, we'll be handsomely rewarded."

"That's why when we see rainbows in the sky, Mama says hello to grand-mama, and grand-papa, isn't it?" Lilli, who shouldn't have been able to hear anything, asks.

Mama swallows what must be a lump in her throat and removes her hands from Lilli's ears. "Yes, my darling. That's exactly why," she utters.

Mama always made light of everything for us. I have to do the same for Alfie and Lilli now. That's what she would want me to do. With Alfie's hands still gripped around mine, I tap my fingertip in his palm, using Morse code to tell him that not everything is as it seems, and it isn't the end but rather the beginning of something much better when we leave here. It would take me too long to share Papa's entire story through finger taps, but Alfie seems to consider what I'm trying to tell him. His eyebrows dip down toward the creases of his eyelids, but I watch as he takes a long breath, then squeezes my hands a little tighter. I don't know if I've helped him in any way, but maybe it will give him something more to think about tonight while he tries to sleep.

As the truck comes to a stop, a pain fills my head as my pulse thumps between my ears, thinking about Lilli, wondering if she made it through the day all right without me. The sun is setting, and the trumpet will play soon, warning us to line up in front of our blocks. In lines, once again, we're herded back into the enclosure where the SS sit in their watch towers, and prisoners who answer to the SS guard the corners. Alfie is in the line for boys and I'm in the one for girls, nearly side by side. He glances over his shoulder toward me and quirks a small smile, mouthing the words, "Good night."

My chest aches as I watch him move in the opposite direction. It would be easier if I could keep him and Lilli with me at all times, but then I'm not here for my life to be easy.

I walk in through the door of my new block, holding my breath as I search around for Lilli. She isn't where we set our blankets down this morning, but our blankets aren't there either. I notice some others nibbling on bread, standing by their wooden bunks.

Quickly turning back around and hurrying to the opposite outside perimeter of the block, I find an older child, serving as a guard distributing bread and the black liquid. A young girl is second to last in line and I'm hoping it's Lilli. I make my way to the end of the line, knowing I don't have my cup. That isn't what I'm concerned about. I touch the little girl's elbow, trying to be discreet so as not to startle her. She peers over her shoulder, and I'm gutted to see she isn't my sister.

"Where's your cup?" the guard shouts at me. I didn't realize I was next in line.

"I—I forgot it."

"No coffee." She hands me the small loaf of bread and I run off in search of Lilli.

She could be in the latrine. I'm running in circles around the block, knowing someone is going to tell me off at any given moment, but I need to find her.

The trumpet's honking sound blares through the air, forcing me to gasp in the musky air, signifying evening roll call.

If I'm not in line, I'll be the next to get a flogging.

Please, Lilli. Please show up to roll call.

By the time I make my way around to the other side of the block, most of the children are already lined up. I realize now that the new block is made up mostly of younger girls around Lilli's age. They all look the same with their shaved heads from behind. I know her number. They must call it. They would have to. She was assigned here with me this morning before I left for the farm.

The night seems to grow darker by the minute as the guards rattle off the list of numbers in no particular order.

Number 512 is called. That's me.

"Present," I say, raising my hand.

"Report to me after roll call," the girl says.

What for? I want to ask my question out loud. Is there something she needs to tell me? Is it about Lilli? She hasn't told anyone else that she needs to speak with them.

She's called dozens and dozens of numbers. I can see her finger scrolling down the page, reaching the bottom.

My pulse throbs in my ears and along my temples.

A girl coughs relentlessly, making it hard to hear the remaining numbers being called. The words "be quiet" are rolling off my tongue but I bite my lip to make sure I don't say something stupid.

"513," Lilli's number is finally called.

There's silence for the longest second. A never ending second.

"Present," I hear her say, her voice mousy and soft.

A sob bursts up through my chest, and I clutch my hand over my mouth, suffocating the air to stay inside of me. I cry silently, my chest trembling with every heartbeat. I need her. I need Lilli. I can't be without her. I'm supposed to be the big sister. I am. I'm older by a lot, but I need her so badly right now.

"Report to the block for lights out," the snitching guard tells us all.

All the girls scatter and scamper, running into each other, tripping, pushing, shoving, anything to do what we've been told.

"Jordie," I hear a meek voice, a name she hasn't called me in so long. Her arms reach between others and loop around my waist, squeezing me with all her might. "You're all right. You're really fine?"

I'm finally able to get my arms around her and hold her head against my chest, kissing her forehead over and over. "I've been so worried about you."

"Your heart is punching me in the cheek," she says with a small laugh.

"Go on inside the block. I'm supposed to speak to the—" I almost referred to her as the snitching guard. I don't want that to accidentally come out of Lilli's mouth.

"The block elder? That's what she's called," Lilli informs me.

"Yes, her."

"I've found us a place to sleep on one of the bunks next to each other. I already set up our blankets. It's in the center of the third row."

"I'm proud of you," I tell her, squeezing her once more.

I walk towards the block-elder and wait for her to lift her stare from her clipboard. "You told me to report to you following roll call," I say.

"You're the girl who worked on the farm today," she states.

"Yes, I did."

"I need to write up a report of the death that took place at the potato field. You were the eldest girl and one of few who speak fluent German. Jot down the information on this piece of paper and return it to me at once. Details are important. They'll be worth an extra piece of bread."

She hands me the paper and a pencil, and I rush to the side

of the block to use the wall as a surface to lean on. There aren't many details to give, but I write out everything I remember, including the incoming rain, the breeze, the thump rumbling through the ground, and the sight of the girl face down in the dirt, pronounced dead within seconds of falling.

EIGHTEEN
DALIA
AUGUST 15TH, 1943 – OŚWIĘCIM, POLAND

My stomach groans and whines as I make my way to my newly assigned labor position at the infirmary. Yet, the pain is dull in comparison to the cloaking shame from not being able to help Magda last night. I keep questioning if there was something more I could have done.

We trudge through the muddy grounds, my body weak and weighed down by my heavy clogs. They squelch with each step. The bird-size helping of bread with bitter coffee I ate and drank this morning isn't enough to keep my body upright for an entire day of being on my feet. I didn't imagine the walk feeling so long between Birkenau and the main camp of Auschwitz.

Not one of the two dozen of us can walk in a straight line, or move many steps without stumbling. Our close proximity to each other only adds to the discomfort as mud splatters and sloshes against my arms and legs.

Finally, we reach our assigned location—two looming buildings guarded by iron gates. "Prisoners assigned to Blocks twenty and twenty-one, report to the SS officer inside the front doors," the kapo tells us. She points back and forth between two red-brick schoolhouse looking buildings separated by a brick wall and conjoined by iron gates, blocking in the exterior courtyard between Blocks 20 and 21.

Shallow stone steps lead up to each of the front doors and I walk toward the building clearly labeled Block 20. The three-story-high building has six windows facing the walkway which are as dark as night, masking what's taking place inside. This is where I'll be working. My stomach snarls as I recall Magda's words from last night. It's *the place where everyone goes to die.* What about the people working here?

My knees shake as I mount the four stairs before reaching for the door handle. I picture Jordanna gleefully climbing the stairs in our apartment building, her infectious laughter filling the stairwell. She would always climb the stairs in pairs, never slowing down, never hesitating, just to make it to the top faster than the rest of us. No one wanted to race her, but that didn't slow her down. I wonder whether she is scared now, if she still possesses that bravery, or if our separation is depriving her of that. I must believe she has enough strength, and I know I must find my own strength for her.

Inside, I squeeze between people in the too-packed space, moving further into the crowd. Groans, moans, cries, and whines fill the air like an out-of-tune orchestra. Dank vile, sweet and rotten chemical stenches fill my nose and burn my throat. I'm afraid to nudge anyone, unsure of how weak they might be, but I slip through every slight opening between people until I spot a wooden desk angled in what looks to be the corner. Another prisoner is at the desk with a pencil and logbook, taking notes while trying to calm the people surrounding her.

"Pardon me," I say, speaking up. "I'm here, reporting for duty. It's my first day. I hold out my forearm for her to see my number in case she knows anything of where I should be.

She points along the shorter end of the space we're in. "An SS officer is by the corner window."

"Thank you," I offer before turning in the direction I need

to make my way through. I trip over someone lying on the ground. I try to avoid the sight, knowing I can't do much of anything to help anyone until I check in. What if it's Max, Jordanna, or Lilli? What if I just stepped over my child's motionless body, just for the sake of reporting to where I need to be? I turn back, trying to spot the body through the crowd, but shoulders shove me in every direction, nearly knocking me over because I'm facing the wrong way.

An opening between people offers me a quick glimpse of a pair of black shoes dragging along the ground. All the children were wearing black boots when we ran from our apartment.

Another shoulder pushes me hard enough that I spin back in the direction I should be moving.

The crowd spits me out between a small desk and the SS guard overseeing the crowd. I've come into contact with many kapos, block elders, and camp clerks while being here—all who report to the SS, but this is one of the few times I've had to speak directly to an SS officer.

I slide my feet together, straighten my posture and hold my hands firmly by my sides. "I'm reporting for duty with nursing experience from Block thirteen in Birkenau." I hold out my forearm to show my number despite the number being displayed on my chest too.

The officer's cold stare sends shivers down my spine. "You will work in triage here, separating prisoners with treatable conditions from those unfit for work. Anyone unfit for work will be moved to another facility for better treatment. You will report to the worker at the reception desk across the way," he says, pointing back toward the woman at the wooden desk.

Treatable versus unfit for work.

With another push and shove through the crowd of sick prisoners, I return to the wooden desk. "I've been ordered to assist you," I tell the woman, speaking over the multiple prisoners trying to ask her questions.

"Are you familiar with the selection process?" she asks.

I shake my head, not sure what she means. "Deciding who needs more than simple care?" I ask.

"Yes, you will report their number, diagnosis, and whether they can stay or should wait for the transport to the other facility." She points over her shoulder toward the ground, where a wooden stacked crate, shorter than the desk, sits. "All minor skin infections, wounds, cuts, common cold, stomach issues or skeletal sprains can be treated with what we have on those shelves. All others must be seen by an SS doctor down the hall in the extermination space."

"Extermination?" I ask with a quiet gasp, covering my mouth. My pulse surges as I stare at her in confusion.

"Examination space," she says as if I must be the one who misheard her. Am I?

"Oh, I see. I—I understand," I tell her, trying to keep note of everything she's just said.

"Simply—you'll decide based on necessary treatment if the person can be treated quickly versus—"

"Yes, of course, I-I do—I understand."

"Also, anyone with symptoms of typhus should be sent to the isolation chamber," she adds. "You should move through people in a matter of seconds." She peers across the room toward the officer, making it clear that her statement is a rule and not her choice. "And I'm Ina." Her introduction comes in a hush of a whisper since we are only entitled to our numbers.

"Of course. I'm Dalia," I reply in a similar whisper to hers.

"Next!" she shouts.

I stand awkwardly beside the desk with nothing in my hands, waiting to play God to whoever walks up to me. This hardly compares to what I've been accustomed to in the past. This is chaos and a mistake waiting to happen.

The people in front of me fight to be seen first and I can't understand why there is so much disorganization here when we've done nothing but line up in rows and columns since arriving.

"Miss, you have to help me." The elderly man's desperate plea for help echoes in my mind as I study his number. His appearance is all too familiar here, a result of starvation and deprivation of the bare necessities. His eyes struggle to stay open and it's hard to know if it's from fatigue or weakness but I can't help wondering how long he's been suffering.

I read his number off to Ina who jots down the digits faster than I've ever seen anyone write, and so clearly too. I wonder how long Ina has been here. I wonder this about everyone I pass. I question what the odds of survival are based on the arrival date too.

"What is it you're ill with?" I ask the man who is pleading with me for help.

He slips his clog off his right foot, pulling out his bare foot. His first three toes are purple and black, sores so deep the tissue is exposed. I can't imagine the pain he must be feeling. The infection has spread too far for ointment to be effective. Amputation may be his only chance at survival. Yet, even with advanced treatment, there are no guarantees, and much less here.

Throughout the Great War, I saw more amputated limbs than I wish to remember, gunshot wounds through a skull, half a face blown off and now, I've also witnessed bodies melding to stone lined streets from a firestorm. Still, my chest aches, my stomach twists and gnarls, and I do the thing where I imagine the pain in order to understand what they must be feeling. I can't help it; it happens on its own. The burn, an infection eating away at healthy skin. He might as well hold a flame over the open injury because it wouldn't feel much different.

I press the back of my hand to his forehead, finding an obvious fever.

"You know—" I gasp for air, trying to hide the raw emotions threatening to spew out of me. "We-we are—" I clear my throat and catch the eyes of a nearby SS officer, feeling the unspoken warning to move faster. "We're going to send you to a different facility for more advanced treatment," I tell him.

"No, no you can't do that. Do you have ointment and a bandage maybe? Just something to help the pain?"

"Gangrene." I shake my head ever so slightly at Ina, telling her without saying the words out loud that he isn't fit for work. "He might not survive much longer without severe intervention."

"You need to step into this line over here," Ina says, pointing alongside the wall to her left.

"I know where you're sending me!" he shouts. "You can help me here. Please, just help me. I don't want to—"

A guard in uniform grabs the man by his arm and pulls him toward the wall. I didn't know there was a guard nearby, listening, but I should have expected so. I watch Ina complete her note on the man, wondering how she controls her expression, not even flickering a hint of remorse.

I could never become numb to human pain. Never.

"Next," Ina shouts.

A young man steps up in front of me, holding his stomach. "I've eaten something bad," he says. "I'll be fine. I'm sure of it." He's young, maybe just over twenty. He's covered in dirt. "I need to get back to work as soon as possible."

I read Ina his number for her to take down. If he has stomach pains from whatever he's eaten, which can't be much, a charcoal tablet would likely take the edge off his pain.

"What is your assigned labor?" Ina asks him before I have the chance.

"Constructing one of the new blocks."

She nods and I squat down next to the wooden boxes

containing various treatments. I spot the tablets and drop two in my hand. "Just one," Ina says. "We are in short supply."

I slip the other back into the small container and replace the contents in the wooden boxes.

"This should help," I tell the man, dropping the tablet into his palm. "You can return to work now."

"We don't have a large supply of charcoal tablets. We can only hand them out to top laborers," she says. "And one likely won't be enough to help him."

I'm unsure of what she's insinuating, whether I should have given it to him or not. There are no written rules to follow here, just an understanding that no one should care too deeply about another's life.

After hours of separating people and barely helping anyone as nothing is simple enough to just bandage, triage begins to thin out. The last three waiting to check in with us are sent to the left, to a "better" facility, whatever that might mean.

Ina slides her finger down her written logs as if checking her work. "It will get easier as time gets on. You stop feeling emotions for others when you realize no one has any for you."

My tongue feels lodged in my throat, listening to her words. They aren't a lie, and they aren't intended to be cruel. I know they're the truth.

Ina glances up at me, recognizing my lack of response, I suppose. "And that's how I know you were a real nurse at some point before arriving at this purgatory."

"I was a nurse during the Great War. I thought I'd seen it all."

"You're a fighter," she says, her words soft though the SS officers have left the area. "I didn't during wartime, but I worked in a hospital before my children were born. My skills all came right back to me, despite thinking I knew nothing other than how to be a mother."

"Do you know where your children are?" I ask, clasping my fists over my chest.

Ina stares at me and her jawline tightens as she sucks in her cheeks. "Almost four years ago, my husband and I decided to find a way out of Warsaw with our two little girls. The fighting in the city was growing worse by the day and we knew no one was safe. We were heading to stay with an aunt who lives away from the city—we left early in the morning, thinking that would be the best time to travel. The Siege of Warsaw. An ambush of nonstop air bombardments trapped everyone in the city. No one knew where to run. There was just complete chaos, and the four of us were pushed and shoved apart. The three of them were hit with heavy shrapnel and died. I found them covered in rubble."

I can't breathe. I can't get air into my lungs as I stare at this stranger looking back at me with hollow eyes. "Ina, I'm so—"

"Please don't. I joined the resistance after that and well, here I am."

"No one deserves to go through what you've been through," I tell her.

"I'm not even Jewish. How can I comment?" she asks.

"Your loss has nothing to do with faith. You're an innocent mother and wife," I state firmly.

"I was." She swallows hard and puffs her chest out, filling her lungs with the air I still can't seem to find. "How about you? Children, husband?"

"Yes, but we were separated, and I don't know where they are, or if they're—"

Ina rests her hand on my shoulder and stares directly into my eyes—hers suddenly aren't as hollow now. "The ability to have hope was stolen from me—hold on to yours for us both."

I nod. "Very well, thank you."

"Pain makes us stronger—it makes us all stronger," she says.

Her words are ones I have lived by and words I will die by

because we can only become so strong before a different choice is made for us.

It's all a lie. Strength means nothing when our survival is based on luck. Everything I've taught the children will only sabotage them now. What kind of mother am I if I can no longer believe the words I used to preach?

NINETEEN
JORDANNA
OCTOBER 7TH, 1943 – ŁÓDŹ, POLAND

Two months and eight days' worth of fingernail markings on the wooden floor track the number of nights since we arrived in this ghetto for juvenile criminals and orphaned children. The Reich don't want to deal with any loose threads of children, so they locked us all up here like zoo animals. But I still don't know why we're here. We're neither orphans nor criminals. My heart tells me Mama and Papa are alive and doing everything possible to find us.

All the while I lost count of the days we've been held here against our will. I forgot to leave a few marks beneath my thin mattress. My memory has always been *sharp as a tack*, Mama would say. I liked to think of myself as the family's memory keeper. In truth, I liked to know what was going on all the time so I would peek at Mama's calendar every day. She had a lot to remember, even with everything written down so I tried to help where I could.

Now, my recent memories feel as though they're covered in dust, which could be entirely possible with how much dirt I've dug in the past two and a half months.

I was desperate to know what month it was, until I received the most beautiful letter in the world.

The words clarified the hours, days, and weeks it's been since we got here. Two months, three weeks, and two days.

Max found a way to have a letter delivered to us. It was waiting on my mattress for me one night after returning from the farm.

I'd seen other children receive letters. I assume their families must still know where they are.

Not us. We were torn apart at the seams.

I'm still trying to understand how Max was able to find us. Now I reread the letter every morning on the truck ride over to the farm. It makes me feel as if he's here beside me. His voice is clear in my head.

My Dearest Sisters and Alfie, a brother, nonetheless,

I don't know when this letter will find you, if it ever does, but I had heard rumors that children without parents are being sent to another area of this Łódź ghetto I'm in, but it's not accessible to anyone here. The others call the place, Little Auschwitz, but I'm unsure of what that means.

I miss you all so much and do nothing but worry about you, and Mama and Papa too, of course. The ghetto is lonely despite the overcrowding. I haven't made too many friends, but know a couple of people who are willing to help each other out. Just after I arrived and went through a bunch of screening tests, a Gestapo assigned me to forced labor while I wait on a 'pending transfer'—whatever that might mean. I spend my days collecting deceased bodies around the enclosed village of broken-down buildings. Food is hard to come by unless we have something to trade, which is rare and impossible unless I find something shiny on the street. We receive bread and soup, but that's about it.

What matters is, I'm healthy, on my feet and still here. I'm praying the rest of you are doing as well as possible.

Poor sweet Lilli must be terrified. I imagine there isn't a glow of light at night when she's trying to fall asleep. I'm hoping she's managed to find a way to sleep in the dark. Make sure she knows how proud I am of her bravery and how much I miss her and love her.

And Alfie, I hope his ears are healing and he can hear better now. I hope he's getting along well too and not starving himself completely to feed the two of you. I know you wouldn't let him, but the two of you are one of a kind with your vow of generosity and kindness. We all need to survive so we can make it back to one another.

Despite whether this letter finds you or not, I will continue to write and I hope that if you read this, you will try to send a letter to me as well. I'm leaving an address for the post here in the Łódź Ghetto.

I'm proud of you, Jordie. I know you're being strong. I can feel it in my heart. I love you so very much. We all have warrior blood. Never forget that.

With all my love,

Max

I sent out a letter the very next morning. I told him all about the cruel labor duties and how many of the other girls have sewing jobs, shoe repairs, nursing the youngest children, or preparing food. But not me. The educators chose to stick me with physical labor, day after day without a break. But at least I'm with Alfie so I know he's doing the best he can be doing too. I've assured Max Lilli is safest, holding a job of sewing and repairing uniforms. She's falling asleep in the dark just fine, her hand in mine each night. We should all be so proud of her bravery.

I made sure to end my letter confirming that his note has been the happiest gift for the three of us. Since then, I've diligently kept track of the time, and know for certain it's been four weeks and three days since I dropped my return letter into the outgoing post. Nothing has come in for us either. We haven't heard another word from Max, which is almost worse than never hearing from him at all.

* * *

The laboring children surrounding me unload from the truck, spilling onto the field like cloudy marbles. It's another cold, dry morning, my scalp itching from exposure to the sun and the odd length mimicking a rugged leafy root like the ones I pull from the ground. My wrists are extra sore today and blue veins draw lines between my knuckles and elbows, which I always seem to notice more than the effects over the rest of my body. Sometimes, I watch the mechanics of my bones twist and turn as I maneuver the shovel, wondering how the human body became so intricate and fascinating, complicated and still undiscovered by even the most brilliant doctors. I don't think our bodies are intended to sustain the type of work and deprivation we endure everyday though. And I'm glad it's rare to see a true reflection of what I look like now. Although, I see Lilli and Alfie, both skin and bones, sunken cheeks, and sallow eyes. Their heads appear too large for their neck and shoulders, and I feel that weight on mine.

I hit another rock with the tip of my shovel and the vibration rumbles through me, shaking my brain within my skull. My muscles are stiff from the cold wind and falling temperatures even though I continue to sweat through the work. My body must be confused.

A pinch on my side grabs my attention and I whip my head around, finding Alfie staring at me with his big eyeballs popping out of their sockets.

I mouth the words, "What's wrong?"

He begins to tap the ground through code, and I miss the first few letters. He's lost his ability to control the volume of his voice without the ability to hear himself, so he taps out his thoughts to me more than he says them out loud now.

I pick up on the following letters and form them into words, pushing my brain to work harder than I sometimes think I'm capable.

"—you just see that?"

He continues shoveling but holds his stare toward the trees just beyond the field rows. I peer over to the trees too, but I don't see anything aside from swaying branches and leaves falling to the ground in colorful piles.

Delusions are common when starvation strikes us worse than usual. If one of us happens to do something as little as blink the wrong way at the wrong time, the educators will withhold our evening bread. It happens frequently.

Moments pass after Alfie's frantic taps, and I keep peering out to the trees, wondering what he could have seen.

After a minute of nothing, I drop my shovel, sweep my arm across my forehead to stop sweat from falling into my eyes and begin to yank on the stubborn potato root.

Alfie grabs my wrist and rapidly taps the letters: L-O-O-K on the base of my palm.

After the very first tap, I was already looking and this time I see something. A figure. A man. A grown man, one not in uniform. Scrawny but tall, in factory clothes. He looks to be staring right at us but from the distance he's at, he could be looking at a dozen of us clumped in the same area. I've never seen anyone between the trees. It's blocked off and enclosed, or so we've been told.

My sack of potatoes is full to the brim, so I stand and pull the slack over my shoulder, bringing it toward the truck we load the bags onto. It's situated closer to the tree line than where we're digging. I swing the bag with all my might, hoping it clears the rim of the truck bed walls. It does, just barely, following a tumbling disturbance of bouncing potatoes.

With another glance toward the tree line, I see the person has moved, bringing themselves closer to the truck. A kapo guard stands between me and a closer view.

"What are you looking at?" she shouts to me.

I point to her feet, making my way closer to her. "I just saw a large mouse. I know you don't care for—" the guard shrieks. Her fear of mice and working in the fields doesn't make much sense to me but I assume they don't have much more say than the rest of us.

She's dancing in circles, searching for the rodent. As I'm within a close radius of her, I act to search around to help her, pointing every second or two and shouting, "There..." or "over there!"

She's in tears before running for the truck to sweep her legs down.

I take a moment to graze the area by the trees, just close enough to make out details of this figure if he decides to show himself again.

And he does.

"Papa?" The word leaves my mouth as a silent gust of wind.

He presses his finger to his mouth and shakes his head. I want to run to him. My heart flutters in my stomach and tears burn the back of my eyes as I take another step toward him. But he waves at me to stop, fear brightly illuminating in his wide eyes.

"Where's Lilli?" he asks by holding his hand at her head's height compared to his chest.

How can I tell him without making a sound? I point in the

direction of the ghetto and mouth the words, "She's fine," unsure if he can see my mouth clearly enough.

"Bring her tomorrow," he whispers through the passing breeze.

I clutch my chest, wanting to go with him right now, take my chances and run, but I know the risks and I won't leave the other two behind.

Tears fall from my eyes as I continue to stare at what very likely could be nothing more than a hungry delusion.

TWENTY
DALIA
OCTOBER 7TH, 1943 – OŚWIĘCIM, POLAND

If there was no war and I was working in a hospital, I would be treating ill and wounded people every day. I don't think there was ever a time in my life where I pointedly decided that I wanted to be a nurse, but it felt like the only choice when there was nothing else I could do to help those getting injured. Doctors complimented me on my quick-thinking skills and ability to react under pressure. I never saw myself as doing a better job than any other nurse, but it was nice to hear I was living up to expectations at the very least.

There are no expectations here in Auschwitz, only that we don't keep patients around to use up resources if they're going to die anyway. That and the rhetoric of removing Jewish lives from occupied German societies. For the past three weeks I've been assigned to this ward, I've seen more than a fifty-percent turnover rate from the time I leave at night and when I return early in the morning. I don't know who works here at night or what really happens. That's not for me to know.

"Bed four," a woman shouts from across the ward.

Like myself, none of the other three nurses working in this

ward with me spring into action. There's no use in rushing to bed 4.

"I'll tend to him," I say, knowing I'm at least making my way down the line of other patient-filled beds in the direction of bed 4.

I take a man's frail wrist into my hand to check his pulse. His records say he's forty, but he looks as if he's lived three times as long. His mouth hangs open, air flowing freely. His pulse is active, but the damage is done. He'll have to wait out his time now. I take his record, hanging from the end of the metal bed and update his notes.

Male/31 y.o.

October 6th, 43'

Progressed Amoebic Dysentery.

Confusion.

Swollen feet.

Headache.

"You're looking better. How are you feeling, sir?" I ask him. He doesn't look better. I don't know if I should be offering hope but why steal whatever hope is left from them?

As usual, he doesn't respond. I can't tell if he's coherent, but he's still alive. Soon, though, starvation will pull him under, just as it has too many others here in Auschwitz.

In the next bed, a woman with jaundice, a bloated stomach the size of a pregnant woman at full term, and a blue circle around her lips, opens her eyes just enough to spot me. "Mordechai," she utters. "My Mordechai. You've come to rescue me?" Her lips struggle into a shallow curve. "I knew you would be back."

I press the back of my hand against her head, feeling the heat radiate off her skin. Sweat drips down her cheeks and chest, arms, and legs. I retrieve the compress left in the metal bowl of water behind her bed and drape it over her forehead. The sore on her arm is seeping through the last bandage so I remove the old bandage and replace it with a new one. I keep my words to myself since my unfamiliar voice only seems to bring her pain and more discontent when she realizes I'm not her Mordechai.

I mark down her renewed treatment:

Female/52 y.o.

October 6th, 43'

Sepsis.

Cooling therapy.

Redressing wounds.

High fever.

She's not stable so I won't write those words. But she's been treated to the best of our ability. Leo would say there's always something more we can do. He would be right, but only if allowed.

I will always know that Leo would have been safer without me even if it wasn't for his deputy officer. Despite his devotion to the Jewish faith, he only has two Jewish grandparents and therefore, considered a mixed-race per the Nuremberg Laws—luckier, some might say. Whereas I'm a full-blooded Jewish woman, married to Leo or not, and we have raised our children Jewish. Therefore, our family is less "lucky." The comprehension of this science has been impossible to understand.

"I'll never leave your side so there's nothing to worry about, darling," Leo would tell me.

Without Leo, I'm just a Jew.

Everything that happens within this infirmary, the entire Block 20, is strictly for record-keeping purposes. Hitler wants the extinction of all Jews. Our death is his final solution, but his final solution cannot be accomplished in a day, so we wait and make it look like it takes longer than a day. We watch others suffer and perish while wondering how death will find us and when.

Being assigned to a ward could have been a death sentence for me if I was sent to care for the patients ill with typhus, dysentery or tuberculosis, but instead I've been sent to the terminally ill ward, which contradicts the idea of prioritizing patients as they walk in.

But the records need to show a full spectrum of minor to deadly cases. The SS officers don't say so, nor would they ever admit such a thing out loud, but the way they handle these medical records, as if each one will be hand-delivered to the Fuhrer himself, makes it very clear their well-being is on the line to whoever they are hiding the truth from.

The next patient has been uncontrollably shaking and gasping for breath since I arrived this morning. There's a gurgle in her lungs. "I'm going to prop you up a bit to help you breathe better. Tell me if you feel any pain," I say, speaking softly to the middle-aged woman.

"Thank you. Thank you so much," she says. "It's so cold. Isn't it?"

I shove the stuffing of the mattress toward the center on one side then move around the bed to do the same to the other, elevating her just a bit. Her skin is cold to the touch, so I take the blanket from bed 4 and drape it over her body to warm up her blood. "How's that?" I ask.

"Thank you, nurse. Better. Much better."

I add my notes, words in vain:

Female/48 y.o.

October 6th*, 43'*

Pneumonia.

Moderate fever.

Elevation for lung support.

No fluids due to aspiration.

I finally make it to bed 4, take the medical log and mark down today's date under the words "Date of Death." Under "causes," I write: natural. *The end of another story.*

I move behind the man's bed and roll him toward the exit of the ward where other laborers wait for human remains.

A male prisoner lifts the body from the bed and places it down on the top of a growing pile. I turn the bed back around and return it to its position back in the ward.

One more bed in this row before moving on to the next. I grab the chart and review the vitals and updates before even looking over at another poor soul. This one must have come in overnight. I haven't seen anyone with a post typhus recovery status.

Male/18 y.o.

October 6th*, 43'*

Post Typhus – self-treated in barrack.

Possible Relapse.

On and off Delirium.

Signs of Organ Failure.

High Fever.

Just as unpromising as all the others in this ward. I step over to the bed, finding—

The pounding in my chest makes it hard to breathe, reminding me I'm still alive and not in a nightmare.

I touch his ear, needing to convince myself I'm not imagining things. I trace four small red dots in the shape of a check mark. I've done this too many times before. I've seen each of my children's faces in crowds, losing myself to delusions.

But he doesn't just look like Max...I'm not wrong this time. I can't be...

I stare at his ear again—I know those markings.

"These tiny little marks on his ear—that's how we know he's ours—our perfect baby," Leo had said as I held Max in my arms just moments after he took his first breath.

My heart pulsates in my throat and my breath catches as I cry out my son's name, "Max!" I reach for his rosy cheek. "My baby. You're here. You're—" He's here and yet, he's so sick. He's too sick. God, don't let this happen—take me instead.

He struggles to swallow and clenches his eyes. "Mama," he says through a weak exhale.

I grab his medical log from the end of the bed and scan down the page of short, brief notes. Then cup my hands around his face, feeling for his temperature. It's high. His back is incredibly hot—a telltale sign of his fever rising. As a baby, I checked his temperature so often, I could guess the degree by touch. He suffered with ear infections for years and they always brought along a fever—fevers that scared the life out of me as a new mother. *My baby.* I slide my hand under his back, his pajama shirt soaked in sweat, stuck to his blazing skin.

Frenzied and unable to think straight, I spin around, looking for a bowl with a compress. I find one at the empty bed 4 and drape it over Max's head. I tear off part of the thin sheet covering the mattress and soak it in the water next, draping it over his head, neck, and wrists. I would soak him in a little enamel tub when he was a baby, sponging him with lukewarm water to bring his fever down. It always helped, but I'm not certain how effective the scraps of wet fabric will be on my son, the size of a grown man.

"When did you get here? How long—"

"Mama?" It feels like a year since someone has called me Mama. My body threatens to collapse as I hover over him, my chest aching with physical and emotional pain and terror.

"I'm here, darling. I'm here. Mama's here." I whisper every word, praying no one hears or sees me. The cool water isn't enough. I need something more.

I reach for the rolling cart behind me and pull it to my side, grasping at everything inside, unsure if there's anything left to even help him. After a long moment, my hand sweeps over a loose jagged pill. I scoop it up and study it in the cup of my shaking hand. An aspirin. With the pill clenched in one hand, I continue digging through the disorganized contents, removing items and setting them down to make sure I'm not missing a bottle of aspirin or any other loose pills. It isn't long before I reach the bottom, confirming I have the only aspirin left. I toss the supplies back into the bin and spin around in search of water.

A pair of hands rests on my shoulders. "Is everything all right?" Ina's voice whispers into my ear.

"My son," I say, holding my shaking finger out toward him. "He's here."

"Dear God. What can I do?" she utters.

"I don't know. We don't even have aspirin left."

There's nothing for Ina to respond with because we all know there's nothing left to treat anyone with here. She holds in her breath and covers her hand, watching as I helplessly tend to Max.

I spot a tin can by a rusting pitcher and fill the can, bringing it back to Max's side. I push the aspirin into his mouth then cup my hand under his chin to help him drink. "Swallow this, sweetheart. Drink the water."

He's so weak, I don't know if he can maneuver his tongue to swallow the tablet. My only hope is it dissolves and seeps down the back of his throat.

I stroke my fingers along his cheek, hoping it relaxes him enough to swallow the pill. His face clenches and his eyes squeeze shut as if he's trying to push down a bottle cap. He's so frail and thin, I watch a small lump travel down his throat.

"You're going to be all right. I'm here now. I'm going to take care of you, sweetheart. Look at me...I'm here, with you, and I won't leave your side."

Two of us can't witness the same delusion. I've never heard of something like that happening before. The bumpy ride back to the ghetto makes it hard for Alfie and me to communicate with our tapping fingers, but I need to know he saw what I saw. He needs to know I heard Papa tell me to bring Lilli to the farm tomorrow.

"Are you sure that's what he said?" Alfie asks in our code taps. It's the last bit of conversation we'll have before we're separated for the night as we pull up to the front gate.

I nod my head. I am sure.

I need more time with Alfie. I need to think up a plan to bring Lilli along with us.

Icy rain pelts the tarp over the truck's bed, the hollow *plunk...plunk...plunk* starting slow and growing quicker as the seconds pass while we wait for our turn to demount the vehicle.

With nothing but the dark sky above us, the heavy rain patters against us while we wait in our designated lines to return to our blocks in an orderly fashion. At least it held out until now. Working in the mud with slimy hands slows us down so much it's impossible to reach our potato count, which leads to punishment.

"Two children are missing," an SS educator shouts at the head of our lines. "Who is missing?" A kapo holds an umbrella above the educator's head while the rest of us become drenched.

No one has an answer. Each of the faces within the two lines are familiar to me after working with most of them for the last two months, but I'm not noticing anyone who should be here and isn't. No one has died on the farm from heat stroke in the past month with the temperatures cooling, and I haven't noticed anyone taken away.

The urge to reply and tell her no one is missing teases the back of my throat. Mama has always told me to *be the truth above the lies, but not if it will be the source of someone's pain. Sometimes lies are a form of protection for both the giver and receiver.* There's no protection here. My vision blurs while staring at the scarf-covered head in front of me, debating my decision until another one of us speaks up first.

"Madam, no one is missing. We're all accounted for," Rachel, one of the older girls replies.

"Come forward," she says, pointing her whipping stick at her head.

Rachel's standing right in front of me and a sheen of sweat forms on the back of her neck below the knot of her scarf as she clenches her fists by her side. She takes in a shuddered breath, steps to the right and makes her way forward, coming face to face with the blonde woman in uniform.

When this place scares me the most, I try to imagine what these educators must have been like before they arrived here, or even how they looked before becoming these terrible people who abuse children. She might be pretty without the scowl on her face.

For all I know this SS educator could be a mother, going home to her two young children tonight with a smile on her face, hiding the nightmare of a world she takes part in all day. They are probably thrilled to see her and wrap their arms around her for a big hug. All the while, they don't know what she's capable of as a person. They might find out some day and I wonder what they'll think of her then. Will they still love her?

Rachel's fists are still clenching by her sides as the educator stares her down as if she's waiting for her to crack and claim she was lying and knows who is missing from our lines.

"Are you insinuating that I can't count properly?" the SS asks Rachel.

"No, madame."

"There should be twenty-seven of you, and there are twenty-five. But, for the sake of teaching lessons around here, let me confirm how well I can count."

The whip moves so fast in the air, I don't see it swing against her face, but the blood splatters.

Whoosh, whoosh, whoosh... twenty-five times with each slap counted out loud. Rachel falls to the ground after the third whoosh and her backside takes the rest of the beating.

"As for the rest of you," the SS woman shouts through heavy breaths. "No evening bread unless someone has an answer about the missing children."

Our two lines are released and move forward, some stepping over Rachel's body. I stop to help her up, her body heavy and weak. I hardly have the strength to carry much more than my own weight, but I won't leave her here. I would hope someone wouldn't leave me here.

Rachel lives in the same block as me, the one that seems like an hour's walk from where we're starting. She whimpers but doesn't cry and I worry my arm under hers is adding to the pain from the lashes.

We make it to the block just as the other girls are waiting in line for the latrine and washroom, so the bunks mostly are empty. Lilli must be in one of the lines.

Rachel shrugs away from me, limping toward the other side of the block. "Thank you for not stepping over me," she says, her words trailing behind her.

"If there's anything I can do, I'm here," I say.

She doesn't respond.

I turn back for my mattress, close my eyes and make a wish that an envelope is waiting for me. "Please, Max," I beg silently.

But just as it's been every day since hearing from him that one and only time, there's no envelope.

If I can talk to Papa again—if he can help us, I can tell him where Max is. He can save him too. I wonder if he knows where Mama is. All these questions and I don't know how I'm going to manage to sneak Lilli to the farm without being caught.

I make my way to the latrine, finding the line shorter than expected. The trumpet will sound soon. There isn't much time to wash up and use the toilet.

My underwear is around my knees when the trumpet's howl berates my ears between the wooden walls.

There are still others beside me, trying to make use of the allotted toilet time. I jump up, pull up my paper-textured fabric underwear and make a run for the line-up next to the block.

Lilli has been standing in the same spot most days, making it easier to find her than the first day I returned from the fields. She purposely takes up just a little too much space on the side so I can squeeze in beside her.

Our hellos are silent, felt only by the brush of our fingers clinging to one another. We're not allowed to do anything aside from stand at attention and wait to hear our numbers called. We've seen lashings and floggings because some of the younger girls were giggling about something while waiting here.

Following roll call, I return to the block while Lilli collects her bread and coffee juice, as we call it. We're still not sure what we're drinking.

She finds me inside on the straw mattress beside hers, still in the corner on the ground where we've managed to remain since entering this block back in August.

"Where is your bread and coffee juice?" Lilli asks, easing down onto her mattress.

"None tonight. Two people were missing upon returning from the farm. We were all punished. It's fine. I'll be all right." I know what's coming next. Our sisterly argument that occurs far too often here.

She tears her bread in half and hands it to me. "Take it, Jordie."

"No. I refuse. It will go to waste. Eat your dinner." She places the bread onto my lap, and I return it back onto hers. We'll continue the back and forth until the lights go out but I need to talk to her. "Hold it for a moment. We need to talk."

"What's happened?" she asks, her eyes big and round, staring at me with dread.

I glance around the block, searching for the block elder, ensuring she's not near us and listening to anything we might say. I spot her scolding a little girl toward the other end of the row.

"What I'm about to say...you can't react. Not at all. We need to be smart and think up a plan quickly."

"For what? What is it?" Lilli presses in a harsh whisper.

"I saw Papa today. He was in the wooded area that squares in the potato field."

Lilli's hand flies up to her mouth. Her eyes bulge even more somehow. "Where is he now?" she utters from beneath her muffling hand.

"He told me to bring you with me to the field tomorrow so he can—"

"He's going to rescue us?" Lilli asks, mouthing the words more than whispering.

"I think he's going to try. But I don't know how we can get

you to the farm without being noticed. Do you have to check in when you arrive at the sewing block in the morning?"

"Yes, but then we all go to our tables. That's the only time we have to check in during the day because there are kapos all over the block."

"So, you can't leave once you're inside," I state.

"I know a way," she says. "I've watched other girls escape the block through a closet window vent."

This plan is becoming more dangerous the longer we talk about it, and my head is throbbing with pain from hunger and thirst.

"Trust me, I can make it to the front gate without being seen. That's where the truck meets you, right?"

"Yes," I say, wishing I had a good reason to tell her not to try this. It could be our only chance to escape. Or we could wind up like Rachel or worse.

We're all shoved onto the truck. There's no formality after we're counted in line. Her timing will have to be perfect to avoid being seen by one of the kapos. "You will have to listen for them counting heads behind the administration building—stay out of view by staying in the shadow beneath the building's slight overhang. You'll be able to reach the end of the line from that edge of the building. The kapos count then shove us into the tight space on the truck. We're herded like farm animals. They don't see who they're pushing to move faster."

"I can do this," she says. "I can."

I try to smile, wanting to be proud of her bravery. But I'm terrified of her newfound confidence. "I love you," I tell her, leaning over to kiss her on the cheek.

"I love you," she says.

I close my eyes but squint just enough to make sure she eats the bread she was offering me. She shoves it into her mouth like a hungry mouse then grabs her cup of coffee juice with both hands and swishes the dry texture down her throat. Her knuckles are all bruised, scratched and raw. And her wrist bones are sharp, more prominent than they were the last time I studied her drinking from that cup. She finishes the bread and coffee juice then lies down and reaches for my hand. I take a hold of her fingers and curl mine around them. Papa would never steer us wrong. We have to trust that this is the right thing to do. He wouldn't tell us to do something without having faith it'll work. Except I know he isn't within these gates and there's no way he'd know what risks we face daily. At least I don't think so.

I can't question this. I can't have doubts. This plan might be our only hope tomorrow.

I've had to continue making my rounds within this ward, knowing if I'm caught being stationary too long, I'll be reported to a guard. My bedside manner isn't what it's been. I've been moving as quickly as possible to make it back to Max's side so I'm not away from him for long.

The aspirin seems to have brought his fever down a bit and he's asleep now. I don't want to wake him, but I'm terrified of losing minutes of his life too.

God, let him pull through this. He's too young to die. He has his whole life ahead of him.

I close my eyes as the tears spill out.

"Mama, don't cry," he says, his words gruff and scratchy.

I take his hand and hold it up to my cheek, still praying and pleading with God. Ina comes up behind me and presses the side of her body to mine. "Take the tin from my hand and pour it into his mouth," she whispers.

"What is it?" I respond in the same hush.

"I stole a few lemons. It's lemon water. I've seen it help others."

I haven't seen a lemon anywhere in the confines of Auschwitz. I don't know where she got it, but it may help.

"Max, sweetie, you need to drink this down as fast as you can," Ina tells him, keeping her voice as quiet as possible.

I reach over him, cupping my hand beneath his chin and pour the contents into his mouth. His lips pucker, and he sucks in his cheeks, highlighting the prominent, skeletal bone structure of his face, edges I should never have to bear witness to.

Tears dribble from his clenched eyes but he takes down the contents of the can, slowly, but entirely.

Ina grabs the can and rushes away.

"That will help you. It will," I tell him. He nods his head with slight movements.

"All right."

I can't leave him here tonight, but the guards won't let me stay and if I don't return to roll call, I won't stand a chance of seeing another day anyway. I don't even know who watches over the patients at night. It isn't information I'm entitled to.

A retching sound croaks from a bed on the opposite side of the row, and I know I need to move. Max takes in a deep breath and closes his eyes again. "Try to sleep some more, baby. Sleep will help too."

He doesn't respond but he's still breathing.

He's still breathing.

The retching sound ceases before I make it back to the other end of the row. Vomit covers the man's chest, his head tilted back. "No, no, no, no. You need to be on your side," I remind him again. I use the sheet to clean off his face and grab his left shoulder to pull him back to his side, but his body is stiff and doesn't comply with my effort. I slide my fingers up to his neck, pressing against his artery, finding stillness.

I can't help anyone, even my own son. Why am I here, being called a nurse? All I'm doing is watching people die. I take the man's medical log and mark down his date of death, and the cause being malaria. I push his bed forward and roll him out into the hall where another laborer takes the bed and moves him along. No explanation necessary. We know what it means to be rolled into the hall—a transaction between prisoners.

The clock on the wall taunts me, the hour hand moving faster than it has any other day I've worked here. Ina has sneaked two more tins full of lemon juice to Max and he's remained otherwise asleep.

"Listen," Ina says, pulling me aside. "My barrack is just a row away from the infirmary, and I know who works the night shift. I'll switch with them after evening roll call. I'll stay with Max tonight. I'll make sure he's fine. I know you don't have that choice."

My eyes are wide with shock, trying to process everything Ina just offered me. She's offering to risk her life for Max and me. "I can't ask you to put your life on the line," I tell her, my whisper shuddering in my throat.

"He's your child. You would do it for my little girls if-if—"

"I would," I say, gasping for air.

"I know what I'm doing," she says.

I glance over at Max, noticing a bit more color in his cheeks. Maybe it's just the light against the sun setting, changing the colors of everything on this side of the window, but I want to believe it's more color in his cheeks. I touch the back of my hand to his forehead, finding heat, but less. His fever is going down, but it could return at any moment.

"Mama," he says, forcing his lips into a quirk of smile. "Don't worry. I'll keep fighting. My head doesn't hurt as much and I'm not so cold now." It's the most he's said to me since I found him here this morning.

"I don't want to leave you for the night, sweetheart. I don't want to."

"You have to," he says, opening his eyes—his beautiful soulful eyes. "I'll be here in the morning."

I run my knuckles along his cheek and kiss his forehead. "You're going to make it through this," I tell him. He is a fighter.

"I'm sure he'll be even better in the morning," Ina says.

"See?" Max agrees with her.

A strangling sensation tightens around my neck, and I cross my arms over my chest, squeezing my arms so tightly circulation stops. "You don't have a choice," Ina says, reminding me, as if I'm considering a decision.

"Who knows, you might have to send me to the recovery ward tomorrow so I can go back to work soon," Max says.

I don't want to think about that either. I won't see him anymore.

"You're going to be late," Ina says.

I lean down and give Max another kiss on the forehead. "Please—" I didn't mean to beg out loud.

"Mama, I'll be here. I promise. I love you."

"I love you, sweetheart."

Despite sleeping on a straw filled mattress and being poked and punctured several times a night, I usually manage to get some sleep. I'm certain I didn't sleep more than an hour last night though. I've been considering various scenarios of what could go wrong today while trying to sneak Lilli over to the fields. My gut tells me it's a bad idea. She would be punished severely if caught and it would be my fault.

Papa is risking his life trying to save us though.

My stomach is growling with anger, starving from missing the crumb of food allotted last night, and this morning for that matter since dinner serves as our breakfast too.

Lilli's nerves are clear to me as we stand side by side in our row at roll call. She's wiggling her knees, bouncing enough to be noticed.

"You must calm down," I whisper.

"I'm fine," she says.

"Are you worried?"

"No. I want to see Papa."

"Me too." I wish I could promise her everything will be all

right, and we'll see him, and he'll save us and—then we'll be free. It all sounds like a fairy tale.

Once the kapo is finished with her list of numbers, she dismisses us to report to our labor duties.

What if I forgot something? What if there's something more that I should have instructed Lilli to do while completing this dangerous task? I watch as she disappears out of my sight, around the buildings, heading toward the sewing block.

At a slower pace than usual but not slower than the slowest person to arrive, I make my way toward the front gates. I spot the line of others waiting to check in and I want to look over my shoulder again, but I might draw attention to my behavior. My heart pounds so hard I can hear it between my ears just like I could when I passed out on the field on my first day of labor.

The kapo, who must receive rewards for every heroic action in favor of the educators, spots my badge number, draws a check mark beside my name and continues to make her looping rounds among the columns we've been directed to stand in while waiting for the truck to pull up.

Alfie is up ahead in the fourth and last column to the left. He peers over his shoulder toward me but doesn't let his gaze linger. There's no expression I can give him to tell him every-thing is under control. Nothing is under control. My chest tightens and it becomes harder to breathe, despite the nip in the air. I shiver and tense my muscles, refusing to reply to the cold.

The truck pulls up to its usual position and just as it comes to a halt, the lines begin to move forward. I peer to my right, trying to catch a glimpse of the nearest building, the corner Lilli should be rounding if our plan has any merit.

The kapo is grabbing children by the arms and shoving them up into the truck faster than they can move on their own.

Where is she?

I'm stepping forward, nearing the back of the truck. I regret-fully peer over my shoulder in search of her but don't spot any sign of her near the building or toward the end of these lines which are moving quicker and quicker.

She's not going to make it. I won't leave her. I'll have to tell Papa we can't go with him. The fields must be the only way to escape. It must have been how the missing girls from roll call got free yesterday. I wish I could believe the fields aren't the only possible way, but I'm sure many others would have already escaped through these gates by now if it weren't. No one has mentioned a word about anyone fleeing over these walls or through the main gates. No gossip or rumors either. There are always guards here and in the watchtowers.

The watchtowers. The thought didn't cross my mind. There are eyes peering down on us wherever we go.

The clouds are thick today, lower than usual. I can only hope it lessens their visibility. Not that it matters at all because she's not here and I'm next to get onto the truck.

My stomach burns, acidic fumes of bile rise into my throat, and I clutch my arms around my waist as I head for the bed of the truck, ready to make a leap upward to avoid the shoving. The young ones don't have the height to make the jump so they're the ones always thrown around. I'm unsure why there are younger children working on the farms at all. Some are hardly big enough to lift the weight of a shovel.

I wish I had a believable reason to hold up this truck. A cause for delay. That would require luck and I'm quite sure no one has any of that here.

With one last glance toward the nearest buildings, heavy defeat settles over my shoulders. Now I won't know if she's well all day. She could have been caught sneaking out of the storm window. She might be getting flogged at this very moment.

The visual would cause me to vomit if there was something in my stomach, but I retch dryly as I fall to my knees inside the truck. Alfie grabs my arm and yanks me over to him. I knock other children around as he does. I stare at him, trying to hold back my tears.

His brows knit together, and he shakes his head. I grab his hand and tap out a Morse message simply stating I'm sorry. I've let him down too. I want him to go with Papa though. I'll force him to if I have to. We shouldn't both stay back. Alfie will know all the ins and outs of this village and might be of help to Papa finding another way.

He shifts over to give me more space so I'm not leaning any weight onto another child. I close my eyes as the truck bucks forward and Alfie elbows me in the chest. I gasp from the blow and press my hands to my heart.

I look sharply at him, his arms wrapped around a little girl he's pulled onto his lap. She has a scarf on her head, and I reach for her chin, twisting her face toward mine.

"Lilli," I utter.

She holds her finger up to her lips and Alfie leans toward me, his lips nearly against my ear as he whispers: "She was at the corner of the building closest to my line. She spotted me and ran." Alfie is louder than he realizes so I wrap my hand around his mouth, his lips wet against my hand. I smile at him as tears fill my eyes. My heart is still racing, throbbing through me like rolling thunder.

"I did it," Lilli whispers.

I want to ask her where she found the scarf because most of the girls on the farm have either stolen it or had one on them upon arrival. I only had on my pajamas from home when I got here. If I had found one, I'd have given it to Lilli.

Alfie rests his cheek on the top of Lilli's head, squeezing his arms around her tightly. He hasn't seen her since we arrived. The boys and girls are separate within the compound and the only reason I see Alfie is because we both work on the farms.

"Did you get any post from Max?" he whispers in my ear again, softer this time.

I shake my head. His gaze drops just as mine does every night when I look for a stark envelope atop the dirty mattress top.

"Follow my lead when we get off the truck," I whisper into Lilli's ear.

She's going to have to dig along with the rest of us and won't be nearly as quick, I imagine. There's no telling when Papa might appear from within the trees again. If...

As usual, Lilli surprises us with her bravery, never hesitating to do anything Alfie, me, or the others do to harvest the dying potatoes. I don't know how much longer we'll be brought out here with how quickly the cold weather is setting in. I assume until the ground is frozen and there are no potatoes left. I try not to think about what will become of the potato broth soup we're all given for lunch. We'll be left with boiled water and dead grass.

Lilli's begun making quiet grunting noises with each pitch of the shovel. She's red in the face and sweating, despite the cool air. "Slow down," I tell her.

"I have to keep up," she says, breathlessly.

A series of thumps against the ground capture my attention, Alfie's attention, and Lilli's. It was the pattern. It was different from shovel digging.

"Papa," she whispers.

"Shh, shh," I warn her. "We must wait until—"

"I know," she says, glancing at the kapo pacing behind us.

All I can see between the trees is an elbow and the edge of a black boot. He must have seen us looking around. I don't know how we'll get to him while being watched with such scrutiny. We aren't far from the tree line or the dark shadows beneath the long overhanging branches, but if the three of us run at once, it'll be a scene.

Sweat forms on the back of my neck the longer I try to come up with an idea. We've come this far. Alfie is sweating too, more than usual, especially with the cooler air. And I have this awful feeling Lilli is going to throw caution to the wind and go running for Papa. Not that I can blame her, but we can't.

More minutes pass and I keep glancing over my shoulder. I'll likely be noticed doing so sooner or later. Now, I'm the one who just wants to make a run for him.

Another vibration of thuds hits my knees, and I watch the trees as I pick up on the letters being tapped out. Papa's elbow is jerking around. He must have something to hit the ground with. He tells us to wait.

In the next moment, a whistle and a rumbling pop echo between the trees, not the trees directly near us but ones farther away. Smoke plumes out from the woods and the children around us scream and run in the opposite direction. The kapos, too. The smoke infiltrates our area, and I grab Lilli's hand, just as Alfie grabs mine, and we race straight into the thickest part of the smoke, holding our breath, running blindly for what feels like forever. My eyes are still closed when something catches the back of my smock, yanking me backward. I don't release either of the other two from my hand so the three of us fall. "Come on, this way!"

Papa. His deep, calm voice. The I love yous, the promises, the goodnights and good mornings, are all painted with his voice, memories I've longed for since we arrived here.

"Papa," Lilli cries out.

Her hand whips out of mine and Papa's arm wraps around my back. I keep Alfie locked to my side and continue pushing through the smoke until we reach a clearing in the woods.

Papa is standing in front of us, worn, tired, a beard longer than I could ever imagine him having. "My girls," he says, his voice breaking as he wraps the three of us into his arms. "Alfie. Son." We all cry silent sobs of joy, trying for just one second to convince ourselves we're out of danger. I know all too well that the smoke will clear far quicker than the night of the firestorm.

"We have to run," he says, lifting Lilli into his arms. "Keep up."

I tap the message into Alfie's hand because he couldn't have heard what Papa said. The trees are only partially bare, concealing us just enough but also, not enough. Newly fallen leaves cover the tree roots and our footsteps crunch. The farther we go, the bigger the woods begin to feel, and an echo follows us, or are we following an echo?

Papa whips us toward a large oak, caving us in on one side as he searches the area.

"Someone's following us," he says between ragged breaths.

TWENTY-FOUR

DALIA

OCTOBER 8TH, 1943 – OŚWIĘCIM, POLAND

I spend my sleepless night thinking up other natural ingredients that Ina might have access to. Garlic, or ginger. She must know someone working at the SS kitchen. Lemons wouldn't be in the prisoner kitchen. Garlic or ginger reduce inflammation and can help kill viruses. I shouldn't dare ask Ina for anything else after what she offered to do for me last night, but my desperation is becoming larger than my ability to keep a sense of gratitude and manners.

I'm the first in line between Blocks 3 and 4, ready for the kapo to escort us into Auschwitz from Birkenau. The others aren't keeping up today and we've already stopped several times.

"Schneller gehen!" the kapo shouts, stomping her boot to the ground. She wants us to move faster but I'm certain some of us aren't able. "Ich melde dich bei der SS!" I don't know if everyone in the lines behind me speak German, but I'm sure they can take the hint that this woman has no qualms about reporting people to the SS for not moving fast enough.

Her threats seem to work somehow, and today will be the

only day I'm grateful for that. I can't take a full breath until I see Max, alive, in that bed. My entire body is numb with terror, my nerves tingling with a warning that I'm on the verge of not being able to handle much more.

I keep in step, imagining Max awake in bed. If we were at home, Jordanna would be at his side, checking his forehead, teasing him, then force-feeding him soup. She would drape cool compresses over him then tell him he resembles a drowned rat. He would throw a gentle jabbing tease back at her and the two would bicker with insults until I walked into the room. Of course, only after she had the last word. He let her. That was his love for her, and her care for him, gentle or not, was her love for him.

My feet carry me through the front door of the infirmary and down the hall toward the ward where I'm to report to the kapo in the corridor.

My heart burns in my chest as I wait for the kapo's nod to allow me into the ward. A cold sweat covers me from head to toe as I turn the corner, finding Max lying awake, peering around the room.

I press my hand to my mouth and race toward him.

"Mama," he says, greeting me with a smile. "See, I told you."

"Are you better today, sweetheart?" I ask, trying not to fall to my knees at his side.

"No, but it looks like I am, doesn't it?" he asks with a soft snicker.

"Max, that's not funny. Are you better?"

He shrugs. "Yeah, I think so."

"Thank God," I say, releasing a heavy breath as I wrap my arms around him. I rest my cheek on his chest, feeling the warmth of his fever still present, but improved since yesterday. He's less delirious too. He must be on the mend. "When was Ina here last?"

"Uh—" Max says, taking another look around the room. "An hour or two."

"She didn't get in trouble, did she?"

"She said she would be back soon."

"All right." I glance around the room, taking in the work ahead of me while also spotting Marie walk in and head for her row of patients. "Have you had water this morning?"

"Yes, I think so," he says.

I grab Max's medical log and read the status as *stable*.

"I need to make a round and check on the others. I'll be back as quick as I can," I whisper to him.

"Mama?"

I turn back at Max's questioning voice, finding a look of defeat in his watery eyes. "What is it, sweetheart?"

"I did everything I could to protect Lilli, Jordanna, and Alfie. I tried—" he says, taking the breath he needs to continue speaking, "to escape the ghetto so I could find them." My heart cracks, a pain searing through my chest, and I clutch my top, pressing my sharp knuckles against my skin.

"You are the most incredible brother, and those girls love you more than anything." Those girls. My words sound as if I'm talking about someone else's children. It's been so long, can I even call them mine still?

"I—I," Max says, swallowing against his dry throat. "I wanted to rescue them—if it was the last thing I did. But I was caught trying to escape."

"That's how you ended up here?" I ask.

Max nods faintly, his head seeming too heavy to move, already weaker than when I walked in a moment ago.

"I love them—my little sisters. I really wanted to—" his voice croaks and tears fill his tired eyes. "I was supposed to save them."

"None of us are allowed to even save ourselves, sweetheart,"

I whisper to him. "You are your father's son, no doubt about that."

As I turn away from him, tears threaten to roll down my cheeks, but I take a forceful deep breath and trudge toward the beginning of my row to check on bed 1.

Just as I mark off no new updates for this unconscious young woman, a hand clamps around my arm, pulling me out of sight from the open doorway. I whip my head around, finding Ina, pale, her face covered with discernible concern. "Thank you so much for everything—I owe you—"

"Stop," she whispers. "I found more aspirin last night. His fever spiked again, high. It was too high," she says.

I press my finger against my lips and shake my head. "Thank you, Ina. I don't know how I can ever thank you enough—"

"The lemons are gone, and I've lost access to the SS kitchen —the infirmary too."

"Were you caught?" I ask, my breath catching on each word.

"No, but there was a lot of activity in front of the SS infirmary this morning and the overnight workers were being interrogated."

"I'm so so—"

"Don't apologize," she says, placing her hand on my shoulder, her eyes unblinking. "I gave him the last dose of aspirin at midnight."

"It seems he's turned a corner now. He's better," I tell her.

A weak smile forms on her lips. "Good. I have to—" she points to her row of patients.

"Of course. Thank you again. I will repay you, somehow. I will."

She holds on to her tight lipped-smile, nods and turns for her row.

There's no more aspirin or lemons. There's no chance of finding garlic or ginger.

I move to bed 2, focusing on only Ina's few words—words that didn't hold any sound of hope. I mindlessly check the woman's vitals, then her wound, search for a tube of ointment, finding very little left. No one is replenishing our supplies. I hardly have enough dressing to rewrap the wound.

Between each bed, I glance over at Max, watching him try to find a comfortable position. He can't seem to be still, yanking at the sheet, tugging it off his feet. Max has never been one to be in one spot for long. He needs to be busy like Leo. Sitting for too long makes them both restless. That must be what's wrong.

I go through the motions of checking on the patient in bed 3, listening to the patient's rambling and incoherence before I can move on to the next.

Again, I peek down the row toward Max's bed. He has the sheet gripped within his fists, his face red, and his teeth gritted together. He's folding himself in half, groaning. I drop the medical log in my hand and race toward him.

"What's wrong, sweetheart? What's happened?"

"My stomach—head—legs. Make it stop, Mama."

I touch my hand to his forehead, his fever returning, but not to the level it was at yesterday. This must be the aspirin wearing off. Maybe he's had too much aspirin and lemon. "It's from the lemon and aspirin. I'll get you some water."

I spin around until I find a tin cup and pitcher, splashing water as I try to pour it into the cup with a steady hand.

"No, no," he says. "No more."

I take his hand, feeling his grip move from the sheet to my fingers. He relaxes his body and falls back into his pillow, gasping for a big breath. His chest moves up and down as if he's just run around the room.

"Shhh, it's fine. Try to take another slow breath." He struggles to take in air but does. "What's happening right now?" I shouldn't be asking him. He doesn't know. I should know, and I don't.

He twists his head on the pillow to look at me, his eyes studying me as if he wants me to read his silent thoughts.

"Mama," he says, the word covered in phlegm.

"What is it, sweetheart? You're all right."

He's not well. My son is not all right and there isn't anything in this entire godforsaken infirmary that could help him.

"I tried to be a warrior."

My face burns as tears fill my eyes. I fall to my knees. Scooping my arm beneath Max, I pull him against my chest, holding his face with my other hand.

"You are a warrior, Max. You always have been and always will be. You have your papa's blood running through your veins. You will make it through this."

"You're a warrior too, Mama."

I remember gazing into his beautiful eyes the moment the doctor placed him into my arms after he was born. I knew he couldn't see much at just a few minutes old, but he stared right back at me as if he knew me already. My little love. I had never felt so much in my heart at once, joy, fear, pride, and incomprehensible love before that moment. I would give him my last breath. I would do anything to protect him. He would forever be my world—the beginning, middle, and end.

He curled his tiny hand around my index finger. I can still remember the pink of his paper-thin fingernails and the dry skin on his knuckles, the silk touch of his skin.

"I love you so much, Max. You know that?" I say now, clutching his hand. "You made me a Mama. You gave me life when I thought I was already living."

"I love you, Mama. I'm sorry. I thought—" he says, his words floating on a whisper.

"You have nothing to be sorry about," I tell him, silent tears rolling down my cheeks.

"I—" he tries to take a breath, but it's so weak.

"Don't-don't." I weep. "Don't give up—" His eyes close as I plead with him to hold on. *How can I ask him to fight harder when he's already fought through the unthinkable?* "I'm still here. I'm with you. It's all right. It's all right, baby."

A hand touches my back. I peer through the corner of my tear-filled eyes, finding Ina pinching her lips together so hard they're white. "I d-don't know what's happening," I cry.

But I do.

I brush my fingertips over Max's head and press my lips to his cheek. "We're all going to be together soon, my darling."

Max's lips quiver and his eyes open. A tear forms in the corner of his eye. I reach for his other hand that's draped over his chest and curl it into both of mine. His breaths become slow and shallow, and his body weighs heavier against my left arm. "Max, sweetheart, look at me—" I beg. "Just—" I gasp for air, unable to take enough in. "Baby, please. You just need—Max!"

A guttural sob escapes my throat, uncontrollable and raw, holding on to his hands tighter as if that could keep him alive. My body heaves from the cries bursting through me. "I won't let go. No. You can't go. Please, please. Max! Can you hear me?" But I feel him take his last breath. I feel him still in my hands. My cries howl in the quiet room and I don't care. I don't care who hears me. "My son—he's gone. Come back!"

Ina's voice breaks through hopeless wails. "I'm so sorry, Dalia," Ina utters. "I'm—I tried—I did—" She squeezes my shoulder, trying to comfort me but her words float over my head. I can't hear anything but the pounding of my heart, the sound of Max's final breath still ringing in my ears. "I—I'm going to go cover the hallway, make sure none of those rats come in," she says. "Marie!" Ina calls for the other nurse. "Cover."

No mother should have to see their child lying lifeless before them. My hand trembles as I touch his lifeless face, my legs threatening to give out. Every one of my breaths is like a betrayal, each heartbeat, a reminder that I'm here without him. "I love you more than you'll ever know," I whisper into his ear.

But he's gone.

Gone forever.

How long can forever be? I can't survive this. I can't survive forever without him.

"A guard is coming," Marie says. "Shh, shh, dear, shh. I'm so sorry. We can't hold him off." She grabs me from behind and lifts me to my feet as I fight to keep a hand on Max. "You have to get up."

"No, no. I can't. Let me go. I can't leave my son. I can't."

Marie drags me away, my body limp and unable to fight her off. She leaves me against the back wall, not far from Max, but not close enough that I can touch him. An SS guard marches into the room in search of something. They hardly ever come in here due to the fear of contracting something from a patient. He holds a handkerchief over his nose and marches between the rows, studying each patient for a brief second.

"Is that one dead?" he asks, pointing at Max.

I don't answer. I can't. I should, because the guard is looking directly at me. I shake my head, but words don't come out. He grabs the foot of the bed and rolls him away, shoving him across the room, down the row toward the door.

This isn't real. This can't be real. It's in my head. I can't even close my eyes or look away.

"Gehen!" he shouts at me to go, to push Max's bed into the hallway.

Marie steps in and takes the bed—takes my baby—for me. She nods her head at me, directing me to her row, mouthing the words, "Go over there."

I move along, dragging my heavy feet, my numb body, and my bleeding heart. For all the pain of giving birth, raising a beautiful little boy into a man who has become as brilliant, strong and resilient as his papa, watching him prepare to take the world on and do all the wonderful things we could only dream of for him, and then—his life is taken from him before he really got to live.

My world is shattering into a million pieces. I know I will never be whole again.

TWENTY-FIVE

JORDANNA

We've been running as if we're ping-pong balls bouncing from side to side, looping around trees and crouching beneath large, leaning tree trunks. I don't know how much farther I can run. My lungs are burning, and my throat is tight. My legs are merely thin sticks holding me up and this speed is too much. "Papa, I can't."

"We're almost there," he says between gasping breaths, running backward for a few seconds as he searches the area again. "We must have lost him—if there was someone following us. It'll be easier to hide when we reach the field."

Alfie wraps his arm around me, hoisting me around his shoulder to take the burden of some of my weight in addition to his own. He's in no better shape than I am but he doesn't seem to be struggling as much.

He curls his hand around my waist, gripping me tightly as we continue running from whatever might be chasing us. The surrounding sounds are bouncing off the trees, making it impossible to know what direction the source is.

A cloud of glowing fog appears in the distance between some trees. For all I know, these woods could go on and on, but maybe it's a way out. With every heavy step, my organs rattle in my body, my brain sloshes around in my head. Everything aches. We reach the fog and there's a warmth within the cloud, the sun must be shining through on the other side.

A dirt road across from a sprawling field is what finds us on the other side. "Where are we?" I ask Papa.

He pulls out his beloved black compass from his pocket, clicks it open, stares at the markers, then closes his eyes before counting something under his breath. "Through the field. Just another ten minutes or so."

"Until what?" I cry out.

"We get to the train station."

"Papa," I say with a wheeze. "What in the world are we going to do at a train station? We're registered Jews and now escapees of an imprisoned ghetto."

"I'm here, Jordanna. I'll take care of you now," he says, reaching for my chin, taking a long moment to stare into my eyes. My heart aches. We shouldn't be standing here. Someone or something was following us in the woods. "Are you all right, Alfie?"

Alfie doesn't respond. He's studying every direction from where we're standing. He also didn't hear him. Papa wouldn't know about Alfie's ears. We didn't know before he and Mama were taken from us.

"He can't hear you," Lilli tells Papa.

Papa pinches his lips. "I'm sorry," he says, shaking his head. He taps Alfie on the shoulder and gives him a nod, nudging his head toward the field.

From a higher elevation on the dirt road, I didn't realize how tall the wheat was. It isn't tall enough to cover the top of our heads, but we can easily duck down if need be. Papa leads the way, pushing through the wheat to clear a path for us to move through.

It's a harder walk than the woods would have been with

sharp prickly awns whipping back at us. From behind me, Alfie tries to grab the handfuls of wheat roots from Papa's grasp to keep the path open but we're moving too quickly to keep up with one another.

I can't see behind Alfie and maybe it's for the best, but I'm worried someone could be following us and we wouldn't hear them over the crinkles and crackles of the roots we're stepping on.

It feels as if an hour has passed when more trees appear on the horizon. I fear another hike through the trees.

"Don't worry. The woods are shallow," Papa huffs.

Once we reach the shade of the overbearing trees, I stop to catch my breath, holding my hands against my shaking knees. "Where will we take the train to? What about Max? He was taken to Łódź, close to where we were. We need to find him."

"Yes, I know. I—we need to get you to safety first."

"You know where Max is too?" I ask.

"Yes. He'll be fine. Come along."

"He's not fine, Papa. He wrote me a letter weeks ago. They were working him to the bone."

Papa takes in a deep breath and releases the air slowly. "Jordanna, I need to get the three of you to a safe place first. Trust me, sweetheart."

"I miss Max too," Lilli says, resting her head on Papa's shoulder.

Papa swallows hard and presses on through the woods. It isn't long before the sound of chugging steam and the whistling of an engine whirs toward us.

"How are you going to get tickets?" I ask Papa.

"We aren't. The sun is beneath the horizon and the darkness will be in our favor. Once the train begins to move, we're going to make a running leap for the open second-to-last freight car. The conductors don't check tickets there."

What if we're not fast enough? Who is going to get on first? What if Papa goes first and the rest of us can't catch up?

"Jordanna, you and Alfie are going to go first, and I'll make sure Lilli and I get on after you. Just wait until I tell you to run. Can Alfie hear any sound at all?"

"Not really, but I have a way of communicating with him. I'll tell him the plan."

I grab Alfie's hand and begin tapping out Morse code, the instructions Papa just gave us. It takes a moment to get all the words out but it's important he understands completely.

"All right," Alfie says after.

I glance back at Papa, ready to continue toward the station. "Did you just talk to him through Morse code?" Papa asks, his voice scratchy with phlegm.

"Yes."

"You make me very proud. I don't quite have words to describe what I'm feeling at the moment, but you are something special. All of you are."

His eyes fill up, but tears don't escape. He wipes his face on his sleeve and clears his throat. The train whistles again and Papa's gaze darts toward the tracks and he waves us along.

The woods line the tracks, only a dozen steps away at most. The back of the train isn't far from us, just a minute or two's walk to meet the rear-end cars. There are metal steps leading toward the closed freight door. I hope it isn't locked.

The grind of metal against metal warns us the train is about to move. We're still hidden within the shadows of the trees, needing to run the twelve or so steps to the metal railing. Papa's hand is on my shoulder. "Hold on," he says. A whoosh of steam spouts, and Papa nudges me forward. "Go now. Go." I have Alfie by the hand, and we make a run for it, he takes the lead, catching the railing before me and yanks me up onto the step, pushing me back against the car door.

"Stay there. I'm going to help your Papa," he tells me.

Papa is running with Lilli in his arms, needing to speed up a bit more than the pace we were going, but grabs a hold of the railing and flings himself and Lilli up to the steps. Alfie snatches Lilli from Papa's arm and I turn around and silently pray the car door isn't locked. I yank on the lever, the rusty metal groaning and vibrating against my hand. The door slides on its own just a bit, telling me we'll be able to get inside. I push it open the rest of the way and grab the inside wall to twist myself in and against the wall. The other three do the same and Papa secures the car door, closing us inside.

Air pours through an open window at the top of the car, and I look around, realizing we're not in a freight car as we thought, but instead among horses. Brown horses line both sides of the car walls, with troughs and rope, keeping them secure to their spot. They seem to all be staring at us but at the same time don't seem very bothered by our presence.

"Sit down here," Papa says, pointing to the floor beside the door. We do as he says. He follows, leans back against the wall and runs his hands across the top of his head.

"Where's Mama?" Lilli asks.

It's the only question I've wanted to ask Papa, and the only question I'm fearful of an answer to. And he hasn't said a word about her. He would have if there was something to say. Mama has been my guiding light and I can't lose her. I can't go through life without her. I need to believe she's still waiting somewhere for us.

Papa lowers his head as if with shame. "I don't know, little mouse. When we were taken to aid with the aftermath of the firestorm, I was grabbed from behind and dragged to a building still in flames, instructed to go inside and pull out anyone who was still alive. They didn't give me a chance to tell your Mama I had to help elsewhere, and when I returned to the square, she was gone. No one could tell me where she went, and I still don't know. I've been trying to find all of you, all this time, I haven't stopped searching."

"How will we ever find her? And what about Max?" I press.

"We need to go to a refugee camp in Hungary. It's going to take a bit to make our way through Poland, then Slovakia, but Germany has yet to occupy Hungary. I know a place we can go. Once I have you settled, I'll return for the rest of our family."

"No, Papa, I don't want to leave your side again," Lilli cries out.

He pulls her onto his lap and wraps his arms around her. "I don't either, but—"

"No, Papa," she pleads. And it's the most heartbreaking sound in the world.

Throughout the blurry hours and night following Max's death, I laid awake on the wooden board in my barrack unable to move while tears streaked down my face and soaked my clothes. The stench of sour body odor, bodily fluids, rotting flesh, and oak floated around me, adding to my nausea. The repeated sounds of coughs, moans, and rustling across wood came in patterns and waves, never ceasing for more than a minute. The visions in my head of Max's last moments, it's all could see—it's all I may ever see again...All I can do is consider the idea of giving up.

I'm ashamed of the thought now, as I stare at the clock in the ward, realizing it's been an entire day since Max died in my arms. I'm already dead inside.

"If we can make it through this, we can make it through anything," Leo said to me upon returning home after the Great War ended. It was so easy to believe those words. The odds were not in his favor of returning, and yet, he did. Of course, not without telling me it was his lucky compass that got him through the war. I know it's just superstition, but I should have given the children compasses too. Maybe I wouldn't be mourning my eldest child's death right now.

If Leo's right and that compass does bring him back to me, somehow, it won't matter because a part of us is dead and won't ever be coming back. We've lost a piece of ourselves. How am I supposed to carry on now?

I've watched fellow prisoners purposely run into the electrified barbed-wire fences to rid themselves of misery. If this torture is a test of our strength and endurance, what's left to confirm? How strong will a person become before a higher power decides it's enough to move on to whatever comes next after this life? I don't know if there's a next one. I prefer to believe there is because it offers me comfort, but no one truly knows if there's an oblivion of darkness that follows our last breath. At forty-two, I still can't wrap my head around the meaning of a person's lifetime in comparison to the duration of eternity.

"Bed eight," Marie calls out. Another life. Gone.

More patients are dying today than yesterday. Is that my fault too? Our supplies are gone.

A set of hands rests on my shoulders while rearranging an empty bed between two occupied ones. The gesture startles me, and I gasp.

"I'm so sorry," a woman says from behind me.

I turn around, finding an unfamiliar nurse and fellow prisoner, but not someone I've worked with in this ward or triage. By the badge on her smock, I see she's a Polish political prisoner, not Jewish.

"Is there something I can help you with?" I ask her, staring into her eyes which carry thoughts I'm certain she won't share out loud.

"Your efforts haven't gone unnoticed," she says. "I'm sorry to hear about your son, as well."

I don't know how she knows anything about me unless she's an acquaintance of Marie or Ina who also work in this ward with me. The three of us have formed a nice bond, a quiet one, but a strong one, nonetheless.

"Give me your hands," she says, speaking in a hushed whisper. I do as she says, confused and unsure what to expect. She dips her hand beneath the collar of her smock and pulls out a small handmade satchel. "Take this, wear it around your neck and keep the satchel between your breasts."

Her filled hands are already resting in mine, but I cup my palms around her fists this time. She releases the fabric filled with lumps made of different small sizes and shapes.

"What—"

"Put it on now," she says, pulling her hands from mine. I slip the thin strap around my neck, sliding it beneath my collar and fold the satchel down the center of my chest. "We're rewarded for reporting infractions, but we'll live longer if we don't."

I don't know what's inside the satchel, but I understand her statement. Friendships are rare in Auschwitz because it's every person for themselves. Survival is a one-person job. We've come to learn that reporting unacceptable behavior can result in extra food. We're rewarded for turning on each other. Desperation can alter a person's ability to navigate their morals.

I wouldn't be able to live with myself if I caused anyone here more pain, grief, or worse for the sake of my personal gain. But I understand when someone else can't stop themselves from falling victim to desperation. We're all weak. We all have a breaking point. I might be beyond that but I'm unsure if anyone ever knows where that point is, was, or might be.

"Thank you," I whisper. I'm thanking her for whatever she's given me, for her warning. For her sympathy.

"You're still standing after losing a child. I know strength when I see it, and strength is what many of us need. There are more of us who have gone through the same." Her eyes narrow but don't blink, and her words are vague. Yet, I think I understand what she's saying.

"How can I help—"

"Notes. I need notes. On everything you've seen, experienced, and live through in Birkenau. There is paper and a pencil in the medical supply bin. I can pick up the notes tomorrow."

The movement of her lips is louder than her voice but somehow, I manage to make out what she's saying. The hair on my skin rises, fear strikes a nerve, and I don't know whether I should trust this woman or consider the thought of being set up. "For whom?" It's my only question.

"Everyone on the other side of these walls. Every chain requires links. And every lock requires a—well, you have what you need if you choose to do so."

Her words are cryptic, but she speaks so eloquently, and with a form of confidence I haven't come across here before. The slightest of smiles touches her lips and she places her hand on my shoulder. "Take care."

As she slips away, a shiver runs down my back and I search around the ward, seeking Ina or Marie, wondering if they saw the woman I was speaking with.

They're both busy with patients so I turn to face a wall, unfurl my hand and loosen the fabric wrapped ball of goods, finding loose aspirin, a slim box of iodine swabs, Benzedrine sulfate tablets, bandages, a scrap of paper with a combination of a dozen numbers and letters, and hard candy. My eyeballs feel as if they might fall out of their sockets, so I rewrap the package, tighten my fist around it and shove it beneath my smock collar to drop it in the satchel. I'm overwhelmed by the idea of everything I have on my person now. Clearly, I need to find out why this woman just handed it all to me. But the aspirin, the aspirin I so desperately needed for Max—would this have been enough to keep him alive?

Before moving on to the next patient's bed, I stop at the medical supply bin and take a few loose sheets of paper and a pencil, adding it to the other supplies in my satchel. As I pull my arm back out from beneath my collar, I realize the danger is writing anything down on paper. The possibility of confiscation is higher than the probability of the correct person receiving the note.

I continue working through my rounds of dying patients, jotting down their statuses and trying to focus on what I'm doing rather than trying to figure out what that woman wants from me.

"How are you doing?" Ina asks after I step away from the last bed in the row.

"I feel dead inside," I tell her. I shouldn't have said that. We're all dead inside at this point.

"That means you're still alive," she says.

Her words don't feel like a blessing.

"Di-did you ah—" I press my hand to my forehead, trying to focus my erratic thoughts, "notice the nurse who came in a bit ago, who pulled me aside to talk?"

I glance over at Marie. Similarly to Ina, Marie is a Polish non-Jewish prisoner. Marie was also arrested on account of so-called resistance, really only offering nursing aid to local Jewish people in her town.

Ina lowers her stare to the ground between our feet. "Yes, I know her."

"She gave me—"

"Shh," Ina says. "She's been made aware you're trustworthy. We've told her you're one of us—a fighter until the end. She might be able to help."

Ina walks away, making it clear she doesn't want to have any further discussion about my interaction with the other nurse, yet she has brought me into a circle of trust and I'm not certain what that might mean. I'm grateful but terrified.

I assume Marie must know her too.

The next row of patients is waiting or lost the battle of waiting, and now need to be moved elsewhere. Some mornings when I arrive, I question if I'm only here to escort people to their death or give them one last inkling of hope before they let go. I'm just watching people die unnecessarily.

Another case of starvation lies before me and the hard candy in the satchel feels heavier as I stare at the person. I couldn't guess how old they might be. It's hard to tell whether they're male or female sometimes. Every skeleton looks the same. The only differentiation between us all now is the cloth badges sewn to our uniforms: Yellow stars for the Jews along with possible accompanying-colored triangles depending on any additional committed crimes. There are red triangles for political criminals, black for anti-social people, pink for homosexuals, blue for emigrants, green for criminals, and purple for Jehovah's Witnesses. This person dying in front of me has a star made from yellow and red triangles, marking them to be a Jewish political criminal. They must have chosen to stand up for themselves, setting aside the understanding that we Jews aren't allowed to do that.

I take a moment to check the record, finding their number and an "F" circled. Date of birth: The 7th day of April 1925. She's only eighteen, born in Le Mans, France.

Malnutrition is the only note listed on her log.

I'm sure that will be altered at some point. Malnutrition suggests she's starving to death. I would give her one of my hard candies if she were conscious.

A whistling tune drawls and drones down the corridor wards. The sound, though muted by the walls, shrills through my ears, knowing whose lips are forming the celebratory tune. I've met him twice, only to answer questions about patients. But Ina and Marie have told me heinous stories of what this high-level doctor is responsible for here at Auschwitz. They've warned me to never look at him without being summoned and never ask questions with him standing within earshot. The man never delivers good news, but is always perky and polite.

The whistling stops just outside the ward's door, and I silently pray he keeps walking. I have stolen items in my satchel, after all.

The whistling continues, the footsteps too, and I release the breath I didn't realize I was holding.

I lift the young woman's arm in front of me and check her pulse for an updated number.

"Bed twenty," I say, my voice hardly loud enough to carry more than a row or two.

Marie passes by, making her way toward the main door. "You're lucky," she says to me. "Took me five months before— before that nurse you spoke to earlier, spoke to me. She must see something in you."

"What do you mean by that?" I ask.

"Do what she said. It won't be long now." Marie nods her head, as if agreeing with her quiet words. "The scrap of paper you have—solve it first."

* * *

I've been staring at this small piece of torn paper for hours. My mind is dizzy from trying to decipher the puzzling meaning of these English words:

FIVE PACK MY LIQUOR JUGS WITH A DOZEN BOXES

BRAVE QUEENS FIXED PICKY DAMAGED WAR JETS IN HAZY LOSS

TVWGCPF NVF QBGVC 15.10.43

The two lines don't even make sense. The other nurses

might refer to themselves as queens. We're all brave. Maybe my English isn't as good as I thought and I'm confusing definitions.

In frustration, I drop my head onto my arms, covering the paper and the hint of light shining in through the window from a nearby watchtower. I didn't write the notes the woman asked me to because she told me to read this note before doing so. It makes me think of a story Leo once told about the war...

"We intercepted these messages sent through carrier pigeons. That's the only reason some of us survived. While under that type of pressure, it took us a long time to decode the memos we were able to get our hands on, and most of the time it was too late to shift our directions, but we were at least prepared for what was coming. The enemy certainly didn't intend for us to know so much," Leo says, lying awake, staring at the dark ceiling just as he does most nights. It's been almost a year since the Great War ended but I'm certain he hasn't slept through an entire night since he's gotten home. I've always told him to wake me up if he can't sleep. It's still early tonight. We only just blew out the candles a few minutes ago.

I have a habit of waiting until he falls asleep before I close my eyes. I worry about him so much and I don't want him sitting up alone with the thoughts and memories that ravage his mind.

"Decode? Were they in a different language?" I ask, resting my hand on his chest.

His heart beats as if he's been running for an hour. It's rare to find him in a calm state. I wish I could help him, do something to ease his burdens. He tells me I keep him at peace just by being here, but I know that can't be true.

"No, the ones we intercepted were written Russian words," he says.

"You knew enough Russian to understand them?" I clarify.

"Oh, no. It wasn't that simple. They were written with the

expectation that the recipient, another Russian, had a mathematical key to decode the message. They're in a ciphertext—an encryption."

"How were you able to decipher it if you didn't have the key?"

Leo wraps his arm around me and pulls me in closer. "You married a smart man," he says with a chuckle.

"Thank God," I say.

"The type of ciphertext the Russians sent used an older method of cryptography which was easier to decode. It was a matter of matching scrambled letters with their alphabet and figuring out how many positions, positive or negative, the alphabet shifted in their original encoding. I'm sure we would have had an easier time with them if they were formulated in Polish or German, of course."

"I wouldn't have known where to start," I tell him.

"We learned some in our basic training. There were only sixty-six possibilities of matching up the letters with the thirty-three letters in their alphabet. Sometimes we found the difference quicker by luck. Other times, it took us nearly sixty-six attempts to finally sort it out."

"I'm confident you would have figured it out too. You don't let much get in your way, and your determination—well, I'm proud to be your husband." Leo kisses my cheek and finally settles into his pillow. "I love you, darling."

"I love you," I tell him, falling asleep to letters and numbers floating around in my head.

I gasp from my half sleep state of distress on the wooden plank. I lift my heavy head, staring down at the paper again. The two sentences have nothing to do with each other. That must be the key.

In silence, I recite the English alphabet, finding one of each letter in the top sentence and the bottom sentence. But there are more than twenty-six letters in each. I write out the alphabet on one of the blank sheets of paper I took from the medical bin, trying not to tap my pencil too hard. No one else needs to sit awake through the night. The daytime is bad enough.

All I see are letters swimming across the page. There are more letters in the second line than there are in the first. The numbers on the bottom line match the date.

I only need twenty-six letters and another twenty-six to line up, if I'm lucky, and this isn't an impossible mathematical equation relying on an actual key I don't have. But what would the purpose of that interaction have been if so?

I reach down toward my feet, finding my infirmary apron and pull out one of the hard candies and pop it into my mouth.

The tart and sugary sweet taste shocks my taste buds, causing a nerve pain to sting my cheek, but then it's a small piece of heaven on my tongue. Drool forms on my lips and I cover my mouth. Oh my...I sigh, reveling in a fantasy of tasting sweets again. Nothing has ever tasted so delicious.

I return my stare to the paper, back and forth between my written alphabet and the nonsensical words. I rewrite the two lines on my paper and begin to underline the alphabetical letters as I spot the letters in the top line. The second instance of duplicate letters, I cross out. Then I do the same to the second line.

FIVE PACK MY L~~I~~QUOR J~~U~~GS W~~I~~TH ~~A~~ D~~O~~Z~~E~~N B~~OXES~~

BRAVE QU~~EE~~NS FIXED P~~I~~CKY ~~DAMAGED~~ W~~AR~~ JE~~TS~~
~~IN~~ H~~AZY~~ LO~~SS~~

~~F~~|~~I~~|V|E|P|A|~~C~~|~~K~~|~~M~~|~~Y~~|~~L~~|~~Q~~|~~U~~|~~O~~|~~R~~|~~J~~|~~G~~|S|W|T|H|D|Z|N|B|~~X~~

~~B~~|~~R~~|~~A~~|~~V~~|~~E~~|~~Q~~|~~U~~|~~N~~|S|~~F~~|~~I~~|~~X~~|~~D~~|~~P~~|~~C~~|~~K~~|~~Y~~|~~M~~|~~G~~|W|~~J~~|T|H|Z|L|~~O~~

A|B|C|D|E|F|G|H|I|J|K|L|M|N|O|P|Q|R|S|T|U|V|W|X|Y|Z

Q|L|U|T|V|B|Y|J|R|K|N|I|S|Z|P|E|X|C|W|G|D|A|M|O|F|H

I stare back at the original note, wondering how I'm supposed to know for sure that I've decoded this correctly. I could be so very wrong.

This part doesn't quite fit in with the other two lines:

TVWGCPF NVF QBGVC 15.10.43

I know the last part is the date, but I match the other letters up to the rough key I just created on my extra paper.

DESTROY KEY AFTER 15.10.43

All I can do is stare in disbelief. I thought for sure I was out of my mind, but I wasn't. This is how she wants me to write my notes. Using this mismatched alphabet that can be decoded later.

* * *

I have dedicated the past two hours to writing as much as I can on these pieces of paper, all coded per the alphabetical key. Once I hear people stirring, I tuck everything away, remembering what the note said about destroying the key. I tear off the top part of the paper with the mismatched letters in the two rows.

I crumple the thin strip of paper and jump when the gong sounds across the compound, shaking the walls and the wooden bunks. Most everyone around moves quickly when the gong rings. I panic and shove the paper into my mouth, hoping I can dampen it enough with my dry, dehydrated tongue—the candy.

My mouth isn't as dry as usual. I chew the paper and grab my belongings.

I turn to leave with the others, but I'm sideswiped and thrashed into the wooden posts. "Watch it," Brygid yips after shoving me. She clearly hasn't warmed up to me at all, despite my attempts to greet her twice a day. She always seems annoyed with my behavior no matter what I do.

I hurry to the latrines and washrooms. With the paper in my mouth, for a moment, I tell myself I am chewing on a piece of meat, something savory I just pulled out of the oven for dinner. My stomach craves to feel something in my hollow stomach, and I swallow the piece of meat, allowing the secret to disappear within me. I tuck the other papers under my smock, now understanding how deadly my words could become if someone knew how to decipher them.

What if this was all a trap? To see if I would comply. Ina wouldn't let that happen to me. We've shared far more secrets than anyone else I've met here. Ina wants justice after losing everything before arriving here. She's made it clear she will continue to fight until all of our lives are put back together, somehow. Except, I don't know if her life could ever be put back together.

The relentless thoughts gnaw at me as I trek through the chilly wind over to the main camp, following a new block elder I'm not familiar with. People come and go from this place as if it's a train station, except the people aren't typically going to a different destination. They're dying and being burnt to ashes. It's a secret that isn't quite a secret.

The orchestra is playing at full capacity this morning, making me wonder what German official must be making an appearance here. The SS officers are under the impression that some lovely music can set a different tune to the torture and suffering endured by everyone here.

I don't know if I'll ever be able to hear music the same way I once did. The scene of a living hell in the backdrop of Bach, Beethoven, and Zimmer's compositional pieces is a dramatic paradox.

Before entering the ward, a cold hand tightens around my wrist and jerks me in the opposite direction. I find the unfamiliar nurse from yesterday to be the one who has a hold of me. "Where are you taking me?" I huff at her, keeping my voice down.

"Be quiet," she snaps under her breath. She pushes me into a small room and closes the door. "Do you have the notes?"

She holds her hand out, a tremor obvious. She's nervous. "Who will be receiving it?"

The woman drops her head. "Did you write them or not?"

"Do you mean, did I solve the code?" I reply.

"Yes," she hisses.

"I will answer you when you answer me."

She leans toward me to whisper in my ear. "I'm a small part of a much larger resistance. We have help on the outside."

I swallow hard, feeling as if the paper has risen back up to my throat. "How dangerous is this?" It's a silly question seeing how each day we're still here is another day longer than we expected to survive.

"No more dangerous than going to sleep at night," she says.

I reach under my smock and retrieve the folded notes. "I followed your instructions," I say, placing the papers in her hand. "Thank you for the—"

"Enough. No thank you is necessary. Our work here is far from complete."

"What ward do you work in?" I ask.

"The one where people return to work later in the day."

"The people with hope?"

"Yes, I suppose that's what we should call it."

"I'd prefer to work there than where I am."

"We all move around. You'll be out of there soon, I'm sure."

TWENTY-SEVEN

JORDANNA

It took a long while for Lilli to settle down and fall asleep on Papa's lap. I was able to get some sleep too and through the air vents above us, sunlight is beginning to seep into the car. The educators must know we're gone by now. I don't want to think about what's happened because of our disappearance. The thought makes my stomach hurt, but my stomach already aches with hunger and it's hard to tell what pain is from where.

I watch the horses eat whatever is in the barrel in front of their noses, feeling jealous of their freedom to breathe fresh air, and eat and drink as they wish. One of the horses seems disinterested in its food, instead cleaning his backside. The thought of taking a handful of his fodder is reeling through my head. These horses are treated so well, I imagine their food must be made from common ingredients to keep them healthy.

I push myself up to my feet, finding Papa with his eyes closed and Alfie too. I'll get enough for all of us to share. The horse is still occupied when I reach the barrel and I'm quick to scoop my hands in, taking a heaping pile to bring back to Papa, Lilli, and Alfie.

I take two careful steps away from the horse, going either

unnoticed, or they aren't fazed by my presence. I take another step away, avoiding sudden movements, but the floorboard creaks, a loud whiny groan. The horses all begin to thrash their necks, their manes wild in the air. Growling sounds echo between the walls. I've never heard horses make such terrifying noises before. The apparent anger follows neighs and horse-shoes clomping back and forth, shaking the car.

Papa jumps up to his feet, pulling Lilli up with him. The movement wakes Alfie and he follows Papa to his feet too.

"What happened?" Papa calls out before spotting the heap of fodder in my hands.

"I'm sorry, Papa," I cry out. "I was—"

"Come here. Come here." He reaches out for me and pulls me to stand behind him, along with Lilli. "The shouts—I hear shouting. The SS are making their way back to this car. They'll find us."

"Where are we going to go?" I ask, shaking against the wall.

Just as my question comes out, the sound of a whistle follows the shouts Papa heard—an officer's whistle, demanding attention and silence. The whistle continues to grow louder and louder.

"There's no time. We need to get off the train!" Papa says.

We're moving so fast now. I don't know how we'll be able to jump and make it off in one piece.

Papa struggles to open the car door, sliding it open as trees blur by us.

The whistles have grown even louder. There's no doubt there are officers heading back here. Papa grabs Alfie's shoulder and gives me a look, one I don't quite understand. Regardless, Alfie does and steps forward to be the first to jump off the train. He pulls Alfie in and gives him a hug and a kiss on the head.

Then he hands Lilli over to Alfie. Papa grabs me, pulls me to his chest, and kisses the top of my head. "We can do this. We're warriors, you and I. Always."

The jump Alfie takes with Lilli is horrifying, watching as they roll away from the tracks. I'm holding the railings, my knuckles straining against my skin as I fear the thought of letting go. There's no time to stall though. I turn back for Papa, waving him along to jump with me.

The whistle blows again. This time it's a piercing loud shrill. The horses let out another wild growl, even more vicious than before. "You there!" a voice shouts.

"Jordanna, you must jump now!" The urgency in Papa's shout makes me squeeze my eyes shut while willing myself to jump. But my legs won't move.

"I'm scared!" I cry out, turning back for Papa's hand. Except, the train door is closing, leaving me with a split second view of his face, void of emotions, pale, then leaving me with nothing more than the sight of a steel panel in his place.

No.

"Papa?" I scream.

The numbing realization that Papa is still inside, and I'm out here causes me to lose my grip on the metal rung, forcing me air bound, away from the speeding train.

My body slams against the unforgiving hard ground, sending me rolling and rolling without the ability to stop.

The world spins around me, trees are upside down, sideways, and every which way.

Once I stop moving, I try to push myself up by my arms, looking toward the train, but it keeps moving, disappearing into a distant fog. There's no sight of Papa reopening the train door to jump. My momentary fear cost us everything. He must have closed himself inside the train, allowing himself, and himself only, to be caught by the officer.

I'm the one who disturbed the horses, and I'm the one who took too long to jump. I should have been the one caught, not him. It's all my fault. "Papa!" I scream, reaching for the train as it disappears into the thin fog. I keep screaming, crawling in the direction of the train, not knowing what else to do. Alfie jumps on top of me and pulls me in, holding me so tightly against his chest I can't scream any more. I open my eyes, finding blood dripping down his hand. Even in the middle of this horrifying moment, as my world is shattering around me, the strong hold of Alfie's embrace numbs the pain. I wish he could numb it forever, but I can't ask him to be that person for me. Not now. Not with our lives in turmoil.

"Where's Lilli?" I pull away, finding her behind Alfie, curled up into a ball, crying.

I'm bleeding too. My legs and hands.

Alfie struggles to stand through his obvious pain, but still grabs Lilli, lifting her into his arms before pulling me up to my feet and wrapping his arm around me. He doesn't take a pause before pulling us toward a small opening in the woods. Another dark entrance that could lead to only God knows where.

TWENTY-EIGHT
LEO
OCTOBER 9TH, 1943 – SOUTHERN POLAND

Twenty-five years ago, I would have pulled out my rifle and taken the two of them down without a second thought. The two of them—being the enemy, not an ally as they once were.

"I'm one of you," I say through gritted teeth. The lie tears at my soul. I've never been one of them and I wish I had never served by their sides.

Two SS officers, neither old enough to say they were alive during the Great War, stand between the columns of horses with rifles pointed at my head.

"Who are you?" one of them demands. "Show us your papers."

I slowly lower my right hand and pat down my pocket. "I'm a former German soldier, who fought in the Great War," I say.

Every moment I continue standing here is another kilometer away from my children who might be injured.

"Show us your papers," they demand again.

I pull them out of my pocket and hold it out in their direction, still holding my other hand in the air.

The officer who grabs my identification opens the booklet

and stares at the information, narrows his eyes then holds it up to his comrade.

"You're a Jew."

"I'm a man who has served his country and yours," I reply.

I can see the look in their eyes. Anything that once made them who they are is gone. They're hollow people, trained to do what they've been bred to do.

If I reach back for the door, they'll shoot.

"I'll get off the train," I offer.

The officer holding my papers reaches them back over to me. I snag them from his pinched fingers and shove them back into my pocket.

"Why are you back here?" he asks.

"I couldn't afford a ticket," I say, reason enough for any hobo to be sitting among equines on a train.

"We loaded the horses in Łódź. No one was in here then, which means you sneaked on after we had secured them, and from Łódź, nonetheless. Where do you live at the current moment?"

I've been a nomad for months, searching for my family through meager connections with former comrades who have either retired from the army or are no longer the person I knew. Through a hole in a wall, I received confirmation that Max had been imprisoned within the gates of Łódź before he was deported to an unknown location, and that orphaned children had been taken to Przemysłowa Street, blocks away from the Łódź ghetto.

"I don't," I say. "I'll get off the train and out of your way."

The officer nods and says, "Get out."

I reach for the door and pull the lever, opening it against the fierce howling wind.

"He's still a dirty Jew," the other officer says. "A dirty Jew who caused our country to lose the first war. He's nothing to us. He's worse than a Jew. He's a traitor and a Jew."

The words are warning, giving me a fraction of a second to jump.

I loosen my tight grip on the sliding door and thrust myself out of the train.

A pop echoes against the interior walls, shattering down my spine. Then another pop follows as the wind slashes against me, stealing the air from my lungs and throwing me against the ground much faster and harder than imagined.

I can't breathe. I can't feel a thing.

With my head flat against the ground, a pool of blood spills out from beneath me in a straight line.

What was it all for? What was the lesson I was supposed to learn in this life? I thought I was supposed to find the answer before now.

God, I plead that you don't let my babies find me here like this.

Their warrior; now nothing but another dead Jewish man.

TWENTY-NINE
DALIA
APRIL 14TH, 1944 – OŚWIĘCIM, POLAND

It takes women approximately nine months from the time of conception to the moment a new life begins. At the beginning of those nine months, one out of a million cells miraculously finds its way through the complex inner workings of a woman's body and secures its place within minutes. Then, the wait begins.

By the time a woman might have an inkling she's with child, the baby is hardly the size of a poppy seed. Minute by minute, day by day, this precious new life takes its time developing: every cell, organ, and single strand of hair. The heart finds a beat, a brain fills with instinct, toes curl, fingers wiggle, and an unknown world awaits their completion.

The unique details and intricacies of every one of us then make up a singular mark on the world's most magnificent painting. Filled with assorted colors, sizes, and shapes, no two strokes the same, resulting in an inexplicable and unimaginable masterpiece.

No one can see this composition as a whole. We can only be a part of it.

Imagine the misfortune of one measly mark bleeding onto

millions of others, making a change that will forever alter the beauty that once was.

The world's painting has been torn and people are falling through the rip into an oblivion. No one will ever know what it felt like to be a part of something whole again.

One in a million chance then nine months to become a life, and yet, it only takes seconds to erase that mark. I've been here nine months and it's impossible to count how many innocent people have been murdered here in that time.

I hate staring up at the smokestack, the plume of charred bodies.

Worse, I hate walking past the line of unknowing victims, promised a shower, only to soon find out the shower nozzles will release a deadly gas that will steal their last breath in minutes. Their bodies will be taken away, toppled on a pile of others and sent to the crematorium. Sometimes I think I see Jordanna and Lilli standing in the line and my heart jumps into my throat, suffocating me until I walk closer and take a better look.

It's always been someone else's children.

I feel empty inside, making me think the worst. I have no sense of intuition or mindful connection telling me the others are fine, or not. Maybe because I'm familiar with the feeling of losing one of them, I might not be able to feel anything else again. This isn't my life.

I've sent so many encrypted messages out into the world through the chain of resistance, facts of what is, indeed, happening within these barbed wire fences from the perspective of Birkenau. So, why has no one come to rescue us?

People might have tried, I suppose. They could be one of us now.

It's becoming harder and harder to remember Leo's words about life after death and that it's something of a reward rather than the end. Nothing makes sense here. Sometimes I wonder if

I'm already dead and this is what came after life—an endless loop of a void.

"Your assistance has been requested in block twenty-eight," one of the newer nurses in the infectious disease ward tells me.

"Do you know what for?" I ask, dropping silver instruments into a tub of disinfectant.

"She didn't say," the young nurse says. "I can take over here for you."

She's quiet and still has hope in her eyes, reminding me of the way I was when I arrived last year. Realization doesn't come all at once here. It steals over you slowly, insidiously.

It's clear, I've lost hope—the one thing I was so eager not to give up. But I have no say over my future, only my past, and I can't change that either.

I shuffle out of the block, heading down the row of others until I reach Block 28, the block I have to be mindful about where I walk because half of the infirmary is for Germans and the other half are for those who shouldn't be breathing the same air as the superiors. They might catch Judaism. That's what they want us to think. We're a contagious disease.

Hate is the only contagious disease that's killed more people here than typhus.

The moans and groans are no different in this ward, the Jewish prisoner half of the ward. The smells mirror the barracks more than anything that would resemble an infirmary. Bodily waste, fresh and old, is so pungent it snakes around my throat. From what I've heard, most of the people here have endured some form of surgical procedure without any relief for pain or anesthesia. I haven't been here often. Only once or twice to pick up supplies.

Marie is sitting at the front admission table, her head down, busy with paperwork. I assume she's the one who called for me. Now that she isn't assigned to the same block as Ina and me anymore, she comes up with excuses to visit us throughout the week. She's been here so long that most don't question her. She does what she's told and doesn't argue.

I place my hands down on the wooden desk, keeping my presence quiet. She glances up and lifts her pencil away from the logbook. Standing, she leans over the desk to my right and whistles affirmatively. Another prisoner nurse stumbles around the corner and approaches the desk within seconds. "Watch the desk," she tells her.

Marie still hasn't said a word to me, making my stomach churn more than it usually does at this hour. It's either something bad or dangerous. There isn't much in between.

I follow her into a stuffy stairwell and down the stairs, feeling the air thicken and stick to my skin. She shoves through another door and then one more. This one releases steam into the corridor and for a moment my heart stops, considering the thought of the steam being gas.

Then I smell the putrid stench of rotten food, cabbage mixed with burnt vegetable broth, with a hint of cigarette smoke —meals being prepared within the clanging metal bins. Still following Marie, we end up in a mint-green tiled room with wet floors. Prisoners peek over makeshift walls but Marie isn't concerned as she begins talking.

"It's happening," she says. "A plan has been put in place for an uprising."

I recognize the smell now. Potatoes and leafy broth, wheat, dirt, smoke. Mealtime.

"Where are we?" I whisper. My voice might not be louder than the commotion on the other side of the barrel stacked wall.

"The infirmary kitchen."

I've heard about this place. It's where the Polish prisoners work, the non-Jewish ones considered political prisoners, marked with their red triangle badges.

"What will the—" I cup my hand around my mouth to

remain discreet despite who may or may not be on the other side. "Uprising consist of?"

Marie glances toward the wall as if she's waiting for one of them to join our covert conversation but then looks back at me. "Our source has secured pistols, and will be obtaining more, as well as gunpowder and other supplies."

"Then what?"

Writing encrypted notes is one thing, going on a murder spree is another. No matter what the situation or shock the SS face, they will be faster, stronger and more powerful.

"The workers at the crematorium are heading this up. If we can blow one of those up, the smoke will surely be seen from a distance. It could bring us a chance to liberate ourselves."

She's so hopeful and I can't seem to find any optimism within myself to join in her moment of high spirit.

Marie grabs my hands, waiting for me to say something more. "If it allows me to see my children again..."

"Me too," she says.

"When will this happen?"

"I'm not certain. It depends on whether we can collect enough of what we need."

"Where will we store it?"

"That's where you come in," she says.

I clench my fists behind my back, unsure of where this conversation is about to go. I want to free us all from this place just as much as the next person, but I've seen what the SS do to the rebellious ones. If they catch anyone doing anything out of order, the punishment could be as severe as death.

"Go on," I tell her, knowing I can't walk away without finishing this conversation.

"In Block twenty, the infectious disease ward on the bottom floor has rooms that aren't being used. The SS will never go down there because they're terrified of contracting typhus. It's their one fear, Dalia, and it's our golden weapon."

I can't argue with her theory but it's a matter of smuggling materials down there that she's yet to suggest a plan for. "And how will I go about doing this? There are kapos who will trip on their way to rat us out, plenty of them meandering around the wards in Block twenty."

"You'll find a moment that's right. We'll keep the loads light so you don't have to take too much at once."

"And if I tell you I don't want to take part in this?" The commotion on the other side of the kitchen wall hushes and I'm scared I've made them mad or worried them that I'll become a loose end in their plan. "I will support this plan, of course, but—"

"We need you, Dalia. Ina will be helping too, of course, and there's more in it for us after."

"More?"

"You want to find your children and husband, right?"

I found one of them, the blessing, short-lived. "Yes, of course."

"Someone can help with that."

But will I be endangering them more by giving someone their names? There is no answer to any question I think up. Everything is a risk and there's more of a chance of losing it all than making even a small gain.

THIRTY

JORDANNA

APRIL 14TH, 1944 – SOUTHERN POLAND

Every single night, as I lie in this cot and the lights go out, I let myself imagine what it will feel like to see Mama again. I wonder if she's fighting to find us. I know she wouldn't give up, and it's the only thing that gets me through every day. On the other hand, despite closing my eyes or having them wide open, I see the look on Papa's face when I turned around to reach for his hand before jumping from the train. I couldn't understand his expression. It was unfamiliar. Now, I know, it was a combination of sorrow, fear, and a final goodbye. He must have known that would be the last time we saw each other, and it's the last memory I have of him.

In the hours following our traumatizing jump from the train, Alfie, Lilli, and I wandered through the woods without a hint of direction or a clue what to do or where to go. I relive those nights in my dreams every night too, hoping for a chance to go back and make things right. In the darkness of my mind, it seems as if we were on that train with Papa just yesterday. But it's been months—one-hundred-eighty-three days of sitting with my thoughts and personal resentment, telling myself everything

I should have done differently. If I had, we wouldn't be here, not without him.

* * *

Six Months Ago – October 9th, 1943

"He must have jumped, but it's impossible to know how long after us," I say for the dozenth time. If we keep following the tracks, we'll surely find him, even in the dark with only the moon shining a weak glow in our path.

"We'll find him," Lilli says. "I'm sure of it." Her feet scuffle behind me, her hand interlocked with Alfie's.

"Papa?" I call out. "Can you hear me?"

I don't know how much time passed before he jumped from the train too. I would think we would have seen him by now if he had jumped, but he could be looking for us the same way we're looking for him.

Lilli suddenly drops Alfie's hand and races ahead of us without saying a word, her sights set on something I don't see.

"Lilli, stop! Come back here. That's too far away!" I shout after her.

"Sunflowers. Do you see them? Sunflowers," she hollers, continuing her hunt.

Just before I catch up to her, she stops running, coming to a sudden stop. Maybe she's realizing whatever she was looking at aren't sunflowers. I don't know how she could have seen them in the dark anyway.

Her attention shifts in another direction as if she isn't concerned about the sunflowers anymore. Something else seems to have caught her eye, holding her feet frozen to the ground.

A chill surges through my limbs, watching the way she's standing, the stillness, it chokes the wind out of me.

"Are you all right, Lilli?" I ask, reaching out to take her arm.

Just as I do, she moves forward, stepping closer to the tracks, not responding to me. I lunge forward and grab hold of her before pulling her back to look at me. "What is it?"

She's staring through me as if I'm not talking to her. Alfie passes by the two of us, walking further down the tracks. I assume he's looking for whatever she might have seen.

Less than a minute passes before I watch Alfie fall to his knees, a hard thud against the dirt.

My body shakes from both cold and fear as I pull Lilli alongside me, stopping at the sight of a man lying dead on the ground.

We've all seen a dead body, too many, especially for Lilli at eight years old. Worse, we've seen charred bodies soldered to the ground. Bodies, engulfed in flames. Bodies, starved to death, worn to the bone, neglected, abused. We've seen so many soulless bodies.

I step in front of Lilli—my body does so on its own—an unexplainable instinct.

Alfie glances back at me and his tears glisten beneath the moonlight.

"No. No. No."

I'm the one speaking but I can't hear my own words as I stumble forward until I can't hold my body up any longer. My legs give out and I fall onto dark-stained dead grass.

Alfie leaps up from his knees, racing back to stop Lilli from coming any closer. I glance back at him for a moment, watching him shield her, protect her from having to witness what's in front of me.

"Papa," I whisper through a silent cry.

They shot him twice—whoever shouted at him as we jumped from the train's steps. I heard them shout but I wanted to believe it was only in my head. I know for sure now it's the last thing I heard before the train door closed, separating my life from Papa's once again.

Even together, as we are in this moment, it seems as if we still haven't found our way back to each other as I thought we had. He is on one side, and I on the other.

He's lifeless, lying in front of me, pale and pulseless. Blue under the thin layer of clouds floating by the moon.

I slide in beside him, cradling my body against his and lift his heavy arm over my side. He used to lie in bed with me at night and wait for me to fall asleep. He would tell me stories about the unicorns and fairies that lived in the forest, the ones who came to grant wishes to good children every night while they slept.

"Papa," I cry out in ragged breaths. "You can't leave me—us. You can't. I need you. I'll always need you. Don't go." My voice is stuck in my throat, not sounding like me at all. I wasn't making any sense.

I know better, but I want to refuse to know better. I want to believe in unicorns and magical fairies. They could come heal him while he sleeps. They were just stories he told me, but I want them to be real. At least just this once.

I press my hand against the unfamiliar sensation of his cool leathery skin. I stare at his closed eyes, praying I see movement beneath his lids. He would always dream a lot. I caught him doing so when I woke up before he did on Sunday mornings. Mama didn't want me to ever wake him because he had more trouble than me falling asleep. Mama told me I wouldn't want to interrupt a dream—no one should do that to another person. I remember asking her how she knew he was dreaming, and she told me when the eyes move beneath a person's eyelids, it means they're dreaming.

There's no movement as he lies here next to the train tracks. Just another minute longer—maybe I'll see something. "Papa?" Mama wouldn't give up. She would keep trying to make him better, somehow. I need to know what she would do. She saved so many people during the Great War, but I don't know how.

My heart hurts. It's as if someone's punching me in the chest again and again and again. And my stomach feels the same way.

A scream comes out of nowhere. It's me. I'm the one scream-ing, but I can't make it stop.

I can't let go of Papa. I won't. I refuse to leave him. He needs me. Mama wouldn't let go. I know she wouldn't.

"Lilli needs you, Jordie." Alfie's voice pulls me out of a blind-ness, my face still buried against Papa's neck.

I push back just enough to look at Papa again, but the clouds are making it harder to see details I know are in front of me—the freckles on the bridge of his nose and the small scar above his right eyebrow.

"This isn't real," I tell myself. "Warriors don't die. So, this isn't real."

I scream again, louder this time, shouting for the real life I was locked out of, to let me back in.

* * *

Current Day - April 1944

I jackknife upright in the dark, screaming at the top of my lungs. Everything around me is hazy and blurry and I'm still searching for Papa's body on the side of the railroad tracks, pleading with him to return. "Papa!"

A nun sits beside me and takes my hands within hers and utters a prayer. "It was a dream, dear. You're here, beneath the church in your cot, not by the railroad with your papa. That was many months ago now."

"No, no, I just saw him—" I argue, mumbling my words.

Alfie jumps out of his cot and rushes to my side, taking my other hand. "Shh. You're all right," he says, lifting my hand to his cheek. He tries to comfort me every night, only waking up because of the vibration of the floor when one of the nuns runs to my side. I stare at him, the slight highlights glowing across his face from the moon shimmering in through the narrow windows above our heads. There's something different about him lately, the way he looks at me with a form of quiet curiosity that aches deep inside. I know the feeling. He takes in his surroundings differently without being able to hear much. He's intense but gentle and consoling without much more than a few words. It's only intensified my feelings for him. I need him like he's the last thread holding me together.

"Your mind is healing from your loss. This is part of the healing process, but rest assured, you will always see him in your mind's eye. Your papa will always be with you as a heavenly spirit."

I don't understand what she means. I just know I've heard her tell me the same thing every night for the months Lilli, Alfie and I have been living beneath a deserted church in the middle of nowhere.

THIRTY-ONE

DALIA

SEPTEMBER 4TH, 1944 – OŚWIĘCIM, POLAND

For six months since I was approached in my ward by the Polish nurse to join in their efforts of resistance, I've been collaborating to hide supplies of gunpowder in a hidden area of the infectious disease ward. My initial fear of taking part in this deadly mission has become a form of empowerment, knowing I'm contributing to the mere possibility of defeating some of the SS.

There's no telling whether any of us will make it out of here alive but if this is the end of the road for me, it will feel better to know I went out fighting.

Throughout my morning walk from Birkenau to the main Auschwitz camp, I take in as many surrounding details as I can, not only for my outgoing notes, but to seek an understanding for why we're all here in this way. Why there's a talented orchestra flawlessly performing pieces that could make a person believe they're entering a lavish ball. I can only assume it's part of the psychological manipulation of confusing us, breaking down our minds to believe whatever we're told. Either that or it's for entertainment purposes to the SS.

At first, I couldn't bear to hear the music when I passed by, but now I'm able to lose myself for a moment, just a moment, and dream with my eyes open wide, telling myself I am walking into a beautiful hall decorated by candlelight and crystal chandeliers with aromas of rich foods and aged wines.

Then static buzz zings through the air and the music stops suddenly as everyone turns their attention toward the prisoner who just took their life by running into the electrified barbed wire fence.

It happens daily now. It's the last bit of control they have over their lives. Other nurses have delivered injections of phenol to give a dying prisoner their final request—to take them out of their misery. What should be inhumane has become a gift to some. It's unfathomable even as I live, breathe and witness the occurrences daily.

I check into the recovery station ward for prisoners who will be returning to their labor duties once cleared by medical orderlies. I hoped this ward would bring me a bit of respite knowing these prisoners aren't in imminent danger. However, despite what most of the patients need to recover from, an illness, injury, or surgery, we can only supply the bare essentials which isn't enough most of the time. They just have a higher chance of surviving longer than those in the other wards.

It's hard to understand how anyone can manage a smile for another, but I've found several patients in this ward who have an unnatural level of determination. Maybe that's the key to survival. I must share the same trait even though I feel as if I'm a walking corpse with a beating heart.

"How are you doing this morning?" I ask the first young woman in the bed closest to the door.

She resembles most of the others in this room, her head shaved, bony cheeks, collarbone protruding against her pajamas. Except she's smiling. Today's her last day in this ward. She'll be sent back to work before nightfall.

"I did what you said to do yesterday," she says with a light-hearted sigh. "Last night, I dreamed of my mama's blueberry blintzes." She closes her eyes and continues to talk, her words a humming whisper. "They were the perfect shade of gold, thin and tender, delicately folded around a sweet soft cheese fresh from the farm. Mama always put a drop of vanilla into cheese to balance the hint of tang, and I could smell it all so clearly. Topped with a blueberry sugar syrup and a handful of the ripest blueberries I've ever tasted—sweet and tart, flavors that exploded in my mouth. Each bite was warm and rich, reminding me of a cool night by the fireplace. My family was there too, everyone in a fit of laughter over a game of charades. And life was perfect." A tear rolls down her cheek. "Thank you for reminding me how to dream."

Her description gnaws at my stomach, but her thin veil of happiness brings a smile to my face. "You're very welcome," I tell her, taking her wrist into my hand to check her pulse.

"Is there anything I can do for you in return?"

Her pulse is good. She doesn't have a fever. I unwrap the dressing on her leg, checking the injury from a loose rotary cutter that bounced off her leg in one of the textile factories. The edges of the wound are still inflamed and pink, but a new layer of skin is beginning to form over the center. The surrounding skin is dry and flaky, which is a good sign. "You should heal just fine as long as you keep the wound covered," I tell her.

"Thank goodness," she says. "But what about you? There must be something I can do—" So many of the patients in this ward ask the same question. I declined the kind offer for the first week I was in here, but then I thought of an idea, something that could help me if ever possible.

"I—there is, and I understand if it doesn't work out, but would you mind if I give you a letter to hold on to? If you make it out of here, maybe it can find its way to my children."

"Of course, but why do you speak as if you won't make it out of here?"

It's hard for me to answer when I gave her hope yesterday. "The letter is for...just in case."

"I understand and would be honored to hold on to it for you. I will do whatever I can to ensure your children receive the letter."

If any of us are given the chance.

I pull the small, folded note out of the satchel and glance over my shoulder, around the ward, before handing it to her. "Thank you," I tell her.

I've written Leo and the children at least a dozen notes at this point and handed them each to different patients who pass through this ward. Living in fear of what might become of me, it seems like the least I can do should my children become motherless, if and when this all ends. There's so much I didn't teach them and it's my responsibility to make sure they know how to survive if they're ever on their own again. Again. They're on their own now. Anything I still wanted to teach them, they've had to learn on their own. Yet, I still want them to know what I would have wanted them to know. I also want them to know how much Max loved them and that he was with me when he passed. It won't be happy news, but it will be better than having to live a life assuming he died alone somewhere.

I've written notes to Leo too. I write of our memories, the words I knew he felt and ones I may not have explicitly said out loud. We always think there will be a tomorrow and there's no sense in ever saying goodbye. I should have known better after what we had already lived through but because of that, I didn't think we wouldn't have the chance to say our goodbyes properly. I hope it's not too late for that and we somehow manage to live on for another fifty years while keeping the best of our memories, especially with Max at the forefront of our minds. But just in case...Just in case.

This ward has become my source for outgoing mail. Each

patient is a thread of hope to me, that they all walk out of this prison in one piece even if I don't.

"Block twenty-eight is ready," a whisper tickles my ear.

I turn around, finding no one in sight. These types of communications come and go like a wisp of fog in the night. I've never known a level of secrecy as I do now.

With a glance around the ward, I spot three other nurses tending to the recovering patients and take the moment to slip out the door with a clipboard in hand and a satchel over my shoulder. A person moving between buildings is a messenger of sorts and without a clipboard and a satchel, I would appear to be working under unauthorized instruction.

My walk to Block 28 is only two blocks down to the left and across the walkway. At this hour, there is less commotion outdoors as everyone is assigned to work. However, no further than ten steps out of the block, I hear the echoing expulsions of ammo fire from a weapon, one after another seven times.

I clutch my chest, the fabric bunching in my hand as I pass the gated courtyards between the rows of blocks. Most everyone knows what the courtyards between Blocks 10 and 11 are used for and when the gunshots blast, we know people are being executed. Sources have mentioned they line up naked prisoners with their noses pressed to a black wall, then each is shot in the back of the head by an SS guard. These are the people caught for participating in acts of resistance and attempts to escape. This is what I'm wagering against with the acts in which I take part.

I move quicker to Block 28, rushing in through the door until I find Marie sitting in her usual spot at the front desk.

"Here for restock?" she asks. She sounds like she's talking about first-aid supplies, but I know what she's truly inferring.

"Yes," I answer quietly.

"Follow me," she says. No one would suspect we've formed

a bond or a friendship with the way we communicate with one another in a location where anyone else can spot us.

Once inside the kitchen, she gives me a hug. "What did you have for dinner last night?" she asks.

"Dumplings and chicken soup with a slice of cake and a glass of wine," I tell her, all in one breath. "What about you?"

"Hunter's stew and cranberry rugelach. The meat was so tender it fell apart before I could chew it up."

"That sounds delicious," I tell her.

"If only," she says with a sigh. "But I come bearing a gift with your daily delivery."

"A gift?"

A hint of mischief glows in her eyes as she pulls something out from beneath the fabric of her smock. I give her my hand and she places a cube-shaped object into it. I unfurl my fingers, finding a paper twisted wrapper. I recognize the packaging. Chocolate. I've dreamed of chocolate, wondering if I've forgotten how it truly tastes.

She unwraps her piece of candy and I do the same. I should be wondering where this came from or what it might cost later. But I don't. I block out the responsible voices in my head with the hunger that might eat me alive.

I shove the entire piece in my mouth at once rather than nibbling or savoring. My cheeks zing from my awakening taste buds. My eyes roll back into my head, keeping the bite in my mouth for as long as I can before it melts into liquid. A moan escapes my lips as I savor each second I can keep this delectable taste on the center of my tongue.

When my mouth becomes empty once again, my eyes reopen, waiting for the consequence of such indulgence. Marie swallows her mouthful too and presses the back of her fingers against her lips before speaking.

"We're getting close to action," she says. "I have a dozen units of gunpowder for you to take back with you today, but also, could you make sure all inventory is organized for quick retrieval?"

"I've kept everything organized all along," I tell her.

"I should have assumed as much," she says with a nod.

"What is the plan?" I ask, knowing my question is broad and possibly unanswerable.

"Your part will be complete. It's like dominoes. We must weaken the SS to start. The following plans will fall into place."

She seems so sure, and I can only imagine she knows more. More of what I don't need to know.

One by one, Marie hands over fabric tied sacks, smaller than the palm of my hand to hide in my pocket. We're just two links of this chain and I'm unsure of where the gunpowder comes from, but I know with as much as we collected, considerable damage should be feasible.

"I'll bring these to storage now," I tell her. "Thank you for the treat."

"It should all take place within the next few days while we're here at the infirmaries. You have nothing to worry about."

"Understood," I tell her, leaving with a heaviness in my satchel that I worry can be seen an acre away.

Upon re-entering Block 20, I find several SS guards standing around the halls, more than typical. The SS usually avoid the infirmaries. Sweat forms on the back of my neck as I pass them with a heavy conscience. They can likely tell I'm hiding something.

I take the stairwell down, passing another guard on the way.

"What ward do you tend to?" the guard asks.

"The-the, uh—the…"

"Well spit it out. Where are you going?" he snaps.

"The recovery station," I say, my voice pinched in my throat.

"What business do you have going down into the infectious disease ward?"

My mind spins to find an answer, one that won't require a follow up question or evidence. "It's midday and I'm collecting the record log." It's a lie. I don't know who is responsible for collecting the record log.

"What's in the satchel?" An icy chill whips around my body as I pat my hands down my front side, knowing the only satchel I have is concealed under my smock. He lifts his hand and points to my neck. I reach up and feel the strap of the satchel peeking out from beneath my collar. It must have shifted.

I can't blink or breathe, and he continues to stare as if he can see through my clothes. "Just a few medical supplies for when I'm moving around the ward."

"Let me see then. Open it," he says.

My hands shake as I reach around my neck. He can see my nerves. He's squinting, trying to discover what I'm hiding—if I'm telling the truth about carrying medical supplies for the work I do here. I don't have any medical supplies in the satchel. This will be the end of my work here. It could be the end of me altogether.

A wheezy wet cough echoes between a connecting corridor with moans of pain following. "Just a bit further," another nurse says, turning the corner with a slight female propped up on her shoulder. The woman is hardly walking on her own and the nurse is struggling to drag her limp body in this direction. "Pardon. I must get her downstairs to the infectious disease ward."

The guard steps away from me and away from the path of the other nurse and patient. He yanks a handkerchief from his pocket and holds it over his mouth and nose.

"I can return to my ward if you'd rather collect the records—"

"No. Ridiculous suggestion," he utters, his words muffled. "Go on then." He shoos me away and scampers along in the opposite direction.

They must smell a rat. I should warn the others, but I won't be able to until I'm relieved from the scrutiny of these guards and officers.

I close myself into the empty spare room on the bottom floor and open the short wall panel to the storage unit, remove one single pin from resting on top of the heap, lift the canvas tarp and add the sack of gunpowder to the rest of the pile. I then replace the tarp and gently rest the pin on top, knowing if I ever find it missing, it's a sign that someone other than the few of us who are protecting this stash has been in here.

Footsteps pound in the stairwell and my heart thunders in my chest as I secure the small door and poke my head out into the hallway, ensuring I'm still alone. No one else is down here, but I don't have a log to return upstairs with.

The nurse assigned to the infectious disease ward doesn't know much about me. She's new and might or might not be hesitant to let me take anything from the ward. I retrieve a torn piece of fabric I can keep in my satchel for the moments I'm exposed to the variety of diseases here and hold it against my nose and mouth.

"Can I help you?" the prisoner nurse asks just as I step inside.

I notice she isn't protecting herself with a cloth or fabric, which tells me she has no will to survive this place.

"I've been asked to retrieve a log from this morning," I lie.

"I only have one. Will you be returning it?"

I can't pass by those officers a second time. "I'll copy down the records so I don't have to take them from you."

"Who sent you?"

Immediately I know, she's a kapo who finds herself rewarded for ratting others out. "Nurse Poloski," I answer without skipping a beat.

"A real nurse?" she questions.

"Yes, from the SS infirmary. I could fetch her?"

Her complexion pales and my racing heart slows just a bit. "No, no, of course not. Take your time."

Her stare burns against the side of my head the entire time I'm copying the log as I'm realizing it's just as bad to have this kapo nurse down here as it would be to have an SS guard. I have to let Marie know before their plan comes to fruition. If the SS are tipped off, these months of planning will have been for nothing, and the outcome will be detrimental for everyone within this compound.

THIRTY-TWO

JORDANNA

We've been beneath this church for just less than a year now. We're somewhere in the south of Poland but I've never heard of the town. I'm not certain this town is even on a map. It's just woodland and this church.

Daily, I watch Lilli sit on the cold, damp floor with a rag doll, its fluff pushing through small tears, sewn x-marked stitches for eyes, a red button for a nose, and no mouth. Sparse threads of brown yarn are scattered along the top of the head, and the doll has no clothes. Sometimes the few other little girls here join her in silence and stare at the doll. On occasion, they might ask to hold it for a moment. Lilli shares well, given she has little to share. The nun who found us in the woods while foraging for berries offered to help us, despite Lilli refusing to follow her to the church because it meant going against all common rules Mama raised her with. Never go anywhere with a stranger. I've asked myself a million times if Mama would have made the same decision as we did by coming to this church with the nun, and I think she would have. I try so hard to channel her strength but more often than not, it feels like I'm just pretending to be as brave as she's always been. If I keep making the "right" decisions, I can just hope it will bring us back to her.

* * *

Eleven Months Ago – October 11th, 1943, Southern Poland

It's been two days since we left Papa's side. Lilli has done nothing but ask when he'll be coming back for us and for every step I take away from his body, the worse I feel for not being honest. I haven't had the heart to tell her the body she spotted in the distance was Papa.

"Jordanna, I don't want to walk any further. Papa will never find us."

I close my eyes for a long blink, stop in my step and turn to face her. My heart feels swollen in my chest as I grab a hold of her hands. "Lilli, Papa isn't going to come looking for us."

She stares at me, her eyes piercing through my soul. There isn't a sense of question or confusion on her face, only anger. I don't want her to be angry with him. "Why are you lying to me?" she asks.

"I'm not lying to you. Papa isn't going to come for us."

"You lied to me. You said you didn't want me to see the man who had died by the train tracks."

"That wasn't a lie either."

"Was it—" she takes in a shuttered breath. "Was it Papa? Is that why?"

She's eight. How can she be this intuitive? Or how can I be so naïve to think I could protect her from the truth?

I close my eyes again. This time, tears spill out and press my lips together as if I can hold in the sound of a cry. I nod my head and swallow against my dry throat.

"You didn't let me see him," she squeaks. "How could you do that to me?" She pulls her hands out of mine and storms past me. "I'm going back to find him. I can help him. I know I can."

Alfie has been watching but not hearing. I'm sure he can make an assumption based on Lilli's sudden behavior though. He grabs hold of her arm as she thrashes by him. "Where are you going?" he asks her.

She screams, "To find Papa," and points in the direction of the railroad.

Alfie turns back to face me, and I lower my head, giving him a nod so he knows I've told her about Papa.

He pulls her into his arms. Her legs go limp, falling to the ground. Alfie goes with her and curls her into his lap. He doesn't hear her screaming out for Papa as he holds her. I wish I didn't have to hear the screams, each a knife to my heart. I don't regret taking her away from his body before she could see him. I wouldn't want that to be her last memory of Papa. It would haunt her as it will haunt me. She doesn't deserve that. I do.

"We can't go back," I tell her. "I'm so sorry, Lilli. We're too far from there now."

I don't think she's listening to a word I'm saying, but even if I were to change my mind and let her see him now, which would be far worse than yesterday, we're too far from there with how much we've walked.

Caves have been our shelter over the past two nights as we've tried to determine where we are and what direction we should be traveling. All we have is Papa's compass, a worn map, a small notepad and pencil that Papa had in his pocket. The map isn't helpful since we don't know where we parted ways with the train. We've been worried about trying to start a fire since the smoke will be a sign of someone hiding in the woods. We've been hunting for berries—ones that aren't questionably poisonous, and a fresh source of water.

The woods spin around us as we wait for Lilli to come to terms with our reality, knowing that might take a while.

The sun begins to poke holes through the trees, the spring humidity and mild warmth weighs over us like a blanket of fog. It seems impossible to keep walking, but we have no choice.

"We're going to have to trek further into the woods," Alfie says. "We need a spring. Drinking rain drops from leaves isn't enough."

We haven't had much rain either.

Lilli stands up from Alfie's lap and wraps her arms around her body, staring at the springs of grass between her worn clogs.

I make my way over to them and rest my hand on Lilli's shoulder, but she pulls away. My chest aches, pushing me to think up an actionable plan. "We need to tag the trees somehow," I say, more out loud to myself than to Alfie who's staring at me.

"Jordie..." Alfie says, standing up from the ground then holding his hands out to the side in question.

I haven't forgotten that he can't hear me. I'm just trying to think everything through. I take his hand and tap the letters out.

"We can't do that. It'll be a bread trail for anyone who might be on the hunt for refugees," he says.

He's right.

Papa had a small notebook and a pencil. I know he used to mark down coordinates but I'm certain I wouldn't be able to do so properly, especially without a starting location on a map.

I nod and pull the compass out of my pocket, turning until I'm facing north.

Alfie spins around as if in search of something. "Three birch trees, two oaks, and—"

Lilli trudges through a few of the trees with her eyes set on something I'm not seeing. She leans down to retrieve whatever it is and returns with a heavy rock in her arms, dropping it by the tree with a loud hollow thud. She returns to where she found the rock and grabs two more to bring back and place next to the other. Lilli shapes them into a triangle. "There. It's just rocks, but this one," she points to the middle-sized rock, "is teardrop shaped."

Alfie and I exchange a smile. He doesn't know what she said about the teardrop, but he can see the triangle, pointing in the direction we're facing. He gives her a pat on the back. "Can I see the notepad and pencil?" he asks me.

I pull them out of my pocket and hand them over. He jots something down and slips the notepad and pencil into his pocket. "Let's make sure we stay heading precisely south for as long as we can. We know Hungary is south of Łódź, right?"

I nod in agreement, though I know crossing a country's border will be impossible and I'm uncertain if we'd want to walk close to a border even if we could. Despite that, we were only on the train for a couple hours, three at most. I don't think we're close to the Slovak Republic border, which would have been the only possible way to get to Hungary.

"I'll count my steps," Lilli says. "Papa always told me it was a good way to know how far I've walked." Her words are full of anger, resentment, but fuel too.

"Great idea," I tell her. It isn't a measurement of accuracy here, but it can't hurt.

I'm unsure if any of this truly matters. If we walk far enough and spot another cave of rocks, there's no sense in returning to where we are now.

We've walked for what I figure must be more than an hour and there isn't a hint of any water source. Alfie has a look of determination and Lilli has definitely stopped counting her steps. My legs ache and I'm sure theirs do too. We're starving and I haven't seen any rock formation that we could consider shelter, which means we might have to walk all the way back to where we came from.

The trees around me spin in a vortex and my limbs become cold. This keeps happening and I don't know why.

"Alf—" My words don't carry sound. At least nothing I can hear. My knees give out and I fall heavily to the ground. A numbing sensation washes over me and I imagine sinking into the dirt.

"Jordanna. Can you hear me?"

I can always hear the voices above me when I faint. The last time Mama and Papa heard me fall to the ground, I remember their footsteps sounding as if they belonged to a giant.

Mama's voice echoed through the apartment. "Oh dear, Jordanna's fainted again," she cried out, pressing her cool hands against my cheeks. "Sweetheart, can you hear me?"

I could hear her just as I hear Alfie now, but my mouth doesn't move. I couldn't tell her about the large spider crawling up my leg, but she knew how I felt about spiders.

"She is a younger version of her mama," Papa told Mama that day, fanning cool air over me. "You know, I remember when you used to fall faint over just about anything, my dear Dalia." Papa chuckled without much concern. "The war hardened you, but I know Jordanna will find her strength in time too."

If only Papa knew that even in war, I would still be weak. Where is the strength I'm supposed to have like Mama?

"Why won't she open her eyes?" Lilli shouts with panic.

Droplets of cold water fall onto my forehead and my neck aches.

"Come on, Jordie," Alfie pleads.

His hand rests on my forehead and more drops of water run down my face.

"Let's pour some water into her mouth," Lilli says. The sound of splashing and Lilli's feet against the dirt grow closer to me and more drops of water splash over my forehead.

"No, no. She can't drink this water. Neither can you. You need to wait," Alfie says.

"I'm thirsty," Lilli utters, "so Jordanna must be too."

Alfie pulls me upright and I fall limp against his chest. His lips press to my forehead and my heart jumps out of its slow beat, forcing me to gasp for air. With Alfie so close, my heart does its typical flutter, the one I've been so keen on hiding from him. He doesn't know how long I've been hiding my feelings for him. I've never been able to convince myself he could think the same way about me. It's been easier just to remind myself that we'll only ever be friends.

"Oh, is that all it takes?" he asks quietly.

My eyes finally open without a fight and I stare up into his, finding myself cradled in his arms. He smiles a small smile, but an Alfie smile. "I need you. We're in this together. You can't leave me."

I nod slightly, so slightly, I can only hope he sees the meager movement.

"We found water, Jordanna," Lilli says from behind me.

"I'm going to have to start a small fire so I can boil it. It's not safe to drink. Lilli, can you find me a rock that has a gully hole, something that can hold water? Stay where I can see you."

Lilli doesn't respond, but sets off where I can see her, searching for rocks around the edge of the pond we're sitting next to. I hate to ask how far Alfie had to carry me to get here. I'm doing nothing but making things harder at this point.

Alfie combs his fingers through my short hair and hugs me a little tighter. His warmth makes me want to cry, but not from sorrow. "Who would have thought it would be you and me left to work together to survive?" he whispers.

We spent so much time teasing each other and I've refused to confess my feelings for him. How could I, when the lines between us have always been blurred by unpreventable circumstances? Everything in my life has changed, but not these moments—not when his eyes linger on mine, or I catch him looking at me for a second longer than he normally might. I still believe it could all be *in my head. I could be imagining it all, but only because I so badly want it to be true. I don't know what I would do without him. He's always been a part of my life, but now he's interwoven in my life.*

"I hope you know how much you mean to me," he says hesitantly. "And not just as Max's younger sister. You've always been there, just out of reach, and even if I didn't think Max might throw me out of a window for having feelings for you, I never wanted to cross a line I couldn't uncross. I wish I had been braver and told you how I felt sooner."

I could swear a swarm of bees is buzzing inside of my chest right now, but it's a familiar feeling, something I've always felt for him. I just never expected to hear him say any of this to me, but it doesn't feel surprising—it's as if I've always known but never knew for sure. I mouth the words, "Me too."

Alfie smiles again and I try to fight the numbness along my cheeks to do the same.

"Goodness gracious," someone says. The sound of feet hurrying across dirt sends triggering alarms down my spine, sending all the feeling back into my body at once. I push myself to sit up on my own and search for Lilli, who is staring wide-eyed at the person speaking behind me.

I scoot out of Alfie's hold and twist around, finding an older woman with a straw basket in her hand.

A black veil over a white cape, and white neckerchief, a rosary. "I'm sorry if we've intruded on your land," Alfie tells her.

"Are you children lost?" she asks, holding her hand up to her heart.

"Yes," I say, not wanting to say anything more. We shouldn't trust anyone, despite the fact that she's clearly a woman of faith, but not our faith and it's hard to know who feels what toward us.

"You look unwell, starved to death, your poor things."

"We're just fine," Lilli says, doing a poor job at telling a lie, and to a nun of all people.

"Let me take you in. I can't offer much, but there are other children similar to you who have come to us in many ways. My sisters and I will do all that we can to help you. You need not to worry."

* * *

Current Day – September 4th, 1944 – Southern Poland

I glance down at the doll in Lilli's hand again. I hate that thing. It reflects each one of us. We're all here without a voice, a way to see beyond these walls, and stripped of the people we once were. I should be grateful to be away from the ghetto, and I am, but all I can wonder is how much longer we will need to live life in hiding. I want to find Mama and Max, and we're left with no choice but to sit and wait until something happens—something that will allow us to walk freely out of this church without a chance of being captured and sent to another ghetto, camp, or just to our death.

Alfie has assigned himself the job of patching leaks in the ceiling. The rain has been relentless and seems to only get worse the closer we come to autumn. There isn't much down here aside from cots, linen, stone for a fire, and metal pots and plates, except for the assortment of unfinished pottery jars left down here before the war broke out. One of the nuns told me the priest who used to run services upstairs was a devoted potter in his free time but never showed off his work because he said it was one particular skill God didn't intend for him to have. The jars aren't exactly symmetrical, but art is art. The priest passed away shortly after the war broke out, but the nuns stayed to offer help in nearby communities.

The leaks had gotten so bad over the summer that Alfie thought up the idea of heating the clay jars to make them back into a moldable substance that he could use to patch the ceiling with. They call him a hero. He is our hero.

It's hard to comprehend what has become of my family in the fourteen months we've been apart. My hope wavers between the nightmares, hunger, and delirium from a lack of daylight, but the three of us are still alive, and I have to believe there's a reason for that.

THIRTY-THREE

DALIA

To know something most others don't know is a heavy weight I don't want to carry around. Fourteen months after arriving here at the gates of hell, today is the planned day for the uprising and whether the SS have been tipped off or not, no one knows. Or at least, I don't know.

With the gong alarming everyone into movement just as it does every morning, I watch and wait for our kapo to follow the first group out to the latrines. Then I scoot out from between the wooden bunks and make my way down a few rows to one of the other women. She's had an infected wound on her arm for over a week and refused to tell anyone. I noticed yesterday morning as we were washing up before roll call. The last thing any of us want is to end up in an infirmary. The odds of walking back out are far too slim.

As she shuffles her coat and metal bowl into a pile on her bed, I grab hold of her arm to inspect the infection, which has grown much worse in just a day. I glance around to make sure the kapo hasn't returned and reach into the satchel dangling from my neck, hidden beneath my smock, for a small bottle of antiseptic I stole from the infirmary. It might not be enough, but it could help. "This is going to sting. You might want to hold your breath to keep quiet," I tell her.

"What is that?"

"Antiseptic."

Before she can get out another word, I twist the top off the brown bottle and pour it over the wound. It bubbles and foams, causing her to clench her eyes and grasp the edge of the wooden bed frame. I release her arm, placing it down gently and secure the bottle and exchange it for the thin wrap of bandaging and a safety pin I brought with me too. I wrap the wound and pull her sleeve down to cover the evidence. "Try your best to keep your arm clean for now."

"Thank you," she utters with a quivering chin.

"Of course," I say, offering her the same forced smile I give every patient who thanks me on a daily basis. I wish I could convince myself they are grateful for something that will keep them safe but nothing I do is ever enough for that.

Across the row on the other side of tiered bunks is a younger girl who's been here as long as I have, if not longer. She's been suffering from a severely sprained ankle all week and she's terrified of being dragged away to the infirmary, which won't do much for her with how emaciated she is. "Give me your hand, sweetheart," I tell her. She struggles to pull it out from beneath the weight of her body. She hasn't moved yet as she should have. I put an aspirin tablet in her hand and then a rolled-up bandage. "Try to support your ankle with this wrap so you can make it through the day."

She clutches the aspirin and bandage and pulls them back beneath her chest.

So many women here are coughing, horrible coughs that will most definitely end up in their lungs. And there isn't anything I can do to help them. We have next to nothing to treat the patients in the infirmary as it is.

I rush outside to the line at the latrine and wait. Every common human necessity requires a wait.

An hour passes before I'm making my way between the rows of blocks in Birkenau toward the gated area between here and the main Auschwitz camp. The walk on the other side is the longer portion of our trek, the more tiresome one.

The lines we walk in shrink each day, or seem to, especially after watching someone weak fall from either tripping, slipping, or giving up. If they don't hop back up to their feet within seconds...

I stop short, waiting for the woman who was walking two spots ahead of me, hoping she pulls herself off the thick, muddy ground. Each second feels like an hour as we wait and watch. But she doesn't move. Too many seconds have passed.

I close my eyes and wait for the blow, the rifle emitting its bullet that becomes lodged in the back of her head.

There is nowhere else to walk to avoid the poor woman's body, forcing us each to step over her as if she's nothing more than a puddle.

I say a silent prayer, as I do for each lifeless body I cross and try to push the thought out of my mind as I continue focusing on the path to the infirmary.

There appear to be fewer SS guards standing around today and I don't know if that's an indication of whether they sense something is about to happen.

On my path to my assigned ward, Ina spots me from around a corner and yanks me to the side. "Did you see anything?" she whispers.

I didn't want to risk peering down toward the crematoriums this morning. No one wants to think about what's happening down there so there's no reason to look.

"No, I didn't notice anything."

"There were SS officers within the gates last night. We saw

them through the block window. They're never here at night. Do you think they know?"

I don't know anything more than she does, but I'm terrified of who can hear us whispering through the thin walls. I hold my finger up to my lips, my brows furrowing with disapproval.

"Shh," I hush.

"I know. I know. I'm just—"

"It's apparent," I tell her, glancing around, hoping no one is within an earshot.

"We won't even know what's happening until it's over. We're too far away."

I'm unsure if she realizes we're safer being farther away from an impending uprising. I can only imagine what will ensue.

"All we can do is wait," I tell her.

My mind has been occupied much of the day to the point where I can hardly recall one small conversation I've exchanged with the patients in the recovery unit.

I wonder how many of them will manage to get out of the gates, if any. Their plan is to blow up at least one of the crematoriums in Birkenau, not only as an act of revolt, but a distraction to allow for escape, and to hinder the process of killing prisoners at the rate they've been doing so.

"Yes, you're right. I don't know who came to remove the gunpowder from the downstairs storage unit, but I checked just a bit ago, and it's gone. I hope it was taken by the right people," Ina says, clutching her hand against her chest. "God help us all. Listen, no matter what happens today—there is no such thing as giving up. You will find a way out of here and locate your family. Where there's hope, anything is possible. Your hope is mine now. Remember that, always, my dear friend."

"Our friendship means more to me than I can ever put into words. I'm grateful for you, Ina."

She glances around, making sure no one is looking in our

direction, embraces me quickly then scampers off around the corner. It amazes me how someone who has nothing can still give so much of themselves to others.

The daylight hours come and go in a blur until the other women of Birkenau and I are directed back to our blocks, still without a clue as to what happened today, if anything at all.

The moment we enter the gates of Birkenau, dust and smoke fill the air, much more than usual. There's shouting from the SS and scrambling prisoners, but it doesn't tell us a story. We just know something is different. I'm quick to return to my block, hoping one of the women who sleep beside me might have insight on what's happened today. But the kapo responsible for our block closes herself in with us, pressing her back against the door as she struggles to take in deep breaths.

"I don't know what's about to happen here but two of the crematoriums have been blown up. There was an uprising earlier and it lasted hours. Some have escaped but they're being hunted as we speak. Others are being gathered for—"

A series of gunshots fire in the distance.

The kapo, whose name we might never know despite having been by her side for over a year, is showing a weakness I haven't seen since our first encounter when she reminded me of Jordanna, her innocent, young view of life. Now, she's weathered and worn to the bone despite the upper hand of authority. She might be questioning if kapos will be held responsible for not having a better awareness of what's been happening around the camp. Maybe she's trying to show us she's more like us than she's pretended to be.

She covers her hand over her mouth. "The SS are executing prisoners. Many of them. Whoever they think might have had a role in the uprising."

The blood drains from my face first, then the rest of my body. A cold chill sweeps across my neck and I take steps backward toward my slight spot within the wooden bunks.

If they interrogate any member of the resistance, will they talk? Will they name names or numbers to keep themselves alive?

I swallow the lump in my throat and take a few deep breaths before straightening the wool blanket over my straw filled mattress.

"If any of you had anything to do with the uprising, turn yourselves in at once. Don't risk the lives of the others in this block. If you were brave enough to take part in this, you'll be brave enough to walk away alone."

I can't blame her for what she's saying. She's as terrified as the rest of us, but not nearly as scared as I am. I won't say a word. I won't leave this block, and I will deny knowing anything that might have happened today. Those are the rules of the resistance. No one talks.

"The explosions were loud. So many people were shot between the crematoriums," someone whispers from behind me. "I wonder if anyone who escaped will make it far enough away from here?"

"Silence, at once," the kapo shouts. "Do you not understand the seriousness of those people's actions today?" More rounds of ammo fire from a place too close to where we are. "Do you not hear that? Those are lives being taken all at once just as they do to those they send into the showers. We're all going to die!"

Kapos are usually naturally reserved as they're privileged with knowing they won't be sent to their death unless breaking a law of some sort. If they follow their rules, they remain as is. I could say something to try and calm her down but by being calm myself, I might appear suspicious. Plus, no kapo wants to appear inferior to any of us and despite the edge of kindness I once saw in her, she's as cold and hollow inside as the rest of them are now.

Maybe the SS are going from block to block and emptying their rounds. If no one is left to blame, they can rest with satisfaction that they're still the ones who have final say regarding who lives and who dies.

A fist pounds against the door as it thrashes open, the kapo shoved to the side. Three SS guards stand in the shadow of the outside light posts, rifles in hand, one in front, two in the back, staring down the center of our block.

THIRTY-FOUR

JORDANNA

There's been a change and I cannot say for sure what it is, but the nuns appear concerned and are held up in private conversations throughout the day. I believe they have a radio upstairs that they take turns listening to. I've heard the simmer of static from the cold basement. I wish I could hear whatever news is being broadcast.

Sister Josephine returned downstairs just a bit ago and since then the four nuns have been moving furniture around, blockading the steps that lead upstairs.

Without drawing too much attention to myself, I coax Lilli closer to the door and take a seat on the floor to entertain her with some guessing games. Alfie is staring at me from his cot with a questioning look on his face, and for a moment, I can still see the boy he once was—the one who would tease me until I'd blush, usually without trying too hard. The months since we've been living beneath this church have changed us—individually and together. Life is nothing but a question mark dangling above our heads. The playfulness between us feels like something I experienced in another lifetime. Now, everything is static, serious, and uncertain. We're waiting to find out what happens next, if hope is even something we can reach for.

I'm sure he's wondering why the nuns seem to be securing the only form of entry too.

I sweep my forefinger along my ear and with a subtle twist of my head, I take a quick glimpse at the quiet conversation a few steps behind me.

"They want the Germans to leave, not us," Sister Margret says to Sister Josephine.

"They don't know we're not German. They will be looking everywhere, high and low, wooded areas and cities," Sister Patricia says.

"Very well, but suppose they do find us? We will tell them we're Polish, as we are, and we are taking care of orphaned children, which we are," another says.

"They've already liberated one of the labor camps. They aren't here to hurt us," Sister Josephine says, the one who found the three of us in the first place. "However, with the number of Germans fleeing Poland, any one of them could easily seek refuge here, in what appears to be an abandoned church. We don't know who is hostile or who is just afraid of the Soviets."

"What about the overhead attacks?" the younger of the four sisters asks. "I'm unsure of how much longer we'll be able to keep these children safe here."

"And where do you suggest we go, Sister Katherine?" Sister Josephine asks.

Sister Katherine doesn't appear to have an answer. It's as if I've woken up every single morning without the comfort of safety and yet, we're still here counting our blessings, scared to death that our luck will soon run out.

"Well, are you going to tell me what game we're playing?" Lilli asks.

I peer at her for a long moment, noticing a change I hadn't noticed before. The shape of her face has become more oval and less round and she's taller, even sitting up. Maybe it's her hair that's grown out just enough to touch the base of her ears, but she sounds older too. She is older. So am I. It's been just over a year since we left Hamburg, but I could easily be convinced it's been five. She's nine going on ten now. I didn't know there was such a dramatic change in a child between those ages. I also wish she were still eight so I could protect her more easily but she's becoming more curious about the future by the day, and also, why we're living the way we are. It's been sweet watching her take more involvement with the younger children here. They all seem to cling to her.

I'm distracted from the conversation between the nuns, staring at Lilli who's staring back at me with big eyes.

Alfie makes his way over and takes a seat between us, forming a small circle. "I know the look on your face," he says in a whisper. He's mastered his ability to whisper at the same volume I whisper. I don't know how he's been able to work it out, but I'm glad he has. We have very little privacy here except for a few makeshift walls separating toilets and changing areas.

How will the sisters take out the buckets of waste if they've barricaded us inside? One of them goes to the nearest town once every couple of weeks to find non-perishable food too. I don't ask many questions of how they do what they do because I'm too grateful for whatever they have been doing to keep us safe.

Alfie rests his hands on the ground beside his legs and I rest my left hand on his, repeating some of what I've overheard from the nuns through finger taps.

He lifts his hand out from beneath mine and places it on top, responding through taps, which means he doesn't want there to be any chance of anyone hearing what he has to say, including Lilli who stares at our hands as if she can read the taps. She might be able to. I wouldn't put it past her.

"I don't know if we're safe here anymore. If other Jews have been liberated, they must have been sent somewhere safe, right?"

We both know there would be no way to find wherever this place or places might be. We hardly made it far enough to find water when Sister Josephine first found us.

Alfie turns his attention toward the nuns, staring up at them from his seat on the ground. "Pardon me, but do you have a radio upstairs?" My eyes bulge upon hearing his question and I'm thankful my back is toward the nuns so they can't see my reaction.

Sister Josephine begins to sign her answer to Alfie. I see her hands waving around from the corner of my eye. She's been teaching him sign language since we arrived here. I've sat alongside him for each lesson so I can learn too, though between the two of us, the Morse code taps are still what we rely on most since it's the only way to have a private conversation.

"I might be able to repair it," Alfie says.

The radio is broken?

I turn to face them as they share a look between themselves. "Even when the radio works, we can only pick up German signals," Sister Josephine replies out loud and through sign language.

Alfie doesn't respond but shifts his stare toward the cement floor between us, his eyes unblinking. He straightens his posture but keeps his hands flat on the ground. Suddenly startled, he begins to sign to Sister Josephine. "There are heavy vehicles nearby. I can feel the rumbling underground. It's not the train."

"Children, children, listen up," Sister Josephine announces. "Remember our game of hide and seek? Well, it's time to see how good we've all gotten. Everyone, follow me," she says. We've practiced this so many times and each time has been a false alarm. Maybe not this time, perhaps. The far left wall has boxed crates stacked up to the ceiling, lining the wall from one side to the other, each row moved in just enough so the top row is flush to the wall but there is enough space for us to move behind the wall of crates. It's the only way to hide down here.

Alfie pulls Lilli up to her feet and urges me along to walk in front of him. He ushers the older children in first then the smaller ones, then Lilli, me, and him before the nuns close us in.

With our backs against the exterior wall of the church, I can feel the rumbling. Alfie takes my hand and begins to tap out his words. "Don't worry. We've been through worse."

A knock on the front door of the church forces gasps out of each of us. Lilli rests her head against my arm and loops her arms around my elbow. Alfie squeezes my hand tighter as someone makes their way inside the church. They must have gotten through the meager lock.

My heart pounds. I can hardly take in a full breath. The familiar sensation of cold sweat returns and I know I can't let my body take me down right now. There's no space to do so.

Alfie wraps his arm around my waist, holding me tightly. "Focus on me," he taps out against the palm of my hand.

I can't see him. It's completely dark within this slim open row of space. He slips his hand out of mine and finds my cheek.

Footsteps thud against stairs. More than one set of footsteps. They might be going up to the attic or down toward us. It's too soon to know.

Alfie's hand moves to my opposite cheek, turning my face in his direction but I'm not certain of what he wants me to see.

A warm sensation presses against my lips. My heart beats even harder, faster, and for very different reasons than a minute ago. His hand is still on my cheek and his lips are on mine, soft, familiar, though this has never happened between us before. I could melt into the wall, forget about the imminent danger. "I love you," he whispers against my lips.

I press my hand against his. "I love you," I mouth back, my lips brushing against his with the words I hope he clearly understands.

Is this a goodbye? Does he know what's about to happen? Can he sense that too? All of his other senses have been on high alert since losing his hearing and I feel as if he knows things before me. He knows we haven't had a chance to experience a true goodbye to anyone we love. Instead, only moments of *it's-too-late.*

A body is pounding against the door that leads down here to the basement, pushing their way through the makeshift barricade—a barricade that will tell them someone is down here.

THIRTY-FIVE
DALIA
JANUARY 6TH, 1945 – OŚWIĘCIM, POLAND

Almost three months have come and gone since the crematoriums were blown up. Nine weeks in which no one has come to our aid. All the time spent preparing and planning for the hopeful end to our imprisonment has done nothing more than elongate the process of death here.

There has always been a clear sense of hatred between the SS officers and guards toward every prisoner here, Jewish or not. A hatred I've struggled to understand, wanting to know where it began and how it might ever end. But now, their anger has surpassed any level I could comprehend from another human being. The beatings I witness daily, they're worse now, happening to twice as many people. The SS look for any reason to punish us and sometimes there's no reason at all. It's as if they look at someone and decide they deserve to be shoved to the ground and kicked repeatedly until blood spews from their mouths. Our food allowances are smaller too, but no one is sure if it's a punishment or lack of resource.

Despite the changes, I'm still standing here, weak, bony, and numb. I don't know why I've survived when others haven't. This isn't a game of luck. Not one of us is luckier than another.

Even worse, it's only just one small step forward in the act of survival.

Since I arrived in Auschwitz, I've been warned by many trying to make newcomers understand that while we might have come here for the same reasons because of who we are, a faith and culture, uniting many of us, the moment we stepped through those gates, we became the only person who cares about ourselves. No one else will fight for my life.

This system of camaraderie is the opposite of Leo's ideals, the ones I wholeheartedly agreed with and understood. It might have been the reason he came home to me. It might have been the reason he was given the fateful opportunity to save another person or many others. Together, they were stronger than one. They were.

I wonder what he might say now, knowing I've participated in the October uprising and despite many who have taken the fall for the acts, not everyone has stepped forward. Because I wasn't involved with the intimate details of igniting the physical uprising that day, there isn't a definitive link back to me. The SS have made threats, scaring every one of us, convincing even the innocent to consider stepping forward just for the sake of making the madness stop.

Yet, I've remained quiet. As I promised the other resistance members I would do. Those who participated from the infirmary blocks aren't in the spotlight. There were many who had to help the final act come to fruition. Even those who escaped were found and murdered before they could get far enough to hide.

The affliction comes in waves, watching the others fear waking up each morning, knowing the actions from the uprising still play a part in our everyday treatment. I have to tell myself that even if I walked forward and admitted to the SS that I took part in what they call a crime, the punishments wouldn't cease.

I'm just one person. They know there are more of us among them.

Everything I've done thus far has been to survive—not for myself but for my children who need me. For Leo. And now for Max, because he wouldn't want me to give up. A spitting image of his father in every way, physically and internally, Max would make me promise him that I would never confess no matter how high the stakes grow.

Upon exiting the latrine, I'm nearly run over by a herd of running women. Everyone is shoving each other, trying to get somewhere faster than most of us can walk.

Brygid, the young woman from my block who warned me how soon I would stop caring about others, the one I called lucky before I understood there's no such thing, and the one who spends her days cleaning up hair from the incoming prisoners' shaved heads, takes a hold of my arm and pulls me with her. "Don't be left behind," she tells me.

"Where are we going?" I ask, my words bouncing in the air as we hobble along. I flinch with every step, trying to ignore the pain from the infected sore on my heel caused by a hole in my sock. No matter what I've tried to help the wound heal, it remains open, growing redder, and riddled with dirt. This one sore on my foot could easily be my demise—the end of the road for me. Then again, anything could be my end.

"Why are you limping?" Brygid asks, locking her arm around mine.

"It's just a sore on my foot. It's nothing," I say, making it out to be a sliver rather than a hole.

"Don't let the guards catch you favoring your foot," she says. I didn't realize I was limping. No one walks around as if they're healthy. How could we?

All the women crash into each other when whoever is up front stops short. Some of us fall, some get back up. Some don't. Heels crunch through the snow-covered grounds, a steady beat I might never forget. The SS are shouting at us to move out of their way, and some aren't moving fast enough, causing a rippling wave through that uneven row of women.

The cold air bites at my face with a gust of snow and wind torpedoing between the buildings. My eyes water in response and I wrap my arms around my cold body as my muscles tense into rock. The crowd of women begins to move again, this time beyond the last wooden block in our row, fanning out into more columns and fewer rows, giving us a full view of the wet wooden gallows posts with ropes tied into nooses, several of them.

My heart plummets into the pit of my stomach.

Whispers become louder but the SS don't seem to have much of a concern for the crowd as four naked women, each cuffed at the elbow by a guard, are escorted barefoot across the snow over to the three wooden steps of the gallows.

Each of them is covered from head to toe with bruises, wounds, bulging contusions, and missing teeth.

"These are just some of the women who took part in the uprising. They've served their punishments, and now it's time to serve yours," one of the SS officers shouts to the crowd of women standing around me. "This could be you." He points to a woman. "Or you." Then points to another. "Any of you."

My stomach quakes while studying each of the four women, my stare catching on the last one in the row. She's as beaten and swollen as the others, but I don't know the others. I know her.

She has children she wants to find. She had a purpose for participating in the uprising. She didn't have a physical hand in the action on October 7th. Just like me. All of her is just like me.

I cover my hands over my mouth to stop myself from crying out her name. I can hear my voice echo from within my head though.

Marie! Marie!
Don't hurt her!

I was hoping she had been transferred to another ward, another job, anything other than this. No one knew where she went, only that she was missing.

Did she confess? Did she give names?

The SS don smiles, appearing to enjoy this activity unlike any sane person would. The four of them look very much alike, their ribs protruding, skeletal figures with loose sagging skin below their midsections. As if in the spotlight, the four of them stand on their platform, waiting for their show of death.

The quiet, somber sounds of violinists and cellists join in harmony in an uplifting piece that feels painfully incongruous with the scene unfolding. There are more musicians than I've ever heard play at once here. With the overwhelming melody circling overhead, each of the four women has a noose placed over her head, and the knot tightened.

I'm staring at Marie, wondering if she can spot me in the crowd and if she could, what she might be thinking. Why her and not me?

The SS shout a command, and the platforms are pushed out from under the women's feet, each falling heavily at the same moment, their necks folding either to the left or right. The ropes all creak in contrasting whines, swinging back and forth just slightly. My insides burn, my stomach shrivels up on itself and I can't bear to wonder how long she'll endure any suffering. I don't know why everyone seems so confused, as if we don't know that they plan to kill us off at some time in some way.

I clench my teeth together, holding my breath inside my lungs as if it will keep the tears from streaking down my cheeks as I continue to stare at Marie. Her fists are clenched, making me wonder if she's still alive. How long will she live with what must be a broken neck?

The music grows in volume again and I fight back the tears that threaten to pour from my eyes. Teeth still gritted, I endure the pain in my jaw. Her fists release, her fingers dangle.

God, guide her into eternal peace.

My chest aches as gasps of horror continue to squeak from others around me. More women keep dying daily for too many reasons to keep track of, and yet, I still don't understand why I'm standing.

The SS have joined together in a semi-circle, chatting between one another as if they're standing in front of an orchestra performing at an evening dinner. Except there are women's bodies hanging dead from ropes just steps away from them.

I didn't realize Brygid was still nearby until she takes my hand within hers. I don't know why, other than for comfort. Unless she knows I was a part of the uprising. But how? Could anyone know? I would be up there with the others if they did. "You're breathing too quickly. You might fall faint," she whispers.

I can hardly hear her words above the orchestra playing more uplifting tunes.

"Did you know one of them?"

I shake my head no because if she thinks I knew one of them, she could suspect I knew what they were doing or worse, was a part of their alliance.

I was.

"Are you sure?" she continues.

I pull my hand out of hers and clench my fists, mirroring Marie's before her heart stopped beating.

"I'm sure," I utter.

She's glaring at me from the corner of her eye. Why is she looking at me this way? Is there something written on my face?

I'm shaking, though I'm trying my hardest to be brave. Lilli can feel my fear, which is the last thing I want for her. Everything I do now though, every choice I make, is for one thing—to get back to Mama. The thought of seeing her in the distance, running into her arms and melting into her warm embrace—it's like a fairy tale—a story with a beautiful ending. I can't tell Lilli this. I need her to still believe in these magical stories because no matter how much effort I've put into shielding her from the terrifying truths that are always footsteps away from us, it feels as if I'm letting her down. Other times, I'm upset that Max isn't here to do the same for me as I do for Lilli. Alfie does everything he can, but I know he can't do all he wants to without the ability to hear what's happening around us.

"I'm in," a man shouts, his words clear and German.

Alfie squeezes my left hand, and I squeeze Lilli's. When I swallow, I wonder if everyone else heard me forcing phlegm down my throat.

Chatter grows from two to four to six or eight German men all within our safe space, leaving us with nowhere to go. They'll force us to surrender to them.

"We can stay the night and continue heading west in the morning," one of them says.

It is only the morning now. There isn't a chance all of us will be able to remain still without making a sound for that amount of time.

"What is it you think you're doing here?" Sister Josephine speaks aloud, stepping out from behind the blockade. My eyes widen, staring against the black wall directly in front of my nose.

The clatter of a weapon fumbles within a hand. I hate knowing the precise sound.

"Are you planning to shoot a woman of God?" she asks, the composure in her voice uncanny for the circumstance. Sister Josephine has revealed herself to be the bravest of the nuns, but no one is fearless in an unplanned encounter with the unknown during a war.

"No, of course not," the man says. "We thought the church was abandoned."

"Who are you running from and where are you going?" she continues.

The questions and answers are unhurried and drawn out, perhaps lies being formulated to convince her of innocence. "The Soviets, sister. That's who we're running from. We're fleeing Poland to return to Germany."

The honesty is unsettling, making me wonder what has shifted within the war—what we don't know or understand after hiding down here for so long.

"You are running from a country Germany is occupying in fear of Soviet liberators. Is that what I'm understanding?" Sister Josephine continues. "Is it the fear of facing an army stronger than what's left of German militants, or fear of the inhumane truth being discovered by the rest of the world—which are you running from?"

Her words are terrifying me. I've seen what happens if

anyone threatens a German in uniform. They remove the threat. Except Sister Josephine isn't threatening them. She's asking a question.

"We're running from it all," the man answers.

"And you think hiding in a house of God is going to protect you?" How can she speak with so much poise to them? It's as if they're naughty boys at a schoolhouse.

"They're on our heels, sister, and there is nowhere else to go," the man says, a plea laced through his words.

"I see. I have made a vow to tend to social justice, caregiving, and spiritual leadership. Allowing you men to stay here would be a sin as you bear your arms, in your uniforms. In this holy house of God, everyone is equal."

"Of course, sister."

What is she doing? I want to ask her, but I have no choice but to keep silent.

Alfie's palm is covered in sweat, and I realize he doesn't know what's happening, so I begin to tap out a short summary of what's happened in the last two minutes. He can't seem to stand still, shifting his weight from one foot to the other and I stop tapping out letters and just squeeze his hand instead.

"Here's how this will work," Sister Josephine says. "All seven of you are going to return upstairs to the chapel, and undress down to your undergarments. You will leave your weapons there as well. I will put all your belongings in a locked closet until morning when you can retrieve them on your way out of the church doors. One word or step out of line, and I will have the Soviets at that door waiting for you before you even know what's happening, and I am a woman of my word."

I've been holding my breath for much longer than I should be able to. I can't make out what I'm listening to or understand what Sister Josephine plans by allowing them to stay here. Are we going to stay back here, unable to move a hair?

There's silence within the cellar. Are they seeking permission from each other, thinking through this agreement, or getting ready to attack Sister Josephine?

"Sister Josephine, a word, if you will," Sister Katherine says, stepping out from behind the blockade. The men out there must only be able to imagine how many people are hiding behind the wall.

"We agree to your terms," the man says. "Men, upstairs and do as the sister said," he orders the others.

The men's footsteps sound frenzied as they take the steps up to the door, which soon closes after the last set of footsteps echo from a short distance.

"Have you lost your mind?" Sister Katherine asks Sister Josephine.

"Without weapons and uniforms, they're nothing. We are here to teach and guide, are we not?"

"Nazis?" Sister Katherine asks, shock electrifying her words.

"These brainwashed, manipulated men are running from their own. It's clear, they have the most to learn of anyone within these walls."

"I will not blink an eye with them here, Sister Josephine."

"Nor will I."

"We are protecting these children."

"As we will continue to do. Nothing will happen to these children under my care, except perhaps to have an opportunity to begin the process of healing from the burdens they've all endured."

"I don't understand what you are talking about. Those men, they have no souls," Sister Katherine says. "We both know they will rid us for their own good."

"We have the leverage," Sister Josephine says. "You are correct though, and if I told them to leave, they wouldn't just walk away. They were looking for a sanctuary."

"They don't deserve our shelter."

"I never said we will be safeguarding them."

Sister Margaret and Sister Patricia step out next and join their conversation. "We need to make sure there is nothing on their bodies before re-entering this space. Can they not sleep in the pews?" Sister Margaret asks.

"We are not to take our eyes off them until they walk out that door tomorrow. Understood?" Sister Josephine affirms.

The agreements limbo in hesitation and I'm still wondering what she plans to do with us children.

"Yes, we will do as you say, Sister Josephine," Sister Patricia says before the others agree.

"Yes, sister."

"Yes."

"I will be waiting for them on the other side of the door to make sure they are down to their long undergarments," Sister Josephine says.

"Bring the children out and keep them behind you on the far left side of the cots."

We're all breathing so hard. It's all I can hear and the heat from everyone's exhausted breaths is creating a thick fog around us within this tight space. I tap my finger against Alfie's hand, giving him the shortened message: we're stepping away from hiding and showing ourselves, and we're to trust all will be well.

"Come along, children," Sister Margaret says. "Everything will be all right."

Not all of us understand the complexities of the agreement just formed. The youngest of us will be just fine. The rest of us, I don't know how well we'll be able to handle being in the same room as the monsters we've been hiding from. We've already faced our fears. It should have been enough.

Alfie and I help corral the children over to the corner behind the cots. "No one needs to speak with these men or even look at them. They will stay on the other side of the room and away from you," Sister Katherine says.

"What if we want to talk to them?" Lilli asks.

"Lilli," I snap at her in a hush. "We do not have anything to say to them."

"I do," she says.

"No, you do not," I correct her. I pull her down to the floor with me between the other children and along Alfie's side.

When the door to the cellar reopens my heart batters against my rib cage. A sour zing shocks my stomach and heat boils through my blood as they trickle in, all in skintight dirty white T-shirts and long johns. If it weren't all children here, I would say they should be forced to sit here, have their heads shaved too, and be beaten every time they say the wrong word. My thoughts are impure and are sinful, especially if any of the sisters were to hear me say such things out loud. However, I believe it's impossible for anyone who didn't see what we saw to be thinking anything different.

None of them are skin and bones, starved, tired, or weak. They're all perfectly healthy or appear that way. It could have been one of them who killed Papa.

What if it was *one of them who killed Papa?*

The seven men appear stunned upon stumbling over the sight of us children sitting in the corner.

"You will stay on that side of the cellar," Sister Katherine says, directing them toward the barricade where we were.

"Maybe they know where Mama and Max are?" Lilli whispers in my ear.

"No. They don't," I say, my words hostile.

"Are you Nazis?" Frank, a nine-year-old boy, asks out loud. Sister Patricia moves to his side and presses her finger up to her lips to quiet him.

"We were, but not anymore," one of the men replies. *I'm unsure of what that means. Maybe they don't either.*

"Does that mean you don't hate Jewish people anymore?" Frank replies.

"That's enough," Sister Patricia says to him. "Not another word. Do you understand?"

Not one of the men chooses to respond to the last question. Instead, they share a look with one another and if I believed there was any good left in humanity among the German Army, I might think there's a sense of remorse. I just don't think that's possible, and it doesn't matter.

One of the men has tears rolling down his cheeks. I want to say: *How dare you?*

Lilli stands up and I try to pull her back down, but she fights me off and slaps my hand. "Stop telling me what to do," she says to me.

"Lilli, sit down," I argue.

Alfie reaches across me to grab Lilli's hand, but she moves to her right, away from the two of us.

"Lilli, have a seat," Sister Margaret tells her, kindly.

"No, sister. I have something I need to say."

"Lilli, could I speak to you—" I try again.

"Let the child speak," Sister Josephine says, returning to the cellar after inspecting the men before entering. "These children should never be silenced again."

I'm so angry with Lilli and I'm trying to hold myself back from tackling her and dragging her back down to the ground, but Sister Josephine is staring at me, not Lilli. She shakes her head ever so slightly, telling me not to do anything.

Alfie must see the look as he stops trying to reach for Lilli too.

"You say you were Nazis but now you're not," Lilli says, stating a fact rather than asking a question. "Does that mean my papa is alive after you killed him?"

We don't know who killed Papa, but it isn't hard to assume it was an SS officer or guard on a manhunt on the train.

"Many people have died who shouldn't have died," one of the men says.

What a foolish response.

"But you can't bring them back to life. Instead, you want to run away from what you did. You took away my parents and my brother. You took away my right to be a child. You have forced me to starve and work until my fingers bled every day. You hurt my friends. You beat them with whips. You made them bleed, cry, and some die. All because we're Jewish. I was born Jewish. What is it that I did wrong? What did any of us children do wrong or do to deserve having our parents taken away from us?"

Lilli's words slice through my chest, making it hard for me to breathe as I struggle to fight back tears. I refuse to cry in front of these men.

"We didn't—" one of them begins to say. But another man throws his arm against the other's chest.

Lilli sits back down on her own and crosses her arms over her chest, squinting her eyes at the group of men, her lips pursed with fury.

"You shot my mother and sister right in front of me then threw me in a wagon for homeless children," Greta says, standing up from her spot on the floor. She's fourteen and has been here longer than most of us. "Before you killed my family, you took away my home and forced us to live in a ghetto where there was no remaining shelter. You laughed at us while we sang and danced in the streets, trying to cheer each other up. You laughed at us when we cried. You laughed when someone fell to the ground from starvation or illness. Laughter wasn't a part of your orders, was it? You did that on your own. Imagine your mother, father, sister, or brother lying on the cobblestones after fighting to protect you. They now have a bullet lodged in their brain; their eyes wide open as they rest in a pool of their own blood. And despite the shock and horror of witnessing the most unimaginable nightmare you will never be able to erase from your memory, you hear laughter all around you."

The men have their knees pulled up to their chests, some

with their heads buried between their legs, others are rocking back and forth as tears run down their red cheeks. Not one of them is sitting there with a blank look on their face, but that's all I had seen among them until now—blank stares, hollow brains and hearts. Yet now they feel something. Now that it's too late.

I stand up without thinking it through and the words come out on their own. "You destroyed this world we live in. You've destroyed each one of us and everything we've ever known. I've learned a lot under the protection of these noble sisters standing between us. They've taught us to forgive and have understanding, to understand that not all people are well enough to make their own decisions." Sister Josephine cracks a small smile, tilting her head as she gazes at me. Her smile might disappear in a moment though.

"Forgiveness is important," one of the men chokes out.

How dare he say such a thing. I open my mouth to speak, unsure if the words will come out, but I must be heard: "My papa, however, the one you murdered while he was trying to save his children, he would tell us that for every sin we commit, there will be a punishment. Those who deal pain will be forced to view life from the inflicted. You might think you're getting away with murder when you walk out those doors tomorrow, but despite what happens to you, you will live forever with your sins. That's your punishment. They will haunt you every minute of every day until you realize you can't run away from it —from yourself."

I wish I felt satisfied following those words but I'm not informing them of something they didn't already know.

"I've changed my mind," Sister Josephine says, her words steady and firm. "You will leave this church at once. The Soviets are not far behind, and this house of God will not serve as your sanctuary."

The men's faces shift from stunned disbelief to raw panic. Without their uniforms and weapons, they look much less intimidating. They fumble to their feet, but instead of a frantic rush for their gear, they hesitate just before their complexions each take on a ghostly white color.

"Are you going to return our belongings to us?" one of the soldiers asks, his question laced with clear concern.

Sister Josephine steps forward, seemingly unafraid of this man as she stares him right in the eyes. "We'll give you your uniforms, but your weapons are locked up in a steel closet. You won't ever find the key. I assure you. I'm not a fool, nor do I trust that any of you are capable of restraint. Your uniforms are upstairs, and you can leave this church dressed as soldiers without arms."

The soldiers exchange nervous looks between one another. One steps, forward, his spine straight, shoulders square. The look on his face hints that he might argue with Sister Josephine. She doesn't step back. She doesn't show a hint of fear.

"You can choose to fight me for your weapons," she says, her confidence faltering, "but don't forget what I said: the Soviets are not far behind, and when they see German soldiers in uniform, they will not hesitate to do what they've come here to do. What happens next is your decision, but I warn you, you will either leave in peace or face the consequences."

The bravery they still held on to is now gone. Fear, a familiar look in a person's eyes, is all I see now. They can't run from what they've done or what's coming for them, but they can still try.

The soldier who stood up to Sister Josephine takes a step back and drops his head, conceding. "We'll leave, sister."

"Good then. Go now. I don't want the Soviets having to deal with you in my church." The men trickle into a line and make their way up the steps to the main level of the church. "You may outrun the Soviets, but never forget that it's impossible to run from your conscience. Let the church always be a reminder of that for you."

No sooner than the last one exits the cellar, Sister Josephine holds up her index finger and nods her head. "I'll be back in just a moment. I want to make sure they find their way out."

I hold my breath, standing in one spot, staring at the door the entire time Sister Josephine is gone.

The door finally reopens, and she steps inside, brushing her hands together. "It's done," she says as if it was no big task. "They won't be back."

The silence following her words offers a sense of relief—an unfamiliar feeling. The war might not be over, but this could mean it's the start of the end. I just hate that we've thought this so many times before too.

THIRTY-SEVEN

DALIA

JANUARY 27TH, 1945 – OŚWIĘCIM, POLAND

We're coming toward an end, but which end is anyone's guess. Artillery strikes rumble the floor beneath us, but it's hard to know what's happening within the containment of Auschwitz versus outside the gates. Another crematorium was blown up yesterday. I don't know if it was an act of resistance, an air strike, or something else. I heard the explosion, stepped outside the block, but could only see smoke and dust in the distance.

No one knows who is fighting whom but many of the SS guards left the camp over a week ago, marching out thousands of prisoners with them. The rest of us left behind can only guess where they were going, not knowing if we're better off here or there, or if it matters at all.

There has been no kapo to take a group of women from Birkenau to Auschwitz in the early morning to report to duty. So, we've remained in our barracks. I'm unsure if anyone is in the infirmaries, and if so, whether they are alive.

Those who are still here seem to be roaming back and forth between the blocks, mindlessly, while others lie still in their wooden bunks, staring blankly ahead.

The kapos are still around but seem to care little about what everyone is doing, or not doing. The kapo from my block sits by the door and stares between the columns of bunks.

I slide off my bunk, trudging down carefully to the floor to check the wound on the bottom of my heel. I unwrap the piece of fabric I've kept secured, finding the shade of red to be the same as yesterday and the day before, the rawness still as severe, but no other discoloration and no growth. There's no more anti-septic. Whether I heal now is up to God.

Every step I take feels as if my skin is tearing open, undoing any form of healing my body attempted overnight. I'm staying off my feet as much as possible except for using the latrine and washroom, as well as the unorganized roll call still in partial effect.

"How's your foot?" Brygid asks, shuffling toward me in slow turtle-like movements. She's so young but could pass for an elderly woman in her final days. She's skin and bones, similar to me, but I try to avoid looking down at the rest of my body aside from my foot. The less I see, the better mindset I can keep, which isn't saying much at this point.

"The same as it's been," I answer.

She struggles to slide down against the wooden posts to sit beside me. "There's a lot of commotion out there. People are flocking in every direction as if a fire is chasing them, but they don't know where the fire is coming from."

The irony of her statement, knowing I ended up here following a fire that was coming at us from every direction.

"Why do you think that is?" I ask her.

She shrugs her shoulders. "Likely a rumor started."

Our block kapo stands up and opens the block door, poking her head outside. There's enough space for us to see others rushing by the block.

"Something must be happening out there."

"Where are you running to?" the kapo shouts outside.

"Soviets!"

Soviets.

Brygid pushes herself back up to her feet and yanks my blanket down from my bunk before moving down to grab hers. Then she offers me her hand. "We should go see for ourselves."

"Yes, we should," I say, giving her my hand, knowing she won't be able to help much with getting me up to my feet. I take hold of a wooden beam and use all my might to push myself up. Brygid swings my blanket around my shoulders, then around her own before wrapping her arm around me. "I'm sure I'm not much help, but you should try to keep the weight off your heel if you can," she says.

Since the day of the hanging at the beginning of the month, she's been kinder to me. I thought she was able to read the thoughts inside my head and knew I had taken a part in the uprising. Maybe she still thinks I did, but all any of us were trying to do was free everyone—do something, anything. The effects of what we achieved were slight, but there was a shift in the way the SS were parading around, then many left the camp. It could all be a coincidence. I might never know.

Brygid and I stay close to the outer walls of the blocks, trudging through the hard snow and brittle gusts of wind until we turn left toward the main entrance of Birkenau where everyone is gathering. Just beyond the electrified wire fences are rows of tanks and trucks, but they aren't German vehicles.

Brygid and I walk nearer to the fence where others are standing, leaning against the wires we'd never step foot near unless it was to end our lives. There mustn't be any more electricity running through the fences now.

The Soviet soldiers of the Red Army stare at us through the fence as if we're a rare species they've never seen before. It's hard to understand the looks on their faces.

Through a bullhorn, a man speaks in Russian, words I don't understand. Most of us don't. When no one responds, they begin speaking in German, saying:

"You are freed, my comrades. Don't be afraid. We've come to liberate you."

My gaze swings to Brygid, wondering if she just heard the same thing I did. "Did they say we're free?"

She doesn't speak German well. I forgot. Just as I'm about to recite the most beautiful words I've ever heard, the man repeats them in Polish. Then again in Yiddish. He's making sure we all understand that they've come to save us.

Brygid clutches her hand against my side but falls to her knees, yanking at my smock. Her howling sobs echo the many others around us, and I wonder why I'm not crying. What's wrong with me? Do I not understand what's happening? Is this my imagination? Am I dreaming? I'm afraid I'm hallucinating. That must be what this is.

The crowds of prisoners all shuffle to the sides, creating open paths for the Soviets to enter the compound, enough of them to move in each direction of the camp to spread the news.

Despite the unsettling looks on their faces, they don't take their eyes off the crowded lines of people welcoming their arrival with wailing sobs, shouts of prayers, and silence as some convince themselves these men aren't just a mirage of our dying minds. I don't know how they'll be able to help so many of us at once. Those of us still on our feet are walking miracles. There are so many who can't move from their bunks.

I watch the Soviets carefully, wondering what their plan might be. We all want to run out of those gates but most of us can't. I doubt there are many who could.

I stare down the row of blocks and all I can think about is Max, knowing I'll likely be freed along with the others, escorted out from these godforsaken walls, but I'll be leaving him here. His body is gone. I know this. But a part of him is here and will always be here, and now it will be without me. What kind of mother am I? How can I just leave him here?

"Max, I need to take you with me," I whisper into the wind. "Can you hear me, sweetheart?"

"Dalia," Brygid says, wrapping her arm around mine, our blankets overlapping one another. "Max will always be with you. He's a part of you, not this place."

My tears come all at once and with the wind striking me as a punch to the face, the tears freeze against my skin. I gasp for air, the cold, a searing knife. "My girls and husband. I don't know where to find them. What if they were here too? Is this the freedom I've been praying for? A life alone without everyone I love?"

"You don't know that they're gone too. We both still have the chance to find our families. We can't give up now," she says. "We've come this far, Dalia."

"We could help one another," I tell her, afraid of being utterly alone in this world I might never learn how to navigate.

"I think that's the most wonderful idea," she says, resting her head on my shoulder.

"If you need medical aid, hold up a hand so that we can assist you," the Soviets announce.

I don't raise my hand, knowing others are in much worse condition than I am. As I limp alongside Brygid back toward our block, she takes my hand and lifts it up. "No, no," I say, pulling against her grip.

"If you don't receive treatment for your foot, you aren't going to make it. Don't try and fool me, Dalia. I saw the wound."

"It isn't so bad."

"There is a hole in your foot. You have exposed tissue."

"I just need some antiseptic," I argue.

"No, you're going to receive proper treatment," she says sternly, still holding my hand up.

I've seen what happens to those who request medical treatment of any kind. Who's to say it's any different with the Red Army. They want to help those who can be helped, rightfully so. I might be beyond help. I'm only fooling myself by thinking otherwise.

THIRTY-EIGHT

JORDANNA

I wonder if the nuns knew there would be more barbed wire fences awaiting our arrival. I was foolish to think there wouldn't be. It's too cold to spend much time outside so we've been restlessly sitting on our three cots, staring at one another, processing thoughts of hopes, fears, and waves of confusion. I used to dream of a beautiful life and the picture I imagined—the idea of beauty—was nothing like this, nothing like anything I've seen in over eighteen months. My mind can only draw in visions from nightmares—the reality of the life we've been trying to survive. I'm trapped here with these thoughts, and I don't want to be. I want to leave them behind. It's not so simple. I know that.

Most of the shallow, wide buildings within the new camp are filled with cots. Thousands of people walk around between the buildings throughout the day. Some appear as if they're looking for something. Others seem lost. I consider the three of us to be lost. Very lost.

Lilli, Alfie and I have been here—wherever here is—for three days. We didn't have a say in whether we wanted to leave the church or the familiarity of the faces we had come to know, especially the sisters. However, upon hearing the words, "You're being rescued," what else is there to say? I don't know what the definition of *being rescued* is yet. No one has told us.

Lilli's shivering, as she's been since we arrived here. She keeps fussing with the wool coat she was given because it's too big and scratching her neck. It's as if the wool is all that's left for her to focus on. When she isn't tugging at the collar, she's staring through me as if I'm a window with a view on the other side.

Before we arrived here three days ago, there was a moment of relief in the cellar of the church. It was moments after Sister Josephine sent the invading Nazis away in their underwear and without their gear.

* * *

Three Days Ago – January 24th, 1945 – Southern Poland

Sister Josephine can fool anyone into thinking she's mentally strong, but after standing up to the soldiers the way she did, something seems to have changed. She's been pacing, talking to the other sisters, and I can only assume, preparing to tell us some kind of news.

"Children," Sister Josephine announces after stopping mid-pace in front of the door. *"Gather round."* She waves us all in closer to her. Each of us hesitates. *"You all know living here beneath the church isn't a permanent home for any of us. We've wanted to keep you children safe for as long as possible until relief—help—arrives. If those nasty Nazis did anything for us, they informed us that the Soviets were nearby. They will be the ones to help us."*

The Soviets. Papa always had stories about how ruthless the Red Army was in the final year of the Great War. They were Germany's enemy then too. I've always seen Russia as a country to fear. Even as natural born Poles, some are perceived as traitors to Russia because of the Great War. It's always been very confusing to me. Papa did explain the difference between countries being at war with each other and a country being at war while also trying to end races of innocent people. He told me a war should never lead to harming innocent civilians. No real soldier would ever intentionally harm the innocent. He also told me we were living in a time where the Third Reich are breaking all civil rules.

I think what he meant was no one knows how this war will turn out for the innocent bystanders.

It's only been a few hours since the Nazis left, but the younger children seem to have bounced back to their usual ways. Most of them, including Lilli, have taken to the wall to work on their mural drawings. We've made it more than halfway around the room since we started the drawings a few weeks ago after one of the sisters found sticks of colored wax in the nearby village.

I'm reading one of the few books we have access to, or I'm giving off the appearance that I'm reading. This one teaches lessons on how to play chess. We don't have a chess board to play with here though. I try to imagine the moving pieces but often lose my train of thought while thinking about Alfie's kiss. His words. The comfort he brought to me in a moment of utter fear— the type of fear that could take me down. We haven't spoken but we're sitting side by side and somehow that feels more important than exchanging words.

The sound of the church door opening and closing forces me to sit up straighter and shut my book, placing it down by my side. I have my hands on the floor, ready to jump up and hide again.

"No need to worry, children," Sister Josephine says as the cellar door opens, revealing Sister Katherine.

I heard several pairs of footsteps though.

Once Sister Katherine moves from the door, a dozen Soviets make their way into the center of our space, all dressed in brown uniforms, not completely dissimilar to the Waffen SS's gray-

green uniforms. A uniform is a uniform and, in this war, it's hard to know who can be considered a source of safety.

At this point, I fear everyone, despite Papa's explanations of war. None of that has mattered here. After all we've been through, it feels impossible to fear anyone more than the Germans in power.

"These soldiers are going to take care of each one of you and bring you to what's called a displaced persons camp to begin the process of reuniting you with family members," Sister Josephine says. Her words show no form of emotion. They're cold and stale, not comforting.

It's the first time anyone has referred to us as displaced children rather than orphans, giving us hope that we aren't, in fact, orphans.

Lilli returns to my side, holding on to my arm as if it's an anchor to the church.

"Be sure to give these men all the information they request of you. They want to help."

"We will help," one of the soldiers says, his accent Russian and thick.

But the war isn't over. We'd know if it was, I think. How can we be safe anywhere?

My question is answered all too soon upon arriving at a compound surrounded by more barbwire topped fencing.

"It's for our protection this time," Alfie tells me. I want to ask him how he's so sure, but I'd rather take his word.

* * *

Current Day – January 27th, 1945 – Southern Poland

We registered, gave them all our details. The soldier who took down our information told us they would be doing everything possible to reconnect us with our family. He didn't say how long it would take.

It's clear Max and Mama aren't anywhere here. I would think they would have matched us up in the last three days if they were. I don't know how many displaced person camps there are or if there are ways to communicate with each other.

All we can do is sit here and wait, and yet, my hope is dwindling after losing Papa. I don't know how Mama will find us, if she's still all right. And if we don't find her, I don't know what will become of us.

Despite all the efforts, the war is still in effect, and I don't know what that means for us either.

"Bergmann," a woman with a Russian accent calls out from the center of the barrack building.

My heart swells and lodges in my throat as I try to make my way up to my feet. My knees shake so hard, I don't know if I'll be able to stand for long. "Jordanna or Lilli?"

"Yes, that's us," I reply.

A woman in an olive drab dress, a matching head scarf and a white apron and a red-cross marked armband approaches us with a letter. Our names are in script on the front of the envelope, but I don't recognize the handwriting.

THIRTY-NINE

DALIA

I'm not as sick as some of the others still here. I keep saying these words out loud and it's as if no one can hear me. I want to leave. I want to walk out of those gates and never return. I must find Leo and the children. There's no time to waste, if there's time at all.

"I'm truly fine," I tell the soldier carrying me into one of the barrack blocks. The stench has changed from body fluids to ammonia or some kind of chemical. It didn't take the Soviets long to set up field hospitals, making use of the rows of buildings within our confinement. I'm sure they didn't have an easy time decontaminating the space. The number of bodies left to rot in these buildings is uncountable. So many died just in the last week. We're all so close to finding a way out and yet the exit feels as if it's still on the other side of the world and impossible to reach.

The soldier continues walking forward, focused on finding an open cot rather than listening to me try and convince him I shouldn't be here. I don't need to take up space. I don't look as sick as the other people here. At least, I don't think I do. I don't really know how I look, and I don't think I want to know.

The Soviets took Brygid elsewhere and I'm not certain we'll be able to find each other with the intense chaos ensuing. She promised to find me. I want to believe her.

"Your foot is infected," the soldier says, his Russian broken into Yiddish. I can't tell if he's asking or confirming my diagnosis. "It needs treatment."

I know my foot is infected. The infection has been growing for far too long. I've done whatever possible to keep it clean, but it hasn't been enough. "A nurse will be with you soon."

Is this supposed to be a life lesson of me watching myself from the other side of a window? I tried to give everyone my full attention. I listened even if there was nothing to hear. Maybe it wasn't enough. I see that now.

"I'm a nurse. I can treat the infection myself if you have any disinfectant and spare dressing." I must sound as if I'm pleading at this point. The nurses are running around rampant in dizzying circles around the cots.

Not much has changed in the past twenty-seven years since the first war. We made do with what we had, the few of us nurses in comparison to the wounded soldiers lying before us on cots.

For many, it was a matter of making them comfortable or holding their hand as they took their final breath. For others it was words of hope. We bandaged up the wounded and moved on to the next. I could hardly remember a single face or name. They all began to look the same, day after day of treating the same injuries. Then there was the part of me scanning faces for Leo, praying he didn't end up in my field hospital, or worse, in another somewhere I couldn't help him. I remember losing faith that it was at all possible that a single soldier would return unscathed. And all I could think was: *What is this all for?*

While treating the prisoner patients in the infirmary until a few weeks ago, I was thinking the same thought. *What is this all for?*

The Fuhrer wasn't standing in my shoes, watching innocent people die for no good reason. He didn't have to watch what I had to. He wants power, selfish power. I was the one who had to watch the others fade away, knowing most people who were in the beds, with the exception of one or two wards, would never leave their bed. And if they did, it was still the end of the road for them. I don't want to be on this side, waiting and watching.

"Miss," the soldier says, interrupting my thought, "I'm afraid we have limited supplies. We've sent for more but we're going to do everything we can to offer you treatment and nourishment."

Limited supplies. I know what that means too.

The Soviets have likely used up whatever supplies they were carrying with them. It's been no secret that they didn't expect to find a compound full of dying prisoners.

There are thousands of us: skeletal, wounded, and disease ridden. There aren't enough people to help us all. I've known this for too long.

The words limited supplies means they will only be able to give me hope after I've come this far, so close to walking away. Without further care for my wound, it will worsen, grow, and spread through my body until I go into septic shock.

I wish I didn't know this.

* * *

The nurses are working through the night but haven't made it to me yet. If they have nothing to treat me with, there's no sense in taking the time to remind me of what I already know.

I'm angry at the brief moments of hope I had today. I'm angry for being in denial about my foot for the sake of trying to give myself false hope.

I'm angry that, for a moment, I truly thought I would be set free.

If we had stayed in our apartment the night of the firestorm, would we have been safe there? We never found out if our building was still standing or if it burnt to the ground. Did we run into the gauntlet just as planned? I should have known better, made Leo think about our plan for an extra moment longer. If I hadn't been helping people in the bunker when the Gestapo found us, they would have left me with the children. I could have known where they ended up. I could have—I should have protected them. Every decision was wrong, but my family shouldn't have to pay that consequence.

Or, this is happening to me so I won't have to live on without them. I don't know whether I'm being punished or spared. There might be worse waiting for me out there than what I've experienced already, when I've been so sure up to now that nothing could ever be more horrific. I don't know if I'm fighting to open the doors to more brutality and pain. If Leo was right, and whatever comes after our death is what everyone is unknowingly working toward, I should let go and see if he's right. See what's next. Because here, there may never be anything next. There's no such thing as freedom when I'm a prisoner of my mind. Again, I wonder why I am here? Why fight? Who is it all for?

It could be worse. I could be fooled into thinking I'm being treated to a shower, only to suffocate in a toxic gas and fall to my death in a heap of other bodies. Then my ashes would snow down over Poland, bringing me back to where my life began. It's a loop. The coming and going. And I'm tired of trying to under-stand the meaningless process of enduring suffrage.

A cold wind blows through the barrack and captures me within its tundra, holding me hostage in an untamed shiver. I turn my head toward the door, wondering why someone might be holding it open so long. We'll all freeze in here. Then I see the door isn't open. No one else around me is shivering. The wind has only come for me.

"Help!" I shout, my voice full of phlegm. "Help!"

A nurse flees to my side, and I should be ashamed that I've stolen her attention from another person who might need her more. But...

"I think I'm dying. How do we know if we're dying? Do I just let it happen?"

I've been asked these same questions before—questions that have kept me up at night, wishing I had a worthwhile answer. I've wondered if people know...if they just know when their time is up, but how soon before? It's one question I've never heard anyone ask. I can't be the first to think of it.

The nurse presses her palm to my head, pulling her hand away quickly as if my face is on fire. She will feel heat when I feel ice forming in my veins. That doesn't make sense. How did I never realize that it doesn't make sense?

Her hand is on my ankle, but I can't feel much else below that spot. She must be inspecting the wound but staying away from the growing bacteria eating my flesh.

The woman shouts something in Russian that I don't understand.

"Dreck!" she shouts.

A nurse shouting through a cuss can only mean one thing.

It's too late.

I try to relax my head, drowning out the panic bleeding out of this nurse's mouth. Haven't we seen it all? An infection shouldn't be something out of the ordinary for her. Unless she isn't a nurse. Many of us had no medical qualifications and yet still treated the imprisoned patients.

"I need an antibacterial medicine. You need to remove the tissue surrounding. Then, I need sutures and clean dressing. I can't feel my foot. Please, help. I'm begging you. Can you keep me alive? I need to see if my children and husband survived. I can't give up on them even though I'm ready to give up on me. I have to tell them I love them and that Max..." My pleas are an echo of the same words from the first patient I tried to help here, pleading for me to keep him alive. I couldn't.

"*Mama, try to breathe,*" Max says. "*It's all right, I'm here with you. Just as you always were for me. But you must listen, Mama. Breathe...for me.*"

FORTY
JORDANNA
FEBRUARY 4TH, 1945 – SOUTHERN POLAND

Alfie sits on one side of my cot and Lilli on the other with me in the center as I pluck open the envelope with our names on the front. My heart has been pounding while we prepare to reveal whatever is inside. I don't know if I'm grateful the handwriting on the front isn't Mama's or scared.

I remove the paper inside with trembling hands. Alfie rests his hand on my knee, keeping it from bouncing up and down. Lilli is staring at my face, waiting for a reaction rather than trying to see what the words are on the inside of the letter.

Several pieces of paper separate from the fold, each numbered by a page in the top right corner.

The handwriting inside—it's Mama's.

My throat tightens as I force my eyes to focus on the top line of words.

29, September 1944

My Sweethearts,

It's me, your mama. I'm writing to you from a place called Auschwitz where I was brought after being separated from Papa the morning after the Gestapo took us away from you. I've spent every single moment since then blaming myself for our separation, wondering where you might be, praying you're together, and most importantly, pleading to God that you are still alive.

I've been working in the infirmary here, watching too many people succumb to ailments. For every patient I've helped, I've questioned whether I've taught you enough to survive without me and I'm still not sure I have that answer. A child should have their mother and it's not fair that you are without me. A mother shouldn't be without her child or children and it's not fair that I'm without you, my loves.

I don't know what will happen tomorrow, or even tonight for that matter. I'm sure you've learned on your own that we have all been deprived of knowing what the future might hold. We can think the worst or hope for the best. I promise you; I've done nothing but hope for the best. However, in the case that my hope isn't enough, I've written a dozen identical letters and hid them with patients who I saw well—well enough to see a chance of walking out of this encampment. That's not to say I won't, but with so much uncertainty, I wanted to be sure I tried every way possible to say what I need to say to you just in case I don't find a way to say it out loud, to your beautiful faces.

Jordanna, you were just a young girl when this war broke out, but even now as I write this letter, you're on the brink of adulthood. I want you to remember everything I've ever taught you about being a strong woman—one who can accomplish anything you set your mind to and also take care of a family and a home, God willing. I know you want it all and you should have all of it. I don't know what you've been through over the last year and a half but I'm sure no one will walk away from this war as the same person they were before. I've always taught you to look for the person in the room who needs the most help and befriend them, love them, be the person you would want if you needed help. If you need help, do not be ashamed to ask someone for a hand. I left that part out of my motherly lectures. To be strong, you need support. I have always seen you as a younger version of myself and in my heart, I know you will find your way through the hard times. You are my warrior.

Lilli, my sweet baby. I spent so much of your life holding on to my last born, treasuring the hugs and cuddles, giving you all I could so you could hold on to your innocence in the confusing world you had been growing up within. I'm afraid I didn't teach you what you might need to know to take care of yourself and I'm sorry if I let you down in that way. I wanted you to be happy. That's all I wanted for you. If you are still by your sister's side, allow her to teach you everything I taught her. Listen and learn, and then become your own person too. You don't have to be like Jordanna to make me proud. You have to be you. And I know you will be. I've seen you as this little girl growing into my high heels, dressing up with my pearl necklaces and long dresses. I also see the way you take control of situations and speak your mind without fear. Never lose that ability, but I hope you understand the importance of self-control and using your words as tools of empowerment rather than power. You may not understand what I mean now, but you will someday. Make sure to hold on to this letter forever. I'm proud of your bravery and your ability to grow up overnight because you had no choice. I will always be proud of you, but know, it's all right to be afraid of the dark and the wind—the things we can't control. Fear makes us stronger.

Alfie, I love you as if you were my own son. I've been as worried about you as the others. You are a good man, raised by wonderful parents who have set you up for success in life.

Despite the obstacles you might find in your path, I know you will overcome it all without batting an eyelash. You are gentle but strong, emotional, and love with all your heart. Stay with the girls. You are family and always will be, however life turns out.

I've written your papa separate letters as I'm quite sure he's not with you. I've had dreams he's found you but I'm unsure of how possible that might be. I'm sure he's looking for all of us and will do anything and everything he can to bring our family back together if possible. Never forget that he is and always will be the strongest of us all and won't give up until his dying day.

The last part of my letter is the hardest, the part I wish I would never have to write to you, your father, or anyone. I'm so sorry to tell you that Max fell ill with typhus. I don't know how unlikely it was to find him in one of my beds in the infirmary, but I did, and it was within his final moments. I held his hand. I told him I loved him. I told him everything I never thought I would have to tell any of you. He wanted to make sure you knew how much he loved you too. He fought so hard to stay alive. I don't know how he made it as long as he did in the condition he was in, but God gave me his final moments and I will forever be grateful for the gift of those brief moments. He'll be watching over all of us, and he wants us to be strong for him. That's where my hope comes from at this moment.

Hope or not, I need you to know all of what I've written. I will fight to survive for you. I will do everything I can to find you no matter where you are. If something does happen to me though, I know the three of you will find Papa and will make it through without me. We're all warriors. We can all get through whatever we're meant to survive. And if we aren't meant to survive, there's something more waiting for us after this life, and I know we'll be together again. You can always talk to me, and I will hear you. I will comfort you even if I can't hold you. I love you more than anything in this world and even if I was *only given the short time I've had to be your Mama, I'm the luckiest Mama in the entire world.*

I love you dearly and always, always will, in this life and beyond.

Love,

Your Mama

Tears have soaked through the blouse and skirt the Red Cross aides gave me. I press my hand to my heart, unsure what it's doing because I can't feel how fast or slow it's beating. I can only feel pain inside every bone of my body.

Max.

Alfie has dropped his head into his hands and lifted his knees to his chest, pressing against the pain.

Lilli is still staring at the letter and I don't know what's going on inside of her head. "Max and Papa are together," she whispers. "They aren't alone like we thought."

I gasp for air, wishing I could breathe freer than my lungs will allow. I wrap my arm around my sister, angry at myself for not knowing how to be stronger in this moment. How much stronger could I be? "You're right," I utter.

"Papa always said life is the hard part and if we can get through it, we can get through anything," Lilli continues.

I don't think that's what Papa said. It doesn't make much sense but if it gives her comfort, I want her to lean on those words. "He was right," I tell her.

"Mama doesn't know Papa died. We have to tell her." Lilli seems sure that Mama is still alive but I'm unsure if I'm able to think the same. If she's alive, is she still in Auschwitz, or has she been released, and if so, where is she now? How will she find us? She wrote this letter months ago. "How can we find her?" She doesn't know I've been checking in with the coordinators at this displaced camp daily, searching lists for names, not finding anything. I didn't want to drain her hope. Max's name hasn't even made it onto those lists. I wouldn't expect Papa's to since I have his papers now. New names come in every day, and I've been assuming they're timely updates.

FORTY-ONE

JORDANNA

"Bergmann children, collect your belongings. You're being transported back to Hamburg to another displaced persons camp. They will be better equipped to help you in relocating relatives," the Russian aide informed us yesterday morning after we'd had some breakfast.

The thought of returning to Germany seems impossible. We weren't wanted there before the fires but now everything is different.

The Fuhrer has died, and the war is over.

In just an instant.

We've been sitting in this displacement camp since January, waiting for a change, a shift in the wind's direction, the world to just end. Not one of us has said: *maybe someday when we're free*...Because for every day longer we sat here as if objects on cots, the thought of someday became a question mark at the end of a confusing sentence. A life sentence.

I've been staring at the front page of a newspaper for days trying to understand what it might mean for us.

VICTORY IN EUROPE! NAZIS SIGN FULL SURRENDER

As if nothing ever happened and so many Germans weren't convinced to rid the world of all Jewish people, now we can all just go back in time and live in harmony. Except it seems as though we've lost everyone aside from the three of us. How can we go back and live as if our world wasn't stolen from us. We won't get it back. No one can give it back to us.

Right after we were told we'd be leaving for Hamburg, I signed a few words to Alfie using the new skills we'd been given by the nuns, curious to see what he was thinking. He still doesn't have an update about his parents either. They aren't on any lists.

"I don't want to go home," I told him, alphabet-signing the word *home* because I still don't know the correct hand gesture for that.

"If we stay here, we will give the Nazis what they wanted. If we go home, we are living proof that they lost the battle. We're stronger than that," Alfie said.

That was the end of our conversation on the subject. We've been traveling by train all day, speeding past unfamiliar land, some destroyed, some still intact but vacant of people, and some unaffected by the war—or so it appears.

We don't know what's left of Hamburg, if much at all. The firestorm might have taken down the entire city for all we know.

Maybe I've just forgotten how it feels to be free. It's as if I've forgotten to blink. Something so natural is foreign to us now.

Flutters in my stomach force my arms to tighten around my waist as the train screams to a stop. We can see the sign for Hamburg outside the window. There is only one stop for Hamburg on this trip, so we know this is where to deboard.

I take Lilli's hand and make our way to the car door. Alfie is behind me with his hand on my shoulder, squeezing gently to remind me that he's here and with me.

There are signs across the platform. The largest of all the signs is for Displaced Persons. We approach the man holding the sign and he points to a pale yellow and blue bus with another sign in the windshield that says: Displaced Persons Assembly Centre.

The bus is mostly full, but we take the second seat in, squeezing in together on one bench. We don't wait long before a driver boards the bus, closes the door and takes us to our next unknown destination.

There is no such thing as home.

Lilli grabs my hand and points out the window. "Hamburg Zoological Gardens?" There's a sign to welcome us. A zoo of all places. I glance over at Alfie, reading the confused look on his face to match my own.

It's not a prison for people. We should be thankful for that much.

A Soviet doctor spared my life with emergency surgery on my foot. The recovery took quite a while and despite wanting to move along faster, I was groggy, weak, and unstable. The Red Cross finally released me last week. One of the nice young ladies from the Red Cross told me the displacement camp in Hamburg would be the best place for me to go if trying to reconnect with other family members. Everyone should be directed home if they're searching for loved ones.

Home; the word meaning very little to me without my children and Leo by my side.

It's only been a few days since I arrived here. I feared what this place might resemble with the word "camp" in its name, but it couldn't be more different than Auschwitz. The people here are kind, warm, and welcoming. Everyone wants to help those of us who have been held captive and went as far as checking through all their lists of registrants for family members. The response was: Not yet. It was more than the hope I might have given myself at that moment, and for that, I'm grateful because I will continue to wait for them, for however long that might take. She also told me that buses full of displaced people arrive throughout the day just at the front entrance of the camp. Each person is registered right away, and if their information matches mine, we'll be reconnected.

Despite the amount of rehabilitation activities that are offered here, the only thing I want to do is sit on a bench near the bus drop-off and watch every single person arrive. If one of my loves finds their way here, I want to be the first to see them.

The door closes on bus number ten today. The gear grinds and the release of the brake screeches as the empty bus pulls away. I grip my fingers around the wooden slats of the bench, urging the pain to stop building. The disappointment is so heavy it's hard to hold my head up.

I've only watched a quarter of the number of buses today that came through yesterday. Each time another pulls away, my heart cracks and burns. One less chance.

The next squeal of brakes pierces the air, followed by a metal rattling from the gears. Then the hiss of air releases before the doors crank open.

It's agonizing to watch anyone step off the bus. We all look the same: emaciated, skeletal, pale, weak, and hopeless. Most everyone is alone, seeking out the idea of someone waiting for them here. Their pain is loud but silent and felt through every bone in my body. Does hope ever truly die? Or does it just dull with time? Do we wake up one day and just say *This is what I'm left with*?

This eleventh bus of the day might be empty. No one else is coming out, but the bus hasn't closed the door to continue on. I grind my teeth, trying to remember to stop doing so when I have so many dental issues to tend to, but it's become a habit I can't seem to break.

A thump thump rattles the bus as another person steps off, followed by two others.

A young girl turns and waits for the other two so the three of them can walk up to the registration desk together.

"My girls..." I call out, my voice raspy and not carrying very far. My heart is cracking. "My girls! Jordanna, Lilli, Alfie?"

The three of them continue to walk forward, not taking a moment to look around. That's them. I can feel it in my bones. It's them.

The girls have much less of a height difference than when I saw them last, and their chocolate brown hair is curled into their chins—a style I've never seen on either of them except for when they were very young. The oldest has the younger one's hand squeezed within hers as if she's never released it in all the time they were gone. And the boy, he stands behind them, guarding them as if he's their protector. He's much taller than he was too, more man than boy. His hair is short but swept to the side as he's always worn it. They all look fairly healthy, healthier than me, thank God.

I push myself up from the bench and will my body to move faster than it usually does now, which the crutch I rely on would help me do more than just lean on it. The limp from my injured foot has created a shift in my body, making it hard to move without sharp pains. I limp toward them. "Jordanna, Lilli, Alfie," I try to shout louder. The wind is stronger than my voice.

Lilli forces Jordanna to stop walking toward registration, demanding she step into the line behind the portfolio book of names beneath a sign that says:

Search registered family members here.

I close in on the few steps between us, recalling the thing I said to them. "It's all right, my sweethearts. We're safe here."

Those words fed me nightmares every night, knowing the last thing I said to my daughters wasn't true—whether knowingly or not. They relied on me to be honest with them and I wasn't because I didn't want them to be afraid.

This wavering moment we're inside of compares to the

trapped air inside of a snow globe, every little piece of us drifting into place as crystal snowflakes.

"My girls," I say again. "Alfie."

Lilli is the first to spin around and step away from Jordanna in search of my voice. Jordanna's shoulders rise and stiffen. I watch as she holds in a breath as she battles with herself whether to turn around too. But of course, she does.

Their eyes are still full of light and life. How could they have been so strong?

"Mama!"

"Mama, is it really you?" The shrill of each of their voices bounce off each other.

Jordanna stops short, tears pouring from her eyes as her hands cover her mouth. Lilli's arms lock around my waist as her head bounces against my rib cage. Jordanna is in shock, her eyes wide, her mouth ajar. I hold my arm out for her, and she trudges to me, wrapping me in her arms so tightly I can hardly breathe.

Alfie's arms fold around all of us. "You're here," Alfie whispers.

"You're alive," Jordanna cries out.

"I am now, sweetheart."

The weight of their embraces reminds me of the crutch beneath my right arm and the heaviness of my left leg that I can't bear weight on.

It takes them a moment to realize I have a crutch holding me up and they carefully take a step back to give me a bit of space. "What happened?" Alfie asks, staring down at my bandaged disfigured foot.

"I'll be fine. I might need this crutch to lean on, but I'm alive."

Jordanna becomes pale, staring at me, pleading for the truth without asking. "Mama."

"It was an infection in my heel. The doctors were able to

save most of my foot but not all. It doesn't matter. We all need to learn to walk again, and we will do it together."

I grab Jordanna's arm and tug her out of her state of shock. I don't want to imagine how many times she might have fallen faint over the last year and a half, and yet managed to remain alive after what I saw happen to so many others.

"We got your letter," Lilli says.

Pins and needles prickle across my cheeks, wondering who managed to deliver a note to my girls. "You did?"

"Yes. We received it in February but we're not sure who passed it along. The writing on the envelope wasn't your hand-writing."

"Do you still have it?" I ask.

A faint smile flickers across Jordanna's face as she pulls it out of her coat pocket. "Of course," she says, handing it to me.

I study the envelope, recognizing the handwriting right away. Ina. She never gave up. If she sent this in February that means she made it out of Auschwitz too. I didn't see her again after we stopped reporting to the infirmary. I didn't know what became of her, if she made it out. I read enough of her notes on charts within the wards to recognize her perfect penmanship. She made sure the children got one of my letters. An angel, that's what she is and will always be to me. I press the envelope to my chest and take in a deep breath. *Thank you, God. Thank you.*

"Let's go to the registration desk," I tell them, nudging my head toward the table set up beneath a white tent.

We walk in silence while questions scream through me, wanting to know if they've heard from their papa. Would they have already said so?

Lilli stops walking as if she forgot something and needs to go back to where we were standing. She turns around, lowers her head and curls her hair behind her ear.

"What is it, sweetheart?" I ask.

She reaches into her coat pocket and pulls something out then returns to us and hands it to me, dropping it into the palm of my hand and holding it there for a long second before releasing it.

I uncurl my fingers, finding the compass I gave Leo many, many years ago.

"You have Papa's compass?" I ask, my words lodging in my throat.

Lilli nods her head as the memory of Leo's words whirl around me.

"So long as I'm alive, darling, I'll carry this with me so I always find my way back to you," Leo said to me after admiring it for the first time.

So long as I'm alive.

I cup my hand over my mouth, trembling, trying to keep myself composed for the sake of the children. "How did you—did he give this to you?" I ask through a whimper.

Lilli peers down between us. "No, but he used it to find us at the children's prison where we were taken. He helped us escape. But—"

"But what? What happened?" I ask, swallowing the lump in my throat.

Jordanna's chin dips and fresh tears fall from her eyes. "It was my fault, Mama. I was so hungry, and I took some horse fodder on a train and the horses got upset. Then the Nazis came after us. Papa made us all jump from the train, but then I don't think I moved fast enough. He couldn't jump with us. We found him by the tracks later that night." Jordanna is crying so hard she can hardly take in a breath, and I'm not crying at all and still feel as if I can't take in a breath.

"He's gone," I say, my voice trailing off in a whisper. "And Max, both of them." I pull them back into my arms as each other's tears fall onto one another. It wasn't supposed to be like this—our life. This wasn't our plan. We were supposed to grow old together and watch all our children go on and have families of their own and then remind each other of where it all started—how hard we fought for what we have. But they're gone. The strongest of our family, the backbones, we're here without them. Forever.

I grab the back of Jordanna's head and lean back enough to look at her. "Listen to me right now. Whatever happened to Papa, it is not your fault. Don't you ever think that way." I know it was not her fault. She didn't ask for this life. "Do you hear me? It's not your fault. Your papa came to your rescue. He found you, then saved you. He would never blame you. Ever. He did what he set out to do. He's the reason we found each other. That's the last thing he did in this world, and he would call that a heroic story if anyone asked."

Jordanna takes in a shuddered breath and says, "He said—he said—the Gestapo took you away from him but when he was able to return, he couldn't find you. He didn't know if the Gestapo had taken you somewhere too. He told us he was doing everything he could to find us all," Jordanna says.

"That's what warriors do. They give up everything for the ones they love, even if that means we must live without them."

EPILOGUE

DALIA, JANUARY 27TH, 1975

The students sit in silence, their eyes set on me as I stand behind the lectern podium. The curiosity and anticipation in their faces tell me they're waiting for my final remarks as the period comes to an end.

My gaze shifts to the row of picture frames on my desk, each one holding a memory from before and after January 27, 1945. The first frame captures the radiating love and joy between Leo and me on our wedding day. The promise of forever in unspoken words, encumbered between our unbreakable embraces. In the next frame, I'm holding Max in my arms, beaming with pride and joy on the day he became a part of my life—the day he made me a mom.

A gap between the two frames symbolizes the purgatory we lived in from the onset of World War II to my liberation from Auschwitz before starting a new life in America.

As life goes, we carry on despite our pain, grief, and the hurdles we'd need to overcome, even after the unimaginable horrors we faced. Just as the flowers that bloom after a brutal winter, we found ways to heal and move forward.

Jordanna and Alfie's framed wedding photo is next to the

one of them holding their twin sons, Max and Leo, the day they were born. And then there's my fierce Lilli in her graduation photo from Yale University, holding her Humanities and Social Sciences degree with a smile that mirrors her papa's.

"In conclusion, a date could be just a date, but a date might also signify the beginning and end. January 27, 1945, was the day thousands of prisoners were liberated from Auschwitz. Many went on to start a new life or find what was left of what they were forced to leave behind. All of them had to navigate a world in a new light without any direction. It's a day of joy and sadness, a fresh start, a release from our suffering, and a defining moment of remembrance, reminding us all to be grateful for what we have today. Even for those who perished before that date, many believe they too found their peace. I remember a wise man once said: 'Those who died didn't have their life cut short, but instead, were set free—to a place where war doesn't exist, where unimaginable happiness and beauty awaits beyond the precipice of our fearful last breath. We're here to find our way to the next place by enduring challenges until we eventually succeed.'"

As the students jot down notes on my conclusion, my gaze sweeps along my desk at the row of picture frames encasing memories from before and after January 27th, 1945, I consider how I ended up here in this classroom when I was sure I wouldn't make it out of Auschwitz.

I never imagined leaving my home in Europe, but after the war and our losses, we felt we didn't belong anywhere. It was only me, Jordanna, Lilli, and Alfie left.

Alfie was the first to lose his parents and the last to find out if they had survived. The days wondering about their status kept him awake at night as he struggled between the feelings of hope and acceptance. When he received a letter in the mail, informing him of his parent's fate—that they had perished in Auschwitz upon arrival, Alfie took the news with a reflection of relief. I'll always remember his profound response that day: "I can go on with my life now. Not only were their souls set free with all the others on January 27th, 1945, but they were spared horrors that many of us weren't. I can live with that."

What he didn't say out loud was that we are the ones who have to live with the horrors we endured.

We needed to find a way to recover. To move forward and forge ahead was our only choice. A change and a fresh start in America would offer us a chance to heal. With my background in nursing, I was able to find a job quickly upon arriving in New York. However, I soon realized the medical field would always bear memories I needed to part from after seeing too much.

Jordanna and I, together, enrolled in a university with the desire to become educators. Lilli soon followed, taking her own path. Alfie struggled to find a suitable path for himself with his hearing loss, but eventually found his gift as a therapist for children hard-of-hearing.

We've each found a new path, ones we couldn't have expected to exist if we didn't end up where we did in 1945. Still, I would go back to the life I loved before we were all torn apart. We shouldn't have had to start over with broken hearts and shattered dreams.

"Okay, class, your essays are due next Monday. Your assignment is to answer one simple question." All of them sit attentively, the tips of their pencils pressed to a page in their notebooks. I turn to face the board, pick up the piece of chalk and beneath the date, script out:

What was it all for?

The clink of the chalk against the metal tray is louder than any reaction in the classroom. I brush the chalk dust from my hands and turn back toward the students, finding some with hints of distress or confusion. Others are still staring down at their notebooks.

The question sounds simple. Except, the answer is not something I've been able to define myself, even after all these years. So, I continue to ask.

I find inspiration in the youth of a new generation while lending them my knowledge of the past with hope that together we might find a way to unearth the revelation of world peace.

"How many pages should the essay be?" one of my students asks, his hand raised in the air as he speaks.

"I have no requirement other than a well written response," I say. "Have a wonderful day. You're dismissed."

All at once, they move from their seats, gathering their belongings and shoving them into their backpacks.

I lift my briefcase from beside my chair and place it down on the desk to file my notes. As I reach for a pile of papers, the briefcase falls heavily to the side. "Oh goodness." A few pencils and paperclips spill out, along with Leo's compass. I keep it on me wherever I go to make sure I'm always going in the right direction. I scoop up the engraved compass and press it to my chest.

"Professor Bergman, is everything all right?" a young lady asks, approaching my desk.

"Of course," I tell her. "Can I help you with something?"

She presses her hands down on my desk, tilts her head to the side and stares at me for a long moment as if she has a question that she can't find the proper words for.

"Is that the compass?" she asks.

Her question perplexes me as I never mentioned myself or the compass in the lecture today. I lower my hand and release my fingers, staring down at the compass.

"I—well—"

The young woman offers me a faint smile. "*That*...is what it was all for."

A LETTER FROM SHARI

Dear reader,

Thank you for choosing to read *The Family Behind the Walls*. Each historical novel I write is very near and dear to my heart for the love and remembrance of my family who endured the worst of the Holocaust, leaving me with only my grandmother and great-grandmother who survived.

There's nothing I love more than sharing my books with readers from all over the world. If you would like to keep up to date with all my latest releases, just sign up at the following link. Your email address will never be shared, and you can unsubscribe at any time.

www.bookouture.com/shari-j-ryan

January 27, 1945, was Liberation Day for Auschwitz. Though the members of my family who had been sent to that camp didn't survive, the date marked the start of freeing all Jewish prisoners from the Holocaust. It's a day to reflect on where we were, where we are now, and where we'll hopefully continue to be.

If my grandmother didn't survive, my paternal bloodline would have ended. I wouldn't be here to write these words and keep the stories of what so many lived through alive.

My eldest son wouldn't have been born on January 27th, 2009, sixty-four years later, with the privilege of meeting his great-grandmother. His birth date might be a coincidence, but it reminds me of how grateful I am for us to have the freedom to be who we were born to be.

In 2022, my other grandmother passed away on January 27th after suffering from congenital heart failure. It was a devastating day and possibly, another coincidental date, but I came to realize *she* was set free that day from her suffering.

This book releases on January 27th, 2025, eighty years after Auschwitz was liberated.

I no longer believe the date is a coincidence in my life.

This date is my beacon of hope.

I hope you enjoyed reading *The Family Behind the Walls* and if so, I would be grateful if you could write a review. Since the feedback from readers benefits me as a writer, I would love to know what you think, and it makes such a difference helping new readers to discover one of my books for the first time.

There's no greater gratification than hearing from my readers—you can get in touch on my social media, or my website.

Thank you for reading!

Shari

www.sharijryan.com

 facebook.com/authorsharijryan

 x.com/sharijryan

 instagram.com/authorsharijryan

ACKNOWLEDGMENTS

Writing *The Family Behind the Walls* was an incredibly emotional experience, as I poured heart and soul into every page to bring this World War II story back to life. I'm so thankful to the amazing team at Bookouture for giving me the chance to continue this writing journey—it's a true privilege to grow as a writer with you by my side.

Lucy, my wonderful editor, your eye for detail, skill, and insight have been such a gift. It's been an absolute pleasure working with you, and I'm excited for all the books we'll create together in the future!

Linda, your constant positivity and belief in me means everything. Our friendship is something I hold dear, and I can't thank you enough for always being there.

To Tracey, Gabby, Elaine, and Gosia—my trusted friends and confidants—thank you for your support and friendship. You've been more important to me than I can express, and I'm endlessly thankful for you.

A huge thank you to the ARC readers, bloggers, influencers, and readers who make up this wonderful community. Your enthusiasm, passion, and support are incredible, and I'm so grateful.

Lori, the best little sister in the world—thank you for always being my biggest cheerleader. I love you so much!

To my family—Mom, Dad, Mark, and Ev—thank you for always believing in me and standing by me through everything. You mean the world to me, and I love you all.

My dearest friends—Kelly, Susan, Jenn, Erin D., Erin L., and Carla, you relentlessly give me reasons to laugh, brighten my day, and offer me confidence when I prefer to be hard on myself. I hope you know I'm always here for you too. I don't know what I would do without you.

Bryce and Brayden, my incredible boys, thank you for always believing in my skills to juggle the world while always keeping you on top. You two will always be my greatest pride and joy, and I love you beyond words.

And last but not least, Josh—thank you for your endless support after more than twelve years. I wouldn't be where I am without your motivation. I'm so lucky to have you, and I love you with all my heart.

PUBLISHING TEAM

Turning a manuscript into a book requires the efforts of many people. The publishing team at Bookouture would like to acknowledge everyone who contributed to this publication.

Audio
Alba Proko
Sinead O'Connor
Melissa Tran

Commercial
Lauren Morrissette
Hannah Richmond
Imogen Allport

Cover design
Eileen Carey

Data and analysis
Mark Alder
Mohamed Bussuri

Editorial
Lucy Frederick
Melissa Tran